1

Romance Unbound Publishing

No Safeword

Claire Thompson

Edited by
Donna Fisk
Jae Ashley

Cover Art by Kelly Shorten
Fine Line Edit by Kathy Kozakewich
Consulting Editor – Jamie D Rose

Print ISBN 978-1523431052

CHAPTER 1

Jaime's boot heels clicked on the asphalt as she walked along the back alley toward Asheville's only real underground BDSM club, The Garden. As she approached the unmarked entrance, she took off the denim jacket she'd worn over her leather vest for the long bus ride from her apartment and shoved it into her gear bag. A thrill moved through her as she gripped the large door handle. It had been too long since she'd smelled the heady scent of sweaty, aching desire or felt the sharp sting of leather against skin held tight by soft, strong rope.

Please, please, please, let me in.

She shook her hair from her face and blew out a breath as she pushed the heavy metal door inward. The doorman, Barry, had let her slide once before. With luck, maybe he'd do it again. Jaime's heart sank as she saw, not Barry, but a forty-something woman with dark, short hair framing a narrow face, her lips painted a shiny crimson, standing behind the counter that separated the entrance from the rest of the club.

"Welcome to The Garden," the woman said, her eyes moving over Jaime in subtle but obvious appraisal. "You here alone or with a partner?" She tilted her head slightly, looking past Jaime in case someone else was about to appear.

"Alone." Jaime's nipples were already responding to the thrilling crack of leather and whoosh of cane emanating from the room beyond the entrance. She could hear the breathy cries and squeals of the lucky subs engaged in scenes at the various play stations scattered throughout the club. Though it was only ten on a Friday night, the place was already in full swing.

"That'll be twenty dollars, please." The woman waved toward a framed flyer on the shiny wooden counter that outlined the cost of entry for single men, women and couples. Though single women got a discount, it was still more than Jaime could afford. Beside the price list was a stack of consent waivers that absolved management of responsibility for any mishap during play sessions. "Do we have your waiver on file?"

"Yes, I think so," Jaime replied. "It's been a while since I was here. Uh, is Barry here?"

The woman shook her head. "Sorry, I don't know any Barry. I've been here going on two months now. Did he used to work the door?"

Jaime nodded, her heart sinking as the prospect of a BDSM scene that night slipped away. She turned at the sound of the front door opening. Several people entered, dressed in leather and hoisting gear bags, clearly ready to play. They were talking and laughing as they approached the counter behind Jaime.

Jaime fingered the two folded five-dollar bills in the back pocket of her jeans as if, by touching them, she might make them miraculously multiply. "Uh, the thing is," she said as she turned back to the woman, "I'm a little short tonight. Is there any way I could maybe, uh, skip the cover, just this once?"

Jaime saw the flash of sympathy in the woman's eyes, but after a moment's hesitation, she replied with a shake of her head. "I'm sorry, hon. I don't have that authority." The group behind Jaime had quieted, and she wondered if they'd heard the humiliating exchange. She turned, ready to flee, when the woman reached a hand across the counter, placing cool fingers lightly on Jaime's forearm. Her smile was kind. "Let's just get these folks taken care of and then I'll see if Anthony, the owner, has time to talk to you."

Jaime stepped aside as the woman took the other people's money and their signed waivers. As she watched them enter the club, Jaime felt like a kid with her face pressed up against a candy store window.

"I'll be right back," the woman finally said. "You stay put, okay, hon?"

Jaime nodded. "Thanks. I really appreciate it." Though she was now thoroughly embarrassed, the woman had been so kind, she knew she'd have to see this through, no matter how humiliating it might be to admit her impoverished status to the owner of the club.

It wasn't long before the woman returned, followed by a tall man with silver hair. "Good evening," he said in a deep, sonorous voice as he stepped through the opening. "I'm Anthony Gerace, owner of The Garden. Charlotte informs me you might like to visit the facilities before committing to a play session?"

Though the man was easily over sixty, he remained handsome, with dark eyes in an angular, strong-featured face. He was impeccably dressed in a pale gray tailored silk shirt over broad shoulders, his legs encased in form-fitting dark gray leather pants that looked soft as butter and molded alluringly over his sizable package and muscular thighs. Sixty or not, the guy was a total hunk. "What is your name?" His voice was soft but commanding.

"Jaime. Jaime Shepard."

The man extended his hand and Jaime did likewise. To her surprise, instead of shaking her hand, Anthony lifted it to his face and lightly brushed it with his lips. She could feel power emanating from him like a force field, and the touch of his mouth against her skin sent a shudder through her loins she couldn't control. His dark eyes moved over her like laser beams and she had the uncanny feeling he was assessing not only her features and clothing, but the very depths of her being.

"You are submissive." It wasn't a question.

Jaime nodded, and then found herself adding, "Yes, Sir," the title of respect a natural addition to the sentence.

"It has been a long time—too long—since you have had the opportunity to serve, am I right?"

"Yes, Sir," Jaime whispered, something inside her unfurling like a flower blossom.

Anthony stepped back, breaking the spell, at least momentarily, for which Jaime was both grateful and a little let down. "I would be delighted if you would be my guest at the club this evening," he said.

Jaime's heart lifted as she glanced shyly up at the owner, wondering if he was offering to scene with her? She quickly dismissed the idea as unlikely in the extreme. Anthony Gerace didn't strike her as the type of guy who engaged in casual play at a public club, even if he was the owner.

"I really appreciate it. Usually I would have the cover. It's embarrassing—"

"Not at all." Anthony cut her off with a wave of his hand, his smile kind beneath those dark, compelling eyes. "I well understand how hard it can be to make ones' way in this world. I'm glad you came here tonight. It's my privilege to host you this evening."

Jaime smiled. "Thank you, Sir."

"Before you play," Anthony continued, "I have something I would like to discuss with you, if I might have a moment of your time." As he spoke, he let his eyes move once over her face and body as if she already belonged to him. She nodded, unable to help herself, the thought of refusing an impossibility.

Again he extended his hand, and this time he took hers in his, pulling her gently forward. "In my office, if you please."

Charlotte, who stood nearby, drew in a soft gasp and Jaime turned to regard her. She met Jaime's eyes and smiled, giving a small nod of what seemed to be encouragement. "Lucky girl," she mouthed silently.

Intrigued, excited and a little frightened, Jaime allowed Anthony to lead her by the hand through the club. Longing sizzled over Jaime's skin as they moved past the various play stations, many of them containing new bondage equipment since the last time she'd been at the club.

Anthony lifted a heavy satin curtain to reveal a pocket door, which he slid open. Gesturing for Jaime to precede him, they stepped into a small but nicely appointed space, more like a sitting room than an office, with comfortable chairs and a sofa placed in a conversational configuration in the center of the room. There was a small desk in the corner, a thin, sleek laptop the only item resting on its polished marble surface.

Anthony pulled the door closed, shutting out the sound of the club beyond. "Let me take that for you." He reached for Jaime's gear bag and lifted it from her shoulder. His fingers brushed her bare arm as he took the bag, his touch sending another involuntary shudder through her frame. She looked up at his face. He was staring down at her with a darkly inscrutable yet unmistakably masterful gaze. She stared back, transfixed, her pussy moistening, her nipples hardening into marbles beneath the thin leather of her vest.

She could feel the sexual tension thrumming like an electric current between them. Or was it only on her side? He was, after all, old enough to be her father. Suddenly unsure, she managed to wrench her gaze from his. She moved toward one of the chairs to sit and get her bearings, but Anthony's words stopped her. "You may sit down, of course, but I think you might be more comfortable kneeling on a cushion. I believe that is where you belong."

It was then she saw two large floor cushions set on the carpet between the furniture, in the place where a coffee table might be.

Jaime drew in a breath, her hand fluttering to her mouth.

Where you belong.

"You will remove your boots and pants," he instructed. "You may leave on your panties and your top, for now."

Jaime reached down and tugged at her boots, pulling them from her feet one at a time, along with her socks. Standing straight, she unzipped her jeans and rolled them down her legs. She stole a glance at Anthony, who had taken a seat on the sofa.

He was watching her intently, appraisingly, and the slow heat of a blush moved over her face and neck. He pointed to the cushion nearest him. "Kneel up," he instructed. "Shoulders back, hands clasped loosely behind your back."

"Yes, Sir." The words, again, came unbidden. She settled on the soft silk. The carpet was padded beneath the thin cushion. It felt good—it felt right—to be on her knees after so long. Though she remained nervous, a certain submissive calm settled over her as she squared her shoulders and straightened her spine, her hands finding each other behind her back.

"I've invited you back here, Jaime, because I sense something in you, something I would like to explore further. I appreciate your trust and patience during the process. I have an opportunity that might be something you want to consider, but first I need to find out a little more about you. I apologize in advance for the mystery, but I'll make it all clear soon enough. Is that all right with you, Jaime?"

Anything you want is all right with me, Sir. As long as it involves whips and chains. "Yes, Sir."

"Excellent." Anthony appeared satisfied, as if she'd just passed some kind of test. He leaned back against the sofa. "Before I get down to my proposal, I'd like to ask you a few questions about yourself.

Please just answer them as openly and honestly as you can. There is no right or wrong answer. First, the basics. How old are you?

"I'm twenty-seven."

"In a relationship?"

"I've been single a while now. I was with my last boyfriend for nearly two years."

"A D/s connection?"

"Kind of. Just not the right one. I actually moved down here from Vermont to be with him." She shrugged ruefully.

"What caused the breakup?" He seemed genuinely interested.

Though this was the most unusual setup for a play scene Jaime had ever encountered, she decided to go with it. "When we met, Jake claimed he was a Dom, but by the end of the relationship, he was the one begging to be tied up. It got, you know, really strange. He's a sweet guy, and I tried to make it work in the context of submitting to his desire to be sexually dominated, but it just didn't feel right, you know? We both finally agreed to end it about six months ago. I've been single since."

"And you've met your submissive needs with scenes at clubs? But your finances are constrained at the moment and this limits your ability to satisfy those needs?"

Jaime nodded. "Constrained. Yeah. That's one way to put it." *Dead broke is more like it.* "I, uh, I lost my job a few months back…" She trailed off, embarrassed. This was feeling more like an interview than the prelude to a hot scene with a sexy Master. She shifted on the cushion, her knees suddenly aching.

"What is your occupation? How did you lose your job?"

"Look, I'm not sure—"

"Please." Anthony leaned forward, placing his large hand on Jaime's bare shoulder. Again just his touch sent a powerful current of need through her. "I'm not being idly curious. I need to know about you, Jaime. If you would indulge me a little longer? As I mentioned, I sense something in you. Beyond the physical beauty, which is abundant, I see in you a sensual submission, or at least the potential for submission, that is rare. I've made my fortune by going on my instincts, and my instincts are telling me you have what it takes. Trust me just a little longer, Jaime. Let me find out what I need to know, and then I'll tell you my proposal. No matter what you decide, you are free to use the facilities here at The Garden whenever you like—free of charge, my guest at any time."

Jaime was silent as she tried to process everything the man said. She was hugely pleased at his assertion of her submission, her *sensual* submission—she quite liked the sound of that. His reference to making his fortune intrigued her, and then there was the completely unexpected gift of free admission to The Garden any time she wanted! Her body tingled with anticipation at trying out all the fabulous new equipment waiting just beyond the door, hopefully with Anthony as her Master and guide. If she had to put up with some embarrassing probing into the financial ruin of her life at present, so be it.

"Okay," she finally said. "You're throwing a lot out here. This is all kind of mysterious, but I admit it—you definitely have my attention. What did you want to ask?"

Anthony leaned back again and smiled. "Your job. Tell me what happened."

"I was—am—a paralegal and I was working at this small law firm, Gordon & Chase, I don't know if you've heard of them."

"The name rings a bell," Anthony said.

"Well, you might have seen the stories in the papers a while back. It was right after Jake and I broke up, and he'd moved out. I thought I could carry the full rent myself, since I had a steady paycheck at the time." She snorted derisively in hindsight at her foolishness. "I'd just bought a new car, too, plunking down all my savings on the down payment."

Did he really want to hear this stuff? Since when did one's job status have anything to do with setting up a scene? Jaime, who had been staring at the intricate patterns on the woven carpet as she spoke, glanced up at Anthony. His expression was intent, his focus entirely on her. "Go on," he encouraged.

Apparently he did want to hear it, the whole miserable saga. Jaime shrugged inwardly, somehow sure she could trust this man, and more than a little curious about his proposal, whatever it might be. "Long story short," she continued, "the two partners were involved in some big embezzlement scandal and a whole lot of shady stuff I don't really understand, and the place was closed down. I never even got my last paycheck."

"Insult to injury," Anthony remarked, shaking his head sympathetically.

"Yeah," Jaime agreed, the surreal nature of what was happening suddenly hitting her. When she'd come out tonight hoping to slip into the club for a little BDSM action, she certainly hadn't envisioned herself kneeling with her pants off in the back office and telling the owner about her career woes. It was, she had to admit, somewhat cathartic to tell someone about it—as far as her parents back in Vermont knew, she was still gainfully employed.

"The whole thing was a nightmare, but I figured I would land on my feet, right?" She grimaced. "I hadn't counted on the taint of the place following me."

"How long since you lost the job?"

"Six months. I've been working in retail and trying to hang on, but it's not going so great. In case you were wondering, it's pretty much impossible to live on minimum wage. My credit card is maxed out, my rent is past due and I can't even drive my car because I'm afraid if I take it out of the garage, the repo man will get it." Jaime clamped her mouth shut, aware she was rambling, certain he must be bored and turned off by her pathetic little story. There was no way this sophisticated, erudite gentleman could be interested in her stupid problems. The patterns on the carpet blurred as her eyes filled with sudden, unwelcome tears.

"A lesser woman might have given up." The man's voice was calm but firm, not a trace of pity in his tone. "Gone back home to her parents perhaps, or looked to a man to save her, but you persevered. That takes courage. Courage is an important trait in a submissive."

Jaime lifted her head, blinking away the tears. "Thank you, Sir," she said softly.

"Enough about that," he continued, to her relief. "Tell me about your specific experience in the scene. Beyond what sounds like a rather unsatisfactory relationship with your boyfriend, have you ever been in a Master/slave relationship with a real Master, someone who understood your deep-seated need for submission, for erotic pain, for total sensual subjugation at the hands of another?"

"Ooh," Jaime breathed, the words moving over and through her like a hard but perfect caress.

"Answer the question."

"No, Sir," she whispered.

"But you long for it."

"Yes, Sir," she admitted.

"Have you ever undergone any sort of formal training—positions training, endurance, pain tolerance, sexual service?"

"Formal? Like with a trainer?"

"Yes. With a trainer."

"No, Sir."

"Can you imagine yourself in such a scenario? Living the lifestyle 24/7? Sleeping bound in chains, your every move dictated by another? Your body, heart and soul the possession of a Master who wouldn't hesitate to take what he wanted, but also to give you what you need, what you crave, what you were born for?"

"Oh my god," Jaime whispered, at once shocked and thrilled to her bones by his words. Again she met his gaze. He was staring at her, his expression almost ferocious in its intensity. She found herself falling into those dark, liquid eyes.

"Answer me. I need to hear you say it—to admit who and what you are, slave girl."

Jaime swallowed hard. "Yes," she finally said, her voice hoarse. She cleared her throat. "Yes, Sir. I can imagine it. I have imagined it."

"When you're alone, naked on the bed, your hand between your legs."

"Yes." Her blush confirmed her admission. "Like O," she added, certain he would get the reference.

"Like O," Anthony repeated. "While other girls were reading teen magazines and romances, you found *The Story of O*, and it was like a homecoming."

"Yes," she breathed. *Oh god, yes.*

"You devoured the descriptions of O's complete sexual subjugation, her erotic humiliation, the willful debasement and her joyous acceptance of her servitude. You dreamed of being completely owned by another."

"'Your hands are not your own,'" Jaime quoted. "'Neither your breasts, nor, above all, is any orifice of your body, which we are at liberty to explore and into which we may, whenever we so please, introduce ourselves.'"

"Precisely!" Anthony said, the word exploding into the room and startling Jaime, who had fallen headlong into the pages of *O*, many tracts of which she could quote verbatim from having read them so many times over the years. "I knew it," he continued, excitement in his tone as he rose to his feet. "You were born for this. Please stand up and remove all your clothes."

"I'm sorry, what?"

"You didn't hear me?"

"I heard you. I was just—"

"Then obey."

Jaime hesitated, aware this was a pivotal moment, aware she was making a decision before even being entirely certain of what was being decided. Rising to her feet, Jaime reached for the leather ties that held the front of her vest closed. She was braless beneath it, and the cool air moved over her bare breasts and erect nipples as she let the vest fall. Her eyes on his, she pulled her panties down her thighs and kicked them aside. She was proud of her body, and yet oddly shy in front of this enigmatic stranger—this stranger who seemed already to know her from the inside out.

"Feet shoulder-width apart, hands behind your head," Anthony instructed, moving closer.

Jaime assumed the position, an ache now throbbing between her legs. Anthony lifted his hand. Before she realized what was happening, he slapped her face twice, once on each cheek, the crack of his hard palm reverberating in the small room, followed by Jaime's startled cry. Instinctively, she brought her hands to her face, pressing them against her hot cheeks. Every nerve of her body was screaming as her mind struggled to catch up.

"Hands behind your head," Anthony said calmly, as if he hadn't just struck her. "I didn't tell you to fall out of position."

"But—but you—"

"I struck you, yes. And while you are protesting with your words, your naked need for what I offer is betrayed in your every move, the dilation of your pupils, the parting of your lips, the way your body leans toward me."

Jaime stared mutely at him, unable to deny his words. "Now," the Master said, "assume the position once more, hands behind your head. This time show some control."

Jaime, her cheeks still hot from his palm, did as he commanded. Without asking, Anthony placed his hand between her legs, a single digit pressing into the wetness.

Unable to help herself, Jaime groaned, her hips moving wantonly forward to take more of him inside her. "You are pure potential," Anthony murmured, his warm breath on her cheek. "Not spoiled by poor training and bad habits. You are waiting to be taken, controlled, molded into submissive perfection. You are just what we need at The Enclave." He moved his finger inside her as he spoke, making it difficult to concentrate on his words.

"We?" she managed to gasp just as he touched something inside her that made her jerk forward and then back. He inserted a second finger, the palm of his hand grinding against her throbbing clit. No one had ever touched her like this. It was perfect, almost too perfect, but only almost.

"Fuck," she breathed, only aware she'd spoken after the fact.

He slapped her again, even harder than the first time. Again Jaime cried out, the pain radiating in perfect juxtaposition to the dark magic he continued to work at her cunt, though somehow she managed to keep her hands locked behind her head. "Mind your language. A slave girl doesn't need to resort to such vulgarities." His voice remained soft but she could feel the steel beneath it. "One more outburst like that and I'll have to gag you."

Another *O* quote slipped into the jumble of her thoughts. *"The gag stifles all screams and eliminates all but the most violent moans, while allowing tears to flow without constraint. There was no question of using it that night. On the contrary, they wanted to hear her scream."*

She'd had a question—something he'd said, something she needed to explore, to understand, but his touch was too perfect, too intense. "Spread your legs farther," he ordered. She obeyed. He moved his fingers roughly in and against her, the intensity nearly more than she could bear. She began to pant. He lifted his other hand again and she flinched, expecting him to slap her face, but instead, he reached for her left nipple and gave it a sharp twist.

She yelped in pain, the nipple throbbing and engorged. He reached for the other nipple, twisting it just as roughly, all the while stroking her cunt until she began to shake. "Oh god, oh f—" She caught herself in time.

Anthony's free hand circled her throat, his finger and thumb pressing hard just beneath the jawline, completely cutting off her ability to breathe. "You already belong to me, don't you?" he murmured, his face so close she could have kissed him, if she had been able to move.

Unable to respond, she could only blink her eyes in urgent agreement.

His lips lifted in a slow, sensual smile, perfectly complementing the sadistic glint in his dark eyes as he took over her body and her will. "Come for me, slave. Now."

He released his chokehold and Jaime staggered back a step, held upright only by his hand buried deep in her sex. She inhaled in a shuddering gasp of release as she tumbled headlong into the most powerful orgasm of her life at the hands of this stranger, a stranger she felt she'd known all her life.

Jaime was seated on the sofa, a glass of cold, crisp white wine in her hand, a short silk kimono provided by Anthony around her shoulders. She was a little vague on the time between the endless orgasm, during which she'd traveled somewhere outside her body, into a place as close to Nirvana as she could envision, and now. As her thoughts cleared and her brain clicked back on, a tingling sense of excited anticipation began to take over. If that was the intro, what was next?

Anthony sat across from her, his intent gaze fixed on her once more. "You've proven yourself a good candidate for what I have to offer. I ask that you permit me to explain fully without interruption. Then, of course, you may ask whatever you like."

Jaime nodded, her brain already teeming with questions. "Okay."

"I am a member of a BDSM community called The Enclave. The Enclave is comprised of a group of serious-minded people dedicated to the art and passion of BDSM as a 24/7 lifestyle. We have a compound up in the Blue Ridge Mountains on a large tract of land that affords us complete privacy. Eight Dominants currently live at The Enclave, myself included. We have a full-time slave staff of four women and two men at present."

"Slave staff?" Jaime blurted, then bit her lip. Anthony gave a brief nod and, though it was unspoken, she felt his displeasure at the interruption.

"Slave staff," he repeated. "We're a relatively new community—we only cemented this formal alliance about two years ago, and we're taking our time in recruiting staff as we refine our expectations. Slaves are carefully chosen, based not so much on their current level of training, but rather on an aptitude, if you will. A willingness to learn, an ability, a *need*, to submit with every particle of their being."

"Ooh," Jaime moaned, enthralled, the word pulled from her before she could stop it. Anthony paused, regarding her, and she stiffened, expecting a rebuke.

But he said nothing, offering only the ghost of a smile as he continued. "Each potential candidate, once they've passed the necessary medical and health qualifications, along with a criminal background check, is invited to spend two weeks at The Enclave, a trial period, during which we assess their potential as a full-time staff slave. They undergo rigorous, full-immersion indoctrination—everything from positions training, endurance training, as well as intensive discipline and pain work. There is also basic service, which includes attending to the physical and sexual needs of the Masters and Mistresses, as well as full upkeep of the house. In a word, staff slaves belong to us in every possible context. They serve at our pleasure and suffer at our discretion."

He paused a moment, the laser beam of his gaze directly entering Jaime's soul. She realized her mouth had fallen open and ordered it to close. What this man was describing was surely the stuff of erotic fiction, and yet he seemed utterly sincere. Could such a place really exist, and right here in North Carolina?

Anthony continued. "If you come to us as a candidate, you will sign an initial contract that stipulates your agreement to give up all rights to your body and your actions while at The Enclave. You will agree to undergo the training we provide and promise to obey our every dictate and whim. You will be subjected to whippings, caning, needle play, bondage, sexual torture, deprivation and sexual pleasure the likes and intensity of which I am certain you have never experienced in your life. The training is constant and rigorous, but if it's something you want, something you were born to be, you will welcome the challenge. You will fail, over and over, but you will be given every chance to try again and again and again until you get it right.

"We are sensual sadists, yes, but we do not inflict pain for its sake. Rather, pain is used both as a reward for the true masochist, and as a punishment, when warranted, to teach and reinforce the lesson. If, at the end of the two weeks, both you and we agree it is a good fit, you will be invited to join our community."

"What if I can't get it right? What if it's all too much for me to handle?" Jaime asked, intimidated by his promise she would fail again and again.

"If by that you mean that you determine the training, the total-immersion slavery program isn't for you, you will be free to leave. The contract between us will be severed at that moment, and you will be returned to your former life. No hard feelings between us, hopefully, but you would have no further contact with The Enclave."

"Oh," Jaime said softly, feeling suddenly bereft of something she had yet to even experience.

"I think you have what it takes, or I wouldn't be making this offer."

"Thank you, Sir." Jaime said, warmed by his praise, though not entirely convinced.

"That said, it's a big commitment, not only of service and dedication, but of your time. With that in mind, training candidates receive ten thousand dollars in advance as compensation for the two weeks of service. We recognize you have expenses and needs in the outside world to which you must attend. Whether or not you are invited to join the staff at the end of the two weeks, that money is yours to keep."

Ten thousand dollars! That sure would go a long way to covering her past due rent and car payments, not to mention paying off her credit card. Even more astounding, imagine being *paid* for the training chance of a lifetime!

"I can see your mind working." Anthony interrupted her thoughts. "I've just scratched the surface of the experience, but what do you think so far?"

"Is this real?" Jaime blurted. "This place you're describing—it's real? It really exists?"

Anthony smiled. "Oh yes, The Enclave is very real."

"How do people live there? I mean, is it an enclosed community— no one comes or goes? How do you support that lifestyle? How does that all work?"

Anthony chuckled, shaking his head. "There's time to answer all your questions, and more, if and when we agree you're a fit for The Enclave. The first thing for you to consider right now is whether you're interested in the training." He leaned forward, fixing her with a serious look. "For obvious reasons, we highly value our privacy. Whether or not you sign up for the training, I ask that you don't share anything about The Enclave or the people you may meet there with friends or family."

"I can't just disappear off the grid for two weeks, can I?"

Anthony shrugged. "We are located in the Blue Ridge Mountains. You can just say you're taking a camping vacation, and that your Internet and phone access will be limited. It's a detail, really, in the face of what I'm offering you."

Jaime nodded her agreement. It wasn't like she lived with someone or even had family in the area.

Jaime's mind whirled with all she was hearing. The place sounded amazing—a Shangri La for those in the lifestyle. But was it something she wanted for herself? More to the point, was it something she could handle? Anthony seemed to have faith in her, but did she have it in herself?

"So, what's your initial impression, Jaime? Are you interested in moving forward? One of our members is a doctor. I can arrange a physical for you, including blood work, for this Sunday. Assuming you pass the physical and the background check, you could be at The Enclave by the end of the week. What do you think? Are you ready to embrace your dreams—to make them a reality?"

Jaime swallowed hard. Her mind continued to leap and twirl in excited confusion. She shivered, Anthony's offer touching something deep and essential at the core of her being. Would she be able to handle full-immersion training? He had promised she would fail, again and again. Could she handle that failure? But he'd also promised they would work with her, give her all the chances she needed to succeed, if that was what she truly wanted. Did she truly want it? She couldn't deny the urgent longing his offer had ignited deep inside her. But did she have what it took to succeed? What better way to find out than to try? If she passed up this chance, she knew she would regret it for the rest of her life.

"Jaime." Anthony's voice, authoritative but gentle, cut through the tumult of her thoughts. "I want you to place your hands in your lap, fingers relaxed." Jaime realized she was clutching herself, her fingers digging into her upper arms in a clenched, protective embrace. "Close your eyes and empty your mind of all the clutter. Breathe. Listen to your heart. To your instincts. Let them guide you in your decision. There is no right or wrong answer. There is only what is true for you, what is right for *you*."

Jaime made an effort to comply, willing her cramped fingers to release their death grip on her arms. She let her hands fall loosely into her lap and closed her eyes. She drew in a deep breath and let it out slowly. As the chatter in her mind eventually subsided, a sweetly budding joy sprung from a deep, hidden place inside her that she'd never really permitted herself to explore.

She didn't only want what Anthony offered. She craved it. She *needed* it with every fiber of her being. She understood there was no right or wrong decision. In fact, there was no decision to be made. What was true had always been true. Only now she was being offered the chance to seize it.

She opened her eyes and looked directly at Master Anthony.

"Yes, Sir," she said. "I accept."

CHAPTER 2

The buzzing vibration of Jaime's cell phoned dragged her unwillingly from sleep. Too bleary-eyed to see who it was, she took the call. She was greeted by the unwelcome voice of her latest boss, Junior (what grown man called himself Junior?), who managed the mall shoe store that was her latest attempt at paying the bills.

"Janie," he barked, though she'd politely corrected him at least half a dozen times in the three months she'd been working there, "Matt called out sick, and we've got the whole inventory thing going on and the kids' sneaker sale starts today. I need you in here by eight o'clock."

She was on the schedule for the afternoon shift, and had already been dreading it. The job paid better than the last gig she'd had, but Junior was constantly changing up the schedule on her, and threatened darkly every time she balked that there were plenty of "honest, hardworking folks lined up behind you," ready and willing to take her job if she had a problem.

As she came more fully awake, the amazing events of the night before came pouring like sunlight into her consciousness, and she smiled in spite of the nasal voice buzzing like an annoying mosquito in her ear.

Ten thousand dollars, paid in advance, hers to keep no matter what.

It was so incredible. She almost felt she should be the one to pay the ten thousand to Anthony just for the chance to experience what he was offering. He'd given her his card before sending her home, as well as the address and phone number for the doctor's office. "You'll receive a text with your appointment time. It will be early Sunday morning when the office is closed to the public. If you have a change of heart between now and then, you can just text back that you've changed your mind."

"Janie? You there or what? I need your ass in here pronto."

"I'm sorry, Junior, I won't be able to make it."

Junior was silent for a beat. "I don't think you heard me correctly, Janie. That wasn't a—"

"Jaime."

"What?"

"*Jaime*. I've told you like ten times, my name isn't Janie. It's Jaime."

"I don't care if your name is Tinker Bell. If you don't get your ass in here by eight, there are plenty of other—"

"Yes, yes, I know," Jaime interrupted, a part of her standing back in amazement as she watched herself torpedo her job, "there are plenty of other folks lined up to take my job. So give one of them a call, why don't you? I'm sure they'll be falling all over themselves to get their ass in there by eight. Bye, Junior. Have a nice life."

The air was fresh and still cool in the early Sunday morning stillness. The doctor's office was located in a primarily residential neighborhood, the only thing distinguishing it from a private home, a small painted sign at the curb that read *Asheville Health Services, A. Hershfield, MD.*

Jaime walked up the flagstones that led to the front door of the doctor's office, butterflies batting against the walls of her stomach. She rang the doorbell and stepped back, her heart pattering as she shifted from foot to foot in nervous anticipation. A moment later, a tall man in his mid-thirties with short dark hair and handsome, regular features opened the door. He was dressed in pale blue scrubs, the very picture of a young MD, save for a burgundy leather collar at his throat with a row of silver studs bordering the edges.

He stepped back, gesturing for her to enter. "You must be Jaime," he said. "Come on back and I'll get you set up. The doctor should be here any minute."

"Oh," Jaime said, confused. "You're not the doctor?"

The man smiled. "No. I'm her assistant. My name is Gene."

What must have once been the living room of the house had been converted into a large, comfortable waiting area, with thick carpeting on the floors and framed posters of soothing landscapes and pleasing abstracts on the walls. Gene led Jaime through a door at the back of the room, next to the empty receptionist's counter, and along a short hallway to an examination room.

"Have a seat." Gene gestured toward a chair and settled on a stool nearby. The room also contained a gynecological exam table, complete with stirrups. An old-fashioned metal gooseneck lamp perched on a stand beside the table. Gene reached for a clipboard from the counter. "I'll just take your blood pressure and do a brief medical history while we wait for Mistress Aubrey."

Jaime, who had been reading the doctor's diploma, which hung in a gold frame on the wall, glanced at Gene, who smiled as he answered her unspoken question. "As Master Anthony probably told you, Dr. Aubrey Hershfield is a Mistress at The Enclave. I'm not only her nurse here at the office during the week. I belong to Mistress Aubrey. She is the focus and center of my life, and there is nothing in this world I would not do for her." As he spoke, his face took on a serene radiance.

"Oh," Jaime breathed, aching with longing.

"Now," Gene continued, his tone suddenly businesslike, "What is your full name and date of birth?"

Just as Gene was finishing the last of the medical history questions, Jaime heard the sound of a door opening and closing, and the click of heels along the hallway. A moment later, a short, slightly plump woman in her early forties appeared, with light brown hair in a blunt cut around a pretty face, large blue eyes and a pointy chin.

"Hi there," she said as she entered the small exam room. "You must be Jaime. I'm Dr. Hershfield. You will address me as Mistress Aubrey. Stand up and remove your clothing. Then stand in the center of the room, feet shoulder-width apart, hands behind your head."

Mistress Aubrey was wearing a form-fitting red dress cut low enough to reveal substantial cleavage, her small feet shod in red stiletto heels, no white lab coat or stethoscope in sight. When Jaime didn't react immediately, Mistress Aubrey stepped closer to her and snapped her fingers just below Jaime's chin. "Come on, up, up, up! Anthony told me you were a sub. Was he mistaken?"

Jaime stood quickly, Anthony's name kicking her into gear. Gene, she noticed as she slipped off her sandals and unzipped the back of her sundress, was kneeling on the ground beside his stool, his head touching the linoleum, his arms crossed behind his back. As she folded her dress and took off her bra and panties, Mistress Aubrey crouched in front of Gene and tapped his shoulder. When he rose to his knees, she took his face in her hands, pulling it down to kiss his mouth.

Jaime assumed her position as ordered, fingers laced behind her neck, watching the lovers with nervous excitement. After a moment Mistress Aubrey stood, and Gene rose along with her, towering a good foot over her when on his feet. As Mistress Aubrey stepped back, Jaime couldn't help but notice the full erection tenting Gene's scrubs.

Mistress Aubrey turned her attention to Jaime. Tilting her head, she regarded Jaime appraisingly. Moving closer, she ran her fingertips along Jaime's sides up to her armpits, tickling her in the process. Jaime giggled involuntarily and shifted on her feet.

"Stay still and quiet," Mistress Aubrey snapped. "I didn't tell you to move."

Chastened, Jaime pressed her lips together. Fortunately, Mistress Aubrey stopped tickling her. Instead she cupped Jaime's breasts and then tugged at her nipples. As the nipples responded to the rough but sensual touch, Jaime's pussy moistened and swelled. Though Jaime had never found herself particularly attracted to women, something about Mistress Aubrey's decidedly masterful touch and sense of entitlement, as if she owned and could do what she liked with Jaime's body, was deeply exciting.

Mistress Aubrey turned to Gene. "Gloves," she said.

Gene reached into a drawer and brought out a pair of disposable latex gloves. Mistress Aubrey held out her hands like a doctor at an operating table while Gene pulled the gloves over her fingers. Turning back to Jaime, she kicked lightly at Jaime's ankles. "Spread your legs wider," she ordered.

Jaime obeyed, her heart thumping as Mistress Aubrey brought her hand between Jaime's legs. Jaime gasped as the doctor pushed a finger inside her and probed. "Nice," Mistress Aubrey pronounced. "She's hot and wet, just as a good little sub girl should be." She moved her gloved palm skillfully against Jaime's vulva as she spoke, and Jaime struggled to stay still and silent. After a moment, Mistress Aubrey withdrew her finger.

"Time for the gynecological exam," she announced. "Lie down, ass on the edge of the table, feet in the stirrups. Gene, tie her down."

Tie her down.

Not a typical doctor's instruction to her nurse, but then, this was hardly a typical physical. Jaime lay on her back against the crinkly white paper that covered the padded table and scooted forward to get her feet in the stirrups.

Gene appeared beside her, holding a handful of leather straps with metal clips at the ends. "Hands over your head, arms on the table," he instructed. As she obeyed, he gripped her wrists together and wrapped a strap around them. Pulling her arms taut, he clipped the strap to a discreet metal loop at the edge of the exam table, which Jaime supposed must have been added by the pair for just this purpose. She wondered what Dr. Hershfield's vanilla patients must think of the loop, if they even noticed it.

Moving down, Gene used more straps on Jaime's ankles, binding her to the stirrups. He placed a thicker strap of leather over her midriff and clipped it into place beneath the table.

"Excellent," Mistress Aubrey said, appearing between Jaime's spread knees. "First, the vaginal exam. I imagine you're familiar with the more traditional exam, which I'll conduct before moving on to the rather, uh, less conventional part of your visit today. Speculum, please, Gene."

Jaime lifted her head nervously as Gene produced a shiny silver speculum, which he handed to Mistress Aubrey, along with a tube of lubricant. As unwelcome images of vaginal torture with sharp metal objects leaped into Jaime's overactive imagination, she reminded herself that Mistress Aubrey was, in fact, a medical doctor, and wouldn't do anything to harm her.

Jaime lay back, staring at the ceiling as Mistress Aubrey slowly and carefully slid the gooey, cold metal spreader into her pussy and widened it. The ceiling had been painted light blue, with tiny silver stars swirled in random patterns over it.

"Aim the light for me, Gene," Mistress Aubrey instructed. Jaime felt the sudden warmth radiating from the incandescent bulb. Despite the deeply erotic thrill of the situation, the doctor's actions were brisk and clinical as she conducted her exam. "A quick swab for the lab," she finally said. There was an unpleasant but brief pressure against her cervix. In her peripheral vision she saw Mistress Aubrey hand a small glass slide to Gene, who slipped it into a medical envelope and set it on the counter.

The speculum was pulled gently from her. The exam wasn't over yet, however. A lubricated, gloved finger pressed deep into her anus while Mistress Aubrey's other hand moved against her belly as she felt for whatever it was doctors felt for. "Excellent," the doctor murmured, more to herself than to anyone else. "Very good." Finally the finger was withdrawn. "Now, we need to do your blood work," she said. "I assume you're comfortable with needles. Gene is an excellent phlebotomist."

"As long as I don't look," Jaime said meekly, her stomach dipping unpleasantly at the thought of being pricked. She lay watching as Gene pulled a tray from beneath the counter and placed on it a wrapped needle and syringe, a disposable orange plastic tourniquet and two small glass vials.

Turning back to her, Gene released Jaime's arms, allowing her to rest them at her sides. He cranked the table so she was in more of a sitting position, and then drew up a stool to sit beside the exam table. After pulling on a pair of surgical gloves, Gene prepared the syringe and then reached for the tourniquet. This he strapped around Jaime's upper arm. He instructed her to clench her hand into a fist, while he tapped at the veins rising at the bend in her arm.

Apparently satisfied, he reached for a small plastic container of alcohol and pulled a ball of cotton from a glass container on the counter. He swabbed her arm and then reached for the syringe. Jaime turned away and closed her eyes, concentrating on her breathing. There was a small, sharp prick as the needle entered her vein, but, as Mistress Aubrey had promised, Gene was good at what he did. After a minute or so, she felt a pressure at the spot where the needle had been, and turned to see Gene placing a Band-Aid over a fresh ball of cotton. The two vials were now filled with bright red blood.

Jaime looked away from this, instead searching for Mistress Aubrey, who stood at the end of the exam table watching the proceedings. "Are we done?" Jaime dared to ask.

"No, we are not," Mistress Aubrey replied in a no-nonsense tone. "The medical part of the exam is over, but now you will be subjected to endurance and sensitivity testing, which is just as important as physical health." Without elaborating, she turned to Gene. "Secure her arms again, slave Gene."

"Yes, Mistress."

Gene lowered the table so Jaime was once more lying flat, and re-bound Jaime's wrists. "I think she can handle the number two dildo," Mistress Aubrey said to Gene. "And get me a medium anal plug."

"Yes, Mistress," Gene replied.

Jaime's sphincter muscles tensed. She pressed her lips tightly together to keep from voicing her apprehension.

"Is there a problem, Jaime?" Mistress Aubrey said, her smile belying the steel in her tone. "I've examined your vagina and anus, my dear. You are in excellent condition, with healthy tissue and good elasticity. If this is an issue for you, however, we can end this right now. I'll just let Anthony know he was mistak—"

"No!" Jaime blurted. "I mean," she amended desperately, "Please, I'm sorry, Mistress Aubrey! I just wasn't expecting the anal plug thing. I mean, I'm kind of shy about my bottom and—"

"Your bottom? You mean your asshole? Be explicit, please."

Jaime's face began to burn. "Um, yes. My, um, my asshole. I don't really have a lot of experience with anal play and—"

"Well, get used to it," Mistress Aubrey cut in. "If you join us at The Enclave, that asshole will belong to me, to Master Anthony, and to every Dominant at the compound. If you have a problem with that, now is the time to find out. This isn't a game. If you sign on, your body will no longer be your own. Modesty has no place, none whatsoever, in a slave's repertoire. You will do as you're told, when you're told, or be punished. If this isn't something you think you can handle, you'd better face that right now. If you can't deal with a little anal play in this controlled environment, then I assure you, The Enclave is *not* for you."

Jaime blew out a breath, forcing herself to calm down. She had always hated any attention to her asshole, even though intellectually she realized this didn't make a lot of sense. It was something she didn't really even understand about herself, and no one had ever forced her to confront the issue before—they'd always just accepted "no ass play" as one of her hard limits. But apparently there were no hard limits at The Enclave.

Mistress Aubrey was right. Either she was willing to give of herself completely, to let all the old inhibitions and hesitations go, or she wasn't. And yes, now was certainly the time to find out, before she signed on the dotted line.

"I apologize, Mistress Aubrey. I let old fears get in the way of my desire to submit and obey."

Mistress Aubrey regarded her silently for several long beats while Jaime held her breath, now desperate for whatever Mistress Aubrey wanted to give her. Finally the Mistress nodded. "All right then. We will proceed." She turned toward Gene. "You ready?"

"Yes, Mistress." Gene held a tray with a sizable pink rubber dildo, as well as a forbiddingly large anal plug that appeared to be made of glass. Mercifully, there was also a tube of lubricant on the tray.

"You will be naked for this part of the session, slave Gene," Mistress Aubrey said casually.

"Yes, ma'am!" Gene said eagerly. He placed the tray on the counter and lost no time pulling off his sneakers and scrubs.

"Quite a specimen, isn't he? Definitely easy on the eyes."

Jaime turned her head to focus on the now naked Gene. He was, indeed, easy on the eyes. Gene was well-muscled and completely smooth, not a trace of hair on his body. Her eyes were drawn irresistibly to his cock, which was semi-erect above his shaven balls, a shiny loop of gold glinting just below the crown of his penis. As he turned to retrieve the tray, she saw the stripes, both new and fading, of a recent caning on his small, muscular ass and the backs of his thighs. Her breath caught in her throat at the sight, her skin tingling with sympathy and desire.

Once Gene returned to the foot of the exam table, Mistress Aubrey said, "Crank the stirrups wider for better access to her cunt and asshole."

Jaime's heart kicked into a higher gear as Gene released some kind of mechanism on the underside of the table that caused the stirrups to slowly widen, pulling her legs farther and farther apart and putting a strain on her inner thighs. Jaime was just about to protest it was too much, when Mistress Aubrey finally said, "Perfect. Stop there."

Mistress Aubrey stroked Jaime's spread vulva with gloved fingers. Her touch caused a spasm of pleasure to ripple through Jaime's loins and she was barely able to suppress her moan. The moan escaped as the fingers were pressed into the tight, wet grip of Jaime's cunt.

"You don't need to stay quiet," Mistress Aubrey said. "In fact, I want to hear how you respond." Mistress Aubrey's fingers moved inside her in sensual, stimulating strokes, pulling a deep sigh from Jaime. "That's right," Mistress Aubrey urged. "Hold nothing back. I want to hear every sigh, every moan, every scream. Is that quite clear, young lady?"

"Yes, Mistress," Jaime said, though she could barely hear her own response over the beating of her heart, which was pounding in her ears.

"Good." The hand was withdrawn. Jaime lifted her head, biting back the urge to beg for more. She watched as Mistress Aubrey reached for the dildo, which she handed to Gene.

"You do it, slave Gene," she ordered.

Gene squirted some lubricant on the tip of the bright pink rubber phallus. Mistress Aubrey stepped aside and he moved into position between Jaime's forcibly spread legs. The dildo was huge, much larger than any man Jaime had been with, or any toy she'd ever masturbated with. Despite her trepidation, her cunt throbbed, aching to feel the fullness offered by the thick phallus.

Her stomach muscles clenched with anxious anticipation as Gene pressed the head of the dildo against her entrance and pushed gently forward. She grunted involuntarily as its hard girth filled her. Her cunt muscles gripped the phallus, spasming against it in a shudder of pleasure.

"Fuck her with it," Mistress Aubrey instructed. Jaime, who had closed her eyes, opened them to stare at the Mistress who had given this order to her slave boy. Mistress Aubrey's eyes were bright, the tip of her tongue moving sensually over her full lower lip.

Gene began to move the dildo, pulling it partially out and then pushing it back again, simulating the movements of a penis, and causing a delicious rush of sensation that included both pleasurable stimulation, along with erotic discomfort from its too-wide girth. A masochist to her core, Jaime relished the sensual combination of pleasure and pain as Gene fucked her harder and faster with the surrogate cock. She began to pant, the heat building inside her as her body began its ascent toward climax.

Her pleasure was disrupted by Mistress Aubrey's next command. "That's enough. She isn't to come. Not yet. Leave the dildo in place. It's time to insert the anal plug."

Swallowing her erotic frustration, Jaime watched with mute trepidation as Gene reached for the obscenely large glass plug. Letting her head fall back against the exam table, she closed her eyes, her guts churning with anxiety. When the tip of the cold glass touched her anus, she squealed.

You can do this, you can do this, she told herself frantically, trying to hold onto what was left of her composure. She felt clammy, her breath catching in her throat.

"Unclench your fists." Mistress Aubrey voice sounded beside her ear. The plug had been withdrawn. Mistress Aubrey stood beside her. She placed her hand on Jaime's chest. "Your heart's beating a mile a minute. I want you to breathe. In…and out. In…and out." She stroked Jaime's arm with one hand, the cool fingers of her other hand pressed gently over Jaime's closed eyes. "Nice and slow," Mistress Aubrey urged gently. "You can do this, Jaime. Anthony saw something in you. Show me, too. Show me your courage and your passion. Show me how strong you are."

In spite of her fear, Jaime began to relax at the sound of Mistress Aubrey's soothing voice and gentle touch. Her panic began to ebb away, a deep, accepting calm moving to replace it. When the Mistress removed her hand, Jaime opened her eyes. "Are you ready to continue?" Mistress Aubrey asked.

Jaime opened her eyes. "Yes, please, Mistress."

Mistress Aubrey nodded toward Gene. The cold, gooey glass once more pushed between her ass cheeks. "Breathe," Mistress Aubrey reminded her. Jaime dutifully tried to slow and deepen her breathing. The glass pressed slowly, inexorably into her tiny opening. It wasn't really too bad, she realized with relief. She could do this. She could definitely do—

"Ow!" she screamed, the sudden painful pressure in her rectum making her forget any promise to be courageous. But just as quickly as the pain had struck, now it subsided, replaced only by a sense of utter fullness.

"Not so bad, was it?" Mistress Aubrey asked.

"No, Mistress. Thank you, Mistress."

Mistress Aubrey nodded. She stroked Jaime's cheek, and Jaime had a sudden, nearly irresistible urge to turn her face so she could kiss Mistress Aubrey's hand. The hand was withdrawn, however, as Mistress Aubrey's eyes slid from Jaime to slave Gene, who stood naked between Jaime's spread knees. Gene's worshipful gaze was fixed on his Mistress. Jaime experienced a pang of longing as she watched the brief but loving glance exchanged between the pair.

Mistress Aubrey turned back to Jaime. "You are doing well, Jaime." As Jaime basked in this praise, the doctor continued, "The anus is quite elastic, as long as it's given time to adapt. My slave can tell you, anal torture can be quite erotic. He's learned to climax from anal play alone, isn't that right, slave Gene?"

"Yes, Mistress. Thank you, Mistress," the naked man replied fervently, his erect cock bobbing.

"Now," Mistress Aubrey continued briskly, ignoring her lover's erection as she addressed Jaime once more, "we'll test your sexual endurance, your obedience, and your ability to control your body, more specifically, your orgasm. Gene is going to stimulate you again. You will not come unless or until instructed. Is that all quite clear?"

"Um, I think so," Jaime said uncertainly, her heart skipping several beats.

"You forget yourself." Mistress Aubrey's voice, so kind a moment before, had turned hard. "You must always address your superiors with proper respect. You must always include a Sir, Ma'am, Master or Mistress in your reply, no matter how confused and nervous you might be, or how much whatever is happening distracts you. It must become second nature. Now is as good a time to learn that lesson as any."

To Jaime's shock, Mistress Aubrey struck her right cheek with a well-placed, stinging blow. "Now," she said brusquely as Jaime blinked back tears she couldn't wipe away in her bound position. "We'll try that again. Are you quite clear on your instructions?"

"Yes, Mistress," Jaime replied breathlessly.

"Repeat them to me."

"Um, I'm to take whatever you give me," Jaime said nervously. "I won't come unless or until instructed, Mistress Aubrey," she added hurriedly, hoping she hadn't forgotten anything.

To her relief, Mistress Aubrey nodded. "Better." She looked at Gene, who stood quietly at the foot of the exam table, his expression calm. "Get the wand. Set it on low," she instructed.

Jaime started to lift her head to see what Gene was doing, but Mistress Aubrey, still standing beside the table, pushed her back down. She closed her hand over Jaime's throat and squeezed lightly. Jaime's breath caught in her chest, her nipples aching, her filled cunt throbbing. A hand on her throat had always been a submissive trigger for her—a button, her ex-boyfriend had called it—and now was no exception.

Something spongy pressed against her vulva. The wand clicked to life, its vibrations moving through her stuffed pussy and anus, sending a deep, shuddering tremble through her loins. Jaime began to pant, mews of pleasure pushing up from deep inside.

Her eyes fluttered open to see Mistress Aubrey regarding her with a knowing smile, her hand still circled lightly around Jaime's throat. "You need to be controlled. You need to be tied down, whipped, and thoroughly used, don't you, slave girl?" Mistress Aubrey spoke in a soft, sensual voice, her words sending a rush of hot, sweet desire through Jaime's veins.

"Yes, Mistress," she admitted with a gasp, a hair's breadth away from a climax. "Oh, yes, please…"

You will not come unless or until instructed.

Jaime drew in and expelled a shuddering breath, and then another. She clenched her hands into fists and tried, unsuccessfully, to twist away from the constant barrage of sensation at her cunt and ass. Another sharp smack to her cheek distracted her in her efforts, its sting heating her face.

"Control yourself," Mistress Aubrey admonished.

The stinging pain had counteracted Jaime's impending climax. The respite was short-lived, however, as the wand continued its inexorable pulse against her swollen, aching cunt. It wasn't long before she began to tremble with the effort of resisting the climax that was threatening to roll over her like a twenty-foot wave.

"Oh god," she moaned. Mistress Aubrey placed her hand once more around Jaime's throat, pushing her fingers hard against the jawline. Jaime shuddered, her hips arching involuntarily upward. Mistress Aubrey released her grip, only to slap Jaime's face again. The wand moved up and down her vulva, the vibrations exploding like firecrackers against her poor, swollen clit.

It was too much. She bucked in her bonds, her voice rising in a wail.

"You will come now." Mistress Aubrey's low voice cut through the cries and the blood roaring in Jaime's ears.

Thank god.

"Thank you, Mistress," Jaime managed, before sliding into the second most powerful orgasm of her life.

Mercifully, the wand was removed, as were the dildo and the plug. She was a rag doll, her limbs flopping uselessly as they were released from the stirrups. The end of the exam table was extended, Jaime's legs positioned by capable hands along its length, a soft sheet pulled over her naked body. Mistress Aubrey's cool fingers caressed her once more, stroking her cheek, pushing her hair from her face.

"She'll do," Mistress Aubrey said, and Jaime, eyes still closed, smiled.

Chapter 3

As Jaime entered the small, elegant bistro on Tuesday evening, a tall, slender blonde in a black dress stepped forward with a smile, looking past Jaime, presumably in search of her nonexistent date or husband. "I'm meeting someone," Jaime said. "I see him." Anthony was seated at a small table near the bar. He was watching her, and as they made eye contact, he lifted his arm in greeting.

Jaime made her way toward him, her heart fluttering. Anthony had called earlier that day to inform her she'd passed all aspects of her exam with Mistress Aubrey, as well as the background check. "If you're ready to move forward," he'd said, "I'll bring the contract this evening. We can discuss the details over dinner."

Anthony stood as she reached the table and moved behind her to pull out her chair. As Jaime sat, he expertly pushed it into place. Jaime couldn't remember when a guy had done that for her, and it both charmed her and highlighted the fact they were from different generations.

"A pleasure to see you," Anthony said, his dark eyes moving over her in that soul-searching way he had that made her feel as if her clothing was see-through. A martini glass sat on the table in front of him, two fat green olives skewered on a toothpick soaking in the gin. Following her gaze, he asked, "Would you care for a drink?"

As if waiting for his cue, a waiter appeared. He handed them menus and took Jaime's drink order. "Just some club soda with lime," she said, wanting to keep her head clear for what was to come. They perused their menus silently for a moment. Jaime was too excited and nervous to have much of an appetite. When the waiter reappeared,

Jaime's drink in hand, he regaled them with the specials of the evening, and Jaime chose the pasta dish, Anthony the steak, along with a bottle of red wine for the table.

When the waiter had gone, Anthony reached into his sport jacket and retrieved an envelope, which he handed to Jaime. "Inside you'll find two copies of the candidacy contract." As Jaime opened the flap with trembling fingers, he continued, "As you can see, it's only a single page. But take your time and read it carefully. After we eat, and you've had a little time to process the contents, you can decide if you still feel this is something you want to do. If you decide it's not for you, the invitation to use The Garden's facilities as my guest at any time remains in full force."

Jaime's mouth felt dry. She reached for her soda and took a long drink before focusing on the words in front of her. She began to read, keenly aware of Anthony's steady gaze as she perused the fine print with her legally trained eye. The document had clearly been drawn up by an attorney, with its herewiths and wherefores, and yet this was certainly like no other contract she'd ever seen. Such an agreement between "Master" and "slave" could never be legally enforced.

As if reading her mind, Anthony said, "I'm sure you understand such a contract would never stand up in a court of law, but that's not why this was developed. Rather, we've found when our submissives, and our Dominants for that matter, sign such a document, it makes the commitment between them that much stronger. Expectations and requirements are clearly laid out, and adding one's signature makes the pact more binding than a mere listing of the rules."

Jaime nodded. This reasoning made sense to her, and she agreed with the underlying rationale. Yet she understood, whether or not such a document could be enforced by the courts, if she signed, she would be handing over complete control of her body, her actions and her rights for the next two weeks, without recourse or limits, save for protection from actual bodily harm. She could sever the contract at any time, but that would result in immediate and permanent expulsion from The Enclave, a place she'd yet to lay eyes on, but had fantasized about endlessly in the days since she'd first learned of its existence.

The waiter arrived, food in tow, and Jaime refolded the pages and slipped them back into the envelope, which she set aside. The food was delicious and the wine took the edge off her nerves. By tacit agreement, they didn't discuss the contract or The Enclave during the meal, instead engaging in small talk about Asheville and the BDSM scene there, such as it was.

When the plates were cleared and coffee was served, Anthony placed his hand lightly on the envelope and lifted his eyes to meet hers. "We want you, Jaime. There is no question in my mind you will make an excellent slave candidate. Have you made a decision?"

Jaime swallowed. She reached for her wine glass and took another fortifying sip. Though she'd told herself she wouldn't decide right away, a part of her, the most basic and essential part of her, had made the decision at the club. It was as if she'd been waiting all her life for this. As if her life had only been a rehearsal to this point. The real show was about to begin.

She gave a small nod, and Anthony reached once more into his jacket, this time retrieving a pen, which he set down beside the envelope. Jaime reviewed the contract again, finding as her eyes skimmed the words that she'd already memorized them. Her hand, she was glad to note, was steady as she lifted the heavy gold pen.

She signed her name over the words *slave candidate* on both copies. Expelling a breath, she pushed the pages toward Anthony. He took the pen from her with a nod, and signed above the *Master* on the signature line. "There you go," he said, taking one of the copies along with his pen and slipping them the inside pocket of his jacket. "A copy for you and a copy for me."

He withdrew a second envelope and placed it beside Jaime's coffee cup. "Inside you'll find a cashier's check for ten thousand dollars. I will have a car sent for you on Friday morning. I trust this gives you enough time to prepare?"

Jaime stared at the envelope. As astounding as it might seem, she'd actually forgotten about the money. While it would be an incredible relief to be able to pay off her past due rent and debts, financial gain was definitely not the driving force behind her decision to enter the slave-training program. Still, there was no question it would leave her free to focus on what really mattered. She looked up with a grateful smile. "Yes, thank you. I'll be ready."

Friday morning Jaime stood in the parking lot of her apartment building, clutching the small duffel she'd been instructed to bring as she waited for the driver to appear. The overnight bag contained only her purse, toiletries, birth control pills, cell phone and laptop. Anthony had told her not to pack any clothing, which prompted her to fantasize endlessly about what she would be required to wear (or not wear!) during her training.

She told no one of her real plans, adopting Anthony's suggestion that she tell friends and family she was taking a vacation in the mountains. She'd invented a local tour group with whom she'd ostensibly be traveling. Cell service and Internet would be limited to nonexistent, but she'd be in touch when she returned.

Now, her heart jumped into her throat as a long, sleek sedan pulled up in front of her and slowed to a stop. The driver's door opened and a man dressed all in black came around the side of the car. He appeared to be in his late twenties or early thirties, with thick blond hair and narrow blue eyes over high cheekbones and a wide, sensual mouth. He wore a thick, black leather collar around his neck, which as he moved closer, Jaime saw was made from three strips of braided leather, the effect artfully beautiful.

"You are Jaime Shepard?" he asked with an accent, possibly German.

"Yes," she replied, hoping her voice didn't betray her nerves. She'd spent the past several days fixated on her experience at The Garden with Anthony and at the doctor's office with Mistress Aubrey and slave Gene, reliving each astonishing detail. Each night she'd drifted to sleep with her hand between her legs, images of what life might be like at The Enclave providing endless fodder for her masturbatory fantasies.

The man reached for her bag, and she let him take it. She moved toward the passenger door, but he stopped her with a hand on her arm, his grip firm. "No. You will sit in the back, please." Yes. Definitely German.

He pulled open the back door for her and Jaime slid onto the plump leather of the deep backseat. The man closed the door behind her and moved quickly back around the car. He shifted into gear and drove out of the parking lot and onto the road.

He looked at her in the rearview mirror as he drove. "My name is Hans. I am a slave at The Enclave."

A slave! He said it so matter-of-factly, as if being a sex slave was an everyday, perfectly normal thing. "Nice to meet you, Hans," Jaime said, hoping her voice didn't betray her jittery excitement. A thousand questions leaped to her mind. This was a chance to pump someone who already knew the score, to find out just exactly what she was in for.

But just as she opened her mouth to ask the first of many questions, Hans cut her off. "You will not speak during this journey, except in response to a direct question or order. You will listen and obey. For the duration of our forty-minute drive, I have been given complete authority as your Master. I will be giving a full report of your obedience upon our arrival. This is understood, yes?"

"Oh! Yes."

"Yes, Sir," Hans corrected. "You will address me as Sir during this ride."

"Yes, Sir," Jaime amended, feeling a little foolish and a lot excited.

"First," Hans continued, his eyes flitting from the road to the mirror, "if you are wearing panties, you must remove them at once. These you will hand to me. You will then lift your skirt and sit directly on the seat."

Anthony had instructed Jaime to wear a simple blouse and skirt for the drive to The Enclave. He hadn't said anything about underwear, and she was wearing panties and a bra beneath her clothes, her legs bare on this warm summer day. She glanced nervously at the rearview mirror, but Hans now appeared to be watching the road.

Jaime reached beneath her skirt and lifted her bottom so she could pull her underwear down. She adjusted her skirt as directed, settling her bare ass on the cool, soft leather. Without turning back, Hans extended his hand back toward her. She could feel the beginnings of a blush heat her cheeks as she handed him her panties.

He took them without comment, his eyes still on the road. After a minute or so, he said, "Unbutton the blouse and remove it."

Jaime glanced anxiously out the window. They were still in the heart of Asheville, just pulling onto Route 694 North. "You do not obey at once," Hans intoned in his accented English. "This will be reported."

Shit! Five minutes into the drive and she was already screwing up!

At least the windows were tinted, and would hopefully afford some privacy. "I'm sorry," she blurted. "I'm sorry, Sir!" she amended quickly, her fingers fumbling over the small buttons of her blouse. She yanked it from her arms, somewhat constricted by her seatbelt, very aware of her bare bottom on the leather seat beneath.

She met Hans' eyes in the mirror. "Now the bra," he commanded.

Jaime reached back and unhooked her bra, letting it fall forward from her body. She set it on the seat beside her, along with the blouse. It felt beyond strange to be riding topless in broad daylight, but the exhibitionist inside her—inside every submissive—was deeply aroused. Hans' eyes flickered back and forth from the road to the mirror. "Tweak your nipples," he ordered. "Make them hard."

Jaime bit her lip, but did as she was ordered. Already deeply excited, her nipples responded instantly to her touch. "Hands behind your head," Hans continued. "Keep your lips parted, and never cross or close your legs when seated. From this moment forward, you must always be accessible, every part of you. This is understood, yes?"

"Yes, Sir," Jaime replied, shifting on the seat to obey as she lifted her arms behind her head. She licked her lips, letting them part. Her nipples throbbed, matched by the ache in her cunt.

They drove silently for a while. Jaime's arms began to ache. She tried to catch Hans' eye in the mirror, but he was focused on the road as they slowly ascended into the mountains. Just when she was about to ask him, as politely as possible, if she could lower her arms, he pulled onto an overhang shoulder and turned off the engine.

"Why are we—" Jaime began, but Hans cut her off.

"Arms down. Get out of the car and into the front seat."

"What?"

"Do it!" he barked. "And that's another two reports. Failure to address me properly and questioning your Master."

Jaime glanced through the tinted windows. The passenger side of their vehicle faced away from the road, so it was unlikely anyone would see her. She reached for the door handle and opened the door. Moving quickly, she jumped from the car, pulled open the front door and slid inside, yanking the door closed behind her.

Hans reached for his belt and unbuckled it. His eyes on her breasts, he pulled down the zipper of his fly. "Take out my cock and suck it. You are not to stop until I climax. You are to swallow every drop."

Apparently *Master* Hans planned to take full advantage of his temporary role. He *was* extremely attractive, and Jaime had always loved sucking cock. Though she was sexually submissive, she enjoyed that bit of control over a man, savoring the anticipation when he tensed and squeezed his eyes closed, and her ultimate power as he cried out with pleasure at the moment of release.

Even so, she reached a little tentatively for the stranger's cock. He had no underwear on beneath his black pants, and her fingers curled around his thick shaft. She tugged the growing member from its confines, watching his uncircumcised foreskin slide back as his cock grew fully erect.

Reaching toward her, Hans gripped a handful of her hair, using it to yank her down toward his lap. "Ah," he breathed as she closed her mouth over the fat head of his cock. "*Das is gut. Das ist so lange her.*" Though Jaime didn't speak German, she understood the gist of what he must be saying—*it's been so long*.

Hans kept his fingers tangled in her hair. He used her head like a handle, pushing it up and down in a pumping motion, forcing his cock deep into her throat. She didn't get a chance to demonstrate any of her skills—the man was just fucking her mouth, plain and simple. It was all she could do to keep her balance on the seat and to suck in a breath of air between each gagging thrust. He was hurting her—his grip too tight in her hair, his cock slamming against the back of her throat. Yet, in spite of the pain, or perhaps partially because of it, her cunt throbbed with desire, its juices seeping onto her thighs.

The experience was short-lived. Within two minutes, Hans groaned and stiffened for a second before shuddering, his hips thrusting as he shot his load deep in Jaime's throat. When he released her hair she sat back, gasping for breath against the seat. Without looking at her, Hans rearranged himself. Tucking in his shirt, he zipped his pants and re-buckled his belt.

Finally he looked over at her. "That was acceptable," he said. "You'll need to work on that gag reflex, though." He jerked his head toward the backseat. "Now, please return to the back."

Her own lust unrequited, Jaime did as ordered, flying from the front to the back seat as quickly as possible. Hans started the car and eased back onto the road. "We will be there soon," he informed her. "In preparation, you will remove your skirt. You are to be completely naked upon arrival. When you get out of the car, I will place a collar and leash on you, and I will lead you to the door. You are to kneel up, hands behind your head, knees spread wide in offering while you wait for permission to enter. This is understood, yes?"

"Yes, Sir," Jaime managed, though she could barely hear her own voice over the pounding of her heart.

About ten minutes later Hans turned the car onto a winding dirt road, which they traveled for about half a mile. The land was densely forested on either side of the narrow road and it seemed they were going deep into some kind of wilderness. It was hard to imagine there was a compound situated on the side of this mountain, but Hans seemed certain of his direction.

All at once, they emerged from a thicket of trees onto a large, cleared plateau. In front of them stood a set of metal gates bracketed by high concrete walls, like some kind of fortress. As the car approached, the gates opened slowly inward and they drove through.

Jaime drew in her breath at the sight of the huge house, a mansion really. It was built of a combination of stone and wood, with lots of large windows, the effect at once grand and welcoming. Hans pulled into the curved driveway in the front of the house and turned off the engine. Jaime, naked in the backseat, drew her arms instinctively around herself.

Hans climbed out of the car and walked swiftly around the back of it, a moment later pulling open her door. He held a slim black collar and leash in his hands. Jaime emerged from the car on wobbly legs, dizziness assailing her for a moment. It was quite a bit cooler at this higher altitude, and a soft breeze blew over her breasts, causing her nipples to stiffen. The paver stones of the driveway were hard beneath her bare feet.

"I—" she began, but Hans stopped her with a stern shake of his head.

"Shh. No words. Be silent and obey." He held up the collar by one of the O rings set at intervals along its length. "Lean your head forward and lift your hair," he instructed. Jaime obeyed, a sense of the surreal settling over her as he buckled the collar into place. The leash was also made of leather, save for a small length of chain at its end. Hans clipped the leash to her collar and turned toward the building, indicating with a gentle tug of the leash that she should follow.

As they walked along the stone walkway set in the center of an immaculate, emerald-green lawn, Jaime glanced up at the many windows, opaque against the sun, wondering if they were being watched. At the large double doors of the entrance, Hans stopped and tugged downward on her leash. "Kneel as I instructed you," he said. "You will wait here until someone comes for you."

"Yes, Sir," Jaime murmured. She sank to her knees, still not quite able to get her head around the fact that this place actually existed, and she was really doing this. Hans watched as she lifted her arms and laced her fingers behind her head. The leash hung down between her breasts.

"Wider," he said, nudging the inside of her right thigh with the toe of his boot. "Offer yourself." Jaime spread her knees and thrust her breasts forward. She lifted her chin and focused on the door, her heart doing somersaults in her chest.

Hans bent down suddenly and Jaime flinched, certain he was going to slap her. But he only leaned close, his mouth near her ear. "Good luck," he whispered, and then he stepped inside, leaving her alone as the door clicked shut behind him.

Jaime closed her eyes. The mountain air was so fresh, scented with pine and honeysuckle, and she drew in deep breaths, letting them out slowly. The collar around her neck felt just right. She wanted to stroke the soft, strong leather but she didn't dare move out of position.

Though it seemed much longer, it was probably only about two minutes before the door opened. Two men, neither of them Anthony, stood before her. They regarded her for several long moments. She felt herself blushing beneath their intent gazes, but she managed to hold her position, though her arms were beginning to tremble from the strain.

"Stand up, slave Jaime," said the shorter of the two men, as he reached down and took the end of her leash. His voice was strident, his mouth curved down in a frown. He appeared to be in his mid thirties, with thinning sandy blond hair, pale eyes and thin lips. He was slender with a wiry build, and clad in black leather from head to toe. As Jaime rose to her feet, he added, "I am Master Lawrence. And this"—he waved toward the man beside him—"is Master Mark."

"You may put your arms down at your sides," Master Mark added in a pleasing baritone. He was younger than Master Lawrence, in his early thirties, Jaime surmised. He was about six feet tall, with broad shoulders and dark brown thick, curly hair. His eyes were a lively green-brown over a prominent nose and a generous mouth. Though not in leather, Master Mark was also in black—black jeans, a black knit shirt and black, square-toed boots. There was something familiar about him, as if she'd seen him before. Maybe at The Garden?

The rest of the world fell out of focus, blurring and falling away as she stared at the man, unable to look away, unable to recall where she was or what she was supposed to do. *Ah,* a small but certain voice whispered inside her. *There he is.*

"Let's go." Master Lawrence, still holding the leash, gave it a yank. The peculiar spell was broken and the world resumed its normal activity as Jaime stumbled forward before regaining her footing. They entered a large foyer. The floor was made from wide planked wood stained a rich chestnut. A huge grandfather clock stood against one wall, the wood frame of dark cherry, the large silver pendulum ticking loudly behind beveled glass.

That was where any typical foyer decoration ended, however. Several sets of rusty-looking manacles in various sizes had been hung along the walls, dangling from thick chains. Whips and floggers were positioned in X patterns, much like swords crossed on a coat of arms. An ominous iron device with cruelly curving talons hung above a large chair set against the wall, its base, arms and back covered in pointy spikes. "Some of Master Anthony's medieval torture collection," Master Mark said, following Jaime's horrified, fascinated gaze. "Be a good girl, and we won't have to put you in the Judas chair." He smiled, revealing even, white teeth. Jaime was far too nervous to smile back.

She was led on the leash through a huge living room that contained several distinct groupings of furniture. One wall was almost entirely of glass, opening onto a breathtaking, expansive view across the mountains and down into the valley below. There were two fireplaces, one of them big enough to walk into.

As they moved through the room, Jaime saw a couple sitting on the couch, a man in a chair nearby. Hans was kneeling beside the man's chair, the man's hand proprietarily on his shoulder. Hans was naked, save for his beautiful slave collar. His nipples were pierced with silver barbells, and his gaze was fixed on what Jaime knew in an instant must be his Master, the love light shining from Hans' eyes.

Instead of stopping for introductions, Jaime was marched past them and into a small, windowless room. The space was empty, save for a St. Andrew's cross set against one wall and a metal-barred cage, barely big enough for a large dog. An involuntary shudder of fear moved through her and she looked away. A thick flogger with many suede tresses hung on the wall beside the cross, a canister of whips and canes on the floor on its other side.

Master Lawrence removed the leash. "We received three reports from slave Hans," he said in his stern voice. "Before you are introduced to the others, you will have to be punished. Each transgression has earned you five strokes, for a total of fifteen. You will remain completely silent during the punishment, or we will be forced to begin again." He pointed toward the St. Andrew's cross. "Since you are not yet trained in the art of holding a position, you will be bound to the cross for your punishment."

Jaime stood in the center of the room, her heart slamming against her ribs. "Go on, move," Master Lawrence snapped. "Stand with your face to the cross. Master Mark will secure your wrists and ankles."

Jaime stepped onto the small raised platform at the foot of the cross. Her arms felt leaden as she lifted them against the smooth wood of the X. Hans had warned her she would be punished, but she hadn't expected it so soon.

Master Mark closed the thick nylon cuffs around each wrist, pressing the Velcro into place to bind her arms against the wood. He crouched behind her and tapped at her ankles, directing her to place her legs in position so he could secure them as well.

Jaime leaned into the cross with a sigh, the familiar, welcome sense of comfort at being securely bound offsetting somewhat the jangle of nerves still warring inside of her. She looked at the flogger—her favorite kind of whip. Fifteen strokes wasn't so much. She could certainly handle it. She would probably even enjoy it—she loved the caressing sting of soft suede tresses against her skin. Maybe this was just a symbolic kind of punishment, something designed to put her into the proper headspace, not that she needed it.

Yes, she could totally do this.

"Master Mark," Master Lawrence intoned. "The cane, if you please."

CHAPTER 4

The split-second warning whistle of bamboo hurtled through the air, but it was not enough to prepare her for the fiery stroke of impact. In spite of Master Lawrence's admonition, Jaime screamed.

"I heard a sound," came his voice from behind her. "Did you hear a sound, Master Mark?"

"I did." Master Mark appeared in Jaime's peripheral vision, and she turned her head toward his voice. She was breathing too fast, her head spinning. She'd been caned before, many times, but never like this. Never without the slow, sensual warming of the skin, the steadily increasing intensity that allowed her to tolerate, then accept, then embrace the sting.

Master Mark placed his hand on Jaime's shoulder and gave it a gentle squeeze. Warmth spread through her body at his touch, and her heart eased its rapid beat, at least a little. "Courage," he whispered.

Fortified by his touch and the masterful calm of his tone, she drew in a deep—

The second stroke caught her just as hard as the first, and just as unexpectedly, but somehow she managed to bite back the cry that rose in her throat, emitting only the tiniest of sounds. But was even that too much?

"One," intoned Master Lawrence.

Relief flooded Jaime, despite the fiery sting of the second welt she felt rising on her ass. They hadn't heard her muted cry. She could do this. *Just hang on, let the pain flow through you.*

Another whistle, followed instantly by the searing cut of the cane.

"Two."

Fuck. Oh fuck, fuck, fuck, fuck.

"Breathe."

Jaime tried to draw in a breath, but her lungs seemed to have collapsed.

"Three."

Jaime opened eyes she hadn't realized she'd squeezed shut. Master Mark was still beside her, his gaze steady on her face. She focused on his clear green-brown eyes. He had a dark, thick fringe of lashes, the kind women would kill for. He was really quite—

"Four."

Thought exploded like china dashed on stone.

"Five. Six…"

"Breathe. "His voice was soothing, even just the one word. She reached for it and clung.

"Seven. Eight. Nine."

She could do this. She was doing it. It wasn't so bad, not anymore. The skin was numbing, acclimating, she was more than halfway through. Her lips were sealed, her lungs had regained their ability to inflate, and Master Mark was still there, still watching, vigilant.

"Ten. Eleven. Twelve. Thirteen. Fourteen. Fifteen."

She sagged with relief, her head falling back, her mouth agape. Sweat pricked beneath her arms and at the nape of her neck. Her ass was in flames, but she had done it—she had taken her punishment.

The two men crouched on either side of her, each grabbing the edge of the thick nylon cuffs and yanking at the Velcro in unison. Jaime shifted, causing her leash, which had been hung over the center of the X, to clank lightly against the wood. Master Mark leaned across her back as he reached for both wrist cuffs. She could feel hard muscles beneath the soft fabric of his shirt as his body brushed hers. It took every ounce of self-control not to lean back into his inviting strength and warmth.

Stepping back, Master Mark reached around her and gripped the leash, pulling it up and to the side. He tugged lightly at the leash, directing her to turn so her back was now to the cross. He moved back, drawing her forward off the platform.

"Time to meet a few of our members," Master Lawrence said. Jaime was nonplussed, confused. Her ass was stinging. One of the welts felt as if it might actually be bleeding! Where was the aftercare she received at the clubs—the healing lotion, the soothing words, the praise?

None, apparently, was forthcoming. Without a backward glance, Master Lawrence opened the door and walked back into the living room. Master Mark followed just behind him, Jaime in tow on her leash.

Hans was still there, though he now stood erect as a soldier behind his Master's chair. The man looked to be in his late thirties. He was quite handsome, with chiseled features, a square jaw and wavy brown hair streaked with blond, brushed straight back. There was an end table beside his chair with a tray containing a packet of surgical gloves, a tube of lubricant and a shiny black anal plug. Jaime eyed the tray with dismay, praying it wasn't there for her.

As they moved closer, she got a better look at the couple on the couch. Even seated, she could tell they were both tall, their builds slender but athletic. They appeared to be in their late forties or early fifties.

Behind the couch stood a young woman with curly red hair, round green eyes and a small rosebud of a mouth. She was naked, her large, heavy breasts marked with a crisscross of new and fading welts. A thick slave collar of rich, emerald-green leather circled her neck, sewn so it came together in a V at her throat. She offered the hint of a smile as she caught Jaime's eye. Jaime didn't dare to smile back.

Master Mark brought Jaime to a standstill in front of the gathered group. He removed the leash. "You may stand at ease," Master Lawrence said. "Hands clasped loosely behind your back, legs shoulder-width apart. You may look directly at whoever is speaking to you. You will obey every command without hesitation."

"Yes, Master Lawrence," Jaime said, pleased her voice didn't quaver. Master Mark took a seat on the other side of the woman on the couch. Master Lawrence sat on the empty chair to the right.

"We've heard a lot about you," the seated woman said. She had honey-blond hair cut to her shoulders. Her eyes were a clear, beautiful shade of green. She wore a figure-hugging black satin gown. Surprisingly, around her neck there was a silver leather collar studded with O-rings, a small heart-shaped crystal padlock at its center. While the piece was stunningly beautiful in its own right, it was clearly a slave collar. "I am Mistress Marjorie. Welcome to The Enclave." She smiled, the smile at once easy and somewhat sad, as if she saw the humor and the tragedy in everything at once.

"Thank you, Mistress," Jaime replied.

"I am Master Brandon," the man beside Mistress Marjorie said. His hair was auburn, trimmed short on the sides and swept to the side on top, with a whisper of gray at the sideburns. He was very tan, with rugged features and bright blue eyes. He, like Master Lawrence, was dressed in black leather. "We're pleased to have you as a training candidate. It's unfortunate you had to be punished immediately upon your arrival. Tell me, what did you do to earn that punishment, Jaime?"

"Oh, I, uh"—Jaime glanced helplessly at Hans, her mind suddenly blank. He stared back at her impassively. Her eyes flitted toward Master Mark, who nodded ever so slightly. Jaime's mind clicked back on. "I didn't obey quickly enough when Master Hans—"

"Slave Hans," interjected the man in the chair. "Hans belongs to me. I am Master Julian." Master Julian spoke in a posh British accent that instantly charmed Jaime.

"Slave Hans," she amended. "I failed to address him properly, and I, uh, I didn't obey quickly enough, Sir."

"Turn around," Master Brandon said. "Show us your welts." Flustered, Jaime did as she was told.

"Beautiful," Mistress Marjorie murmured. A sudden rush of pride swelled inside Jaime.

"Remain facing away from us, but come closer," Master Brandon continued. "I want to examine the welts."

Jaime obeyed, stepping backward toward the couch. She jumped slightly as fingers glided over her sensitized skin. She gasped as they stroked the most painful of the welts. "You have delicate skin," he remarked. "We'll toughen that up over the next two weeks, won't we?"

"We will, indeed," Master Lawrence, whom Jaime could see in her peripheral vision, remarked dryly, and there was laughter.

"Step forward and bend over," Master Julian said, once the laughter subsided. "Spread your ass cheeks. I want to inspect your asshole."

Taking a breath, Jaime forced her hands to unclasp as she bent forward. She moved quickly, not daring to risk another punishment. She reached for her bottom and pulled at the welted flesh to expose herself, glad her flaming face was hidden from scrutiny.

"Hans," Master Julian said from behind her, "give me a glove and some lube. Let's see how tight this girl is."

"Yes, Master Julian," Hans replied.

Jaime remained in her awkward, bent position as Master Julian presumably prepared himself behind her. Though she knew to expect it, she jumped when she felt his hands on her—one hand gripping her hip while a thick, hard, but mercifully lubricated and gloved finger pushed insistently into her ass.

"Yes…good…nice and tight," Master Julian murmured approvingly as he probed her most private orifice. "Do you like ass play, Jaime?"

How to answer? *No, I fucking hate any attention to my asshole, please stop at once?* But that wasn't entirely true, was it? While it was humiliating, and not directly sexually stimulating to her, hadn't she experienced the second most powerful orgasm of her life while her ass was plugged on Mistress Aubrey's exam table?

Just answer honestly, a small voice whispered inside her head. "It makes me nervous, Sir. I'm not used to it…yet."

"*Yet*. I like that," Master Julian replied, and she could hear the smile in his voice. "We'll be sure to work on that while you're here, since I only like to fuck slaves in the ass—I'm sure you understand." Some of the others chuckled.

His finger was withdrawn, and Jaime started to rise, but his hand pressed firmly against her lower back. "Remain in position. I didn't tell you to move. Keep your cheeks spread. I'm going to insert the plug. You will keep it inside your ass during the rest of our welcome interview."

"Yes, Sir," Jaime managed through clenched jaws.

She flinched when the head of the plug touched her anus. She felt awkward and uncomfortable, bent over as she was, all eyes no doubt on her exposed asshole. She told herself to calm down, to breathe, but she wasn't really listening. All she could manage was to tough it out.

The plug pushed slowly into her. "Relax," Master Julian admonished gently. His other hand had remained firmly on her back, his touch centering and reassuring. "This is the last bit." There came the sudden but short-lived burst of pain as the fat end of the plug slipped inside her. Jaime gasped and then sighed with relief. The damn thing was in. Master Julian's hand fell away from her back.

"You may stand and face us," he said. As she obeyed, Master Julian returned to his seat. He held out his gloved hand toward Hans, who slipped it off and dropped it into a small trashcan near the end table before returning to his post behind Master Julian's chair.

"Do you like girls?" Master Brandon asked suddenly, peering intently at her with his brilliant blue eyes.

"I'm sorry, Sir?" she replied, confused.

"Girls. Pussy. Sex with other women," he clarified, his tone impatient.

Feeling like an idiot, Jaime stammered, "Uh, not really. I mean, I've never had sex with a girl, if that's what you mean, Sir." Her eyes flitted involuntarily toward the naked girl standing silently behind the couch.

"You've never done it, but that doesn't mean you wouldn't like it," Master Brandon replied. "Love and sex exist along a continuum of desire for most people. It's a matter of learning your true self—of jettisoning all the societal dictates and nonsense that can shut you down before you've even given yourself a chance. An open mind and a willingness to learn are all you need. Isn't that right, Marjorie?" He put his hand proprietarily on Mistress Marjorie's thigh.

"It is, Master Brandon," she said softly, beaming at him.

"Perhaps a brief demonstration is in order?" Master Mark spoke, his question directed toward Master Brandon. Jaime's eyes moved toward the pleasing sound of his baritone. Then her mind processed his words, and she tensed.

"Excellent idea," Master Brandon agreed. He twisted back to the slave girl behind the couch. "A good opportunity for you, as well, slave Katie, to demonstrate your obedience."

Red color seeped like spilled paint over Katie's fair complexion, and Jaime's stomach dropped. Whatever was about to happen, it was going to happen between the two of them, and this girl looked as nervous as Jaime felt.

Mistress Marjorie shifted on the couch, nudging Master Mark to the edge as she made a space between herself and Master Brandon. She patted the cushions. "Come sit between us, slave Katie," she said gently.

"Yes, Mistress," Katie said in a low, pleasing voice. She came from behind the high-backed sofa. She was of medium height with a little extra meat on her bones, though she carried it well. Her pretty face remained beet red as she settled herself between the couple.

"Scoot forward," Mistress Marjorie instructed the girl. "Spread your legs. Jaime is going to lick your cunt to orgasm. You will ask for permission to come, of course."

"Yes, Mistress," Katie said in a small voice.

Master Brandon reached for Katie's arms, capturing both her wrists in one hand. He pulled her arms upward over her head and held them there. "You," he said, pointing with his free hand toward Jaime. "Get on your knees and get to work. I assume you understand the mechanics of the task, even if you've never done it before?"

Jaime swallowed hard. She looked from face to face. They were all watching her—judging her, and no doubt finding her wanting. She felt lightheaded as she sank to her knees.

Katie looked incredibly vulnerable, naked between the Dominants, her arms held high over her head, her thighs parted. The small voice in Jaime's head was whispering furiously now, and she tried to listen. *Don't fuck this up, Jaime Lee Shepard. It's just a pussy, for heaven's sake. You have one. You know what to do. Just do what you like to have done to you. Stop being such a baby. This is a test. They are testing you. Don't fail!*

She took a deep breath and blew it out. She scooted closer to the girl, until she was right between her knees. Carefully, cautiously, she placed a hand on either thigh and gently pushed Katie's legs a little wider. She studiously avoided looking up into Katie's face, and instead focused on the pierced pussy directly in front of her. Katie was shaven smooth. She had piercings along both sides of her outer labia, three to a side, each containing a small, thin gold hoop. Her inner labia were a darker pink than the outer, folded like the petals of an orchid. The hood of her clit was pierced as well, with what looked like a real diamond.

You can do this. You can do this.

Tentatively, Jaime snaked out her tongue and touched the delicate folds of flesh with the tip. Katie flinched slightly. "Offer yourself, slave Katie," Mistress Marjorie said softly. "This is your gift of submission, remember?"

"Yes, Mistress," Katie breathed. Jaime felt suddenly better—even this obviously well-trained full-time staff slave needed encouragement and reminders. She touched the soft folds again with her tongue, and this time drew it up along the curve of flesh. She moved it in a circle around the diamond and Katie sighed softly. Emboldened, Jaime pulled a little on Katie's inner thighs for better access. She licked along the inner labia, fluttering her tongue as she moved. The skin was silky soft. Katie sighed again.

Jaime realized she'd been holding her breath. Her tongue still moving over the now moistening folds, she breathed in through her nose. Katie's scent was a mixture of soap with a hint of something sweet, like honey, and an underlay of spicy musk. To her surprise, Jaime found the smell intoxicating rather than off-putting, as she'd feared. She became aware of her own pussy in that moment; of the gentle throb of desire pulsing at her core.

She licked with more pressure, running her tongue directly over the hard diamond and feeling the rise of Katie's clit beneath it. Katie's moan was more audible now, the scent of her arousal stronger. Jaime focused on and around the hood of flesh until it began to miraculously contract, revealing the hard purple nubbin of Katie's clit beneath it.

Aware of her own sensitivity to too much direct stimulation, Jaime shifted her focus, licking in lazy, sensual circles over Katie's pussy. She even poked the tip of her tongue into the silky wetness of her entrance, and Katie shuddered and shifted beneath her. Jaime held her still, her grip firm on Katie's thighs.

After teasing Katie this way for a while, Jaime realized she was having fun. This wasn't horrible at all. It was similar to the rush she got when pleasing a man, but with something sweeter beneath it, somehow more tender. Katie's responsiveness was thrilling.

Jaime alternated her strokes, flicking lightly at Katie's clit, and then sliding away. Finally Katie began to tremble, her thighs hot beneath Jaime's hands, her clit pulsing against Jaime's tongue. "Oh god, oh Sir, oh Mistress!" Katie cried. "May I, oh, may I come, please?" she begged breathlessly.

"Yes, slave Katie," Mistress Marjorie replied calmly. "You may come."

"And you, Jaime," Master Brandon added. "You are not to stop until you have permission."

Jaime nodded as best she could with her head buried between Katie's thighs, to show she had heard. Katie begun to buck against her, her movement punctuated with breathy cries. After several long seconds, the girl sagged back, her thighs pressing against Jaime's hands as if she would close them.

Jaime kept her grip, however, mindful of Master Brandon's dictate. Holding Katie open, she continued to lick and suckle the engorged, slick folds of Katie's cunt. Katie lay limp at first, but after a minute or so she stiffened and began to squeal, little high-pitched yips. Jaime wanted to stop, worried she was over-stimulating the girl, aware of how easily the pleasure could turn to irritation, even pain, after a certain point. But Master Brandon had been very specific in his orders, and she was determined to obey.

Finally Katie began to shudder. Her whole body trembled, her thighs slippery with sweat beneath Jaime's hands, her clit hard as a glass bead beneath Jaime's tongue. She moaned, the sound low and guttural, and then she went completely limp and silent, not even a rasp of breath audible in the silent room. For a frightening split-second, Jaime thought she'd killed her.

"Breathe," Mistress Marjorie said softly, and, thank goodness, Katie did.

Jaime felt a hand on her head. "You may sit back," Master Brandon said.

Jaime obeyed, leaning back onto her haunches, exultant. She had made a girl come! And not just some wimpy little 'gasm. She'd practically knocked the girl unconscious!

"Proud of yourself, aren't you." Master Lawrence's voice cut across her thoughts. The sentence was declarative, rather than a question. Jaime glanced in his direction, her heart dropping at his stern expression. "Pride has a place in a slave's repertoire," he continued, his voice soft but edged with danger, "but not the pride of power over another. No, your pride should be in obedience and service. In doing what you are told and doing it well."

"That hunger for power will need to be beaten out of her," Master Julian remarked as Jaime's triumph vanished beneath their criticism.

"Indeed," Master Brandon added, his tone dry. "I would say daily beatings are definitely in order for this one."

Jaime was suddenly aware of the plug still embedded in her ass. Her face was soaked with her own saliva and Katie's juices, but she didn't dare to wipe it off. She was hot and sweaty, and suddenly very thirsty. Her jawed ached. This was so unfair! She'd done everything they asked of her. Could she help it if she'd been proud of her accomplishment? She looked down at the ground.

"It takes a lot of courage to be a true slave, Jaime," Mistress Marjorie said quietly. "The most difficult thing to let go of is ego. You're used to a different world, where submission is a game in a carefully controlled scene at a public club. This two weeks is designed to give you a glimpse into our world, and to understand that it isn't for everyone."

Her gentle touch on the top of Jaime's head made the tears fall, and Jaime tried to blink them back. "You are used to having the focus on *you*. You've probably heard it many times before—it's all about the submissive. She remains in ultimate control, because she controls the scene. You are obsessed with your own pleasure and pain, and your effect on your Dom. When do you get a whipping, when do you get to come, does your Dom find you sexy, attractive, submissive, obedient? The underlying theme here is ego."

Mistress Marjorie placed her finger just beneath Jaime's chin, forcing her to raise her head. She gazed at Jaime with sharp, knowing eyes. "If you choose to stay with us, Jaime, and if we choose to accept you, the pride, the vanity, must go. You will learn by observing and experiencing the training process, which, as you're probably gathering, won't always be easy and won't always be fun. But in the process, if you can set aside your preconceptions, your fear, and most especially your ego, you will achieve a level of peace and actualization that is tremendously freeing."

Jaime nodded slowly, Mistress Marjorie's words resonating in her soul. The jittery anxiety and sense of indignation she'd experienced had evaporated, replaced by a fledgling sense of calm that was new to Jaime.

"Yes, Mistress Marjorie," she said. "Thank you." She turned slowly to look at each person in the room, including Katie and Hans. "Thank you all."

CHAPTER 5

Katie preceded Jaime down a set of narrow concrete stairs, the way lit by sconces of brushed nickel set along the walls. Though her leash had been removed, the anal plug was still very much present inside her. "Are we allowed to speak?" she whispered as they descended to what must be the basement.

"Sure," Katie said in a normal tone of voice. "Once you put your foot on these stairs, it's considered the slave quarters. We're permitted to speak freely down here, unless there is a Master or Mistress present." She flashed a shy smile at Jaime. "You said you didn't have experience with girls, but you sure seemed to know what you were doing up there."

Jaime smiled and shrugged. "I tried to do what I would want done, I guess. You were, uh, very responsive." She felt her own face flushing.

Katie beamed. "Thank you. It's been a lot of work for me—the hardest part of my training, by far. Before I got here, I'd never had an orgasm."

"Never had an orgasm?" Jaime blurted, shocked.

They'd reached the bottom of the stairs. Jaime looked around, realizing she'd expected a typical basement—concrete walls and floors—but that wasn't what she found. The space opened into a large, finished room with thick carpeting on the floor, the walls painted a pleasing, pale yellow. The space was softly lit with more wall sconces, and there was a grouping of chairs and a sofa in one corner of the room.

"I love to serve others," Katie explained. "But sex"—she wrapped her arms protectively around her torso, her voice dropping to a whisper—"I mean when I'm the center of attention, it makes me uncomfortable. I've lost a lot of weight since I got here, but I'm still kind of dumpy, you know, and—"

"You're not dumpy," Jaime interjected. "You have a lovely body." It was true. Though she was heavyset, Katie was curvaceous, her skin creamy smooth.

"Thanks," Katie said softly, her cheeks still pink. "Mistress Marjorie tells me that every day. Hopefully, I'll actually believe it one day."

Her hand fluttered to her slave collar, prompting Jaime to ask the question that had been in her mind since she'd entered The Enclave. "Your collar, it's so unique. All the staff slaves have such beautiful collars." Jaime's hand went to her own collar, which, while simple, was buttery soft, the O-rings expertly hand-stitched into place. "Even this collar they've given me feels like such quality."

"That's my Master's handiwork." Katie beamed. "Master Brandon makes all the collars for The Enclave. It started as a hobby for him—he loves to work with leather—but word's gotten out in the BDSM community. Apparently people are always pestering him to make custom collars. He's thinking of starting a cottage industry, now that he's retired from banking. He's been teaching me a little about the process, and even lets me do some of the cutting and stitching." She stroked her collar lovingly as she spoke, her green eyes sparkling with pride.

The distant sound of a clock's chime from upstairs made Katie move her hand from her collar to her mouth. "Come on," she said, quickening her pace. "We only have fifteen minutes before lunch. Our quarters are back here. I'll show you."

"Um, this plug?" Jaime said. "Can I take this thing out? I was afraid to ask up there, but it's bugging me."

Katie shook her head. "It can come out, but you're not to do it.

Mistress Marjorie told me I was to remove it for you when we came down. Let's go to the bathroom first and take care of that."

"You're to remove it?" Jaime asked, dismayed. "But I can do it myself…"

She trailed off in the face of Katie's expression. "No," Katie repeated firmly. "You cannot. Unless you were specifically directed to do so?" She lifted her eyebrows skeptically. Jaime reluctantly shook her head.

"That's what I thought. Be careful, Jaime, about doing something like that without permission. I mean, don't even think about it. Forget everything you ever knew or thought you knew about D/s scenes. For the next two weeks at least, you are in one long, continuous training scene and the rules are very exact. Your job is to listen and obey to the best of your ability. Don't ever make assumptions or decide to do something on your own without express direction or permission. That's a sure way to get punished, and fast."

As Jaime absorbed the warning, Katie led her down a hallway, the floor of smooth, polished wood. They moved past doorless rooms, four on each side of the hallway, each containing a full bed set in a wooden frame and a small bureau. The beds were neatly made with quilts in pastel colors. Despite the lack of windows, the rooms were bright from indirect lighting, the walls painted in soothing blue. Jaime had envisioned some kind of bunk bed, dormitory type arrangement and was pleasantly surprised by the accommodations.

The end of the hallway opened into a spacious bathroom. The bathroom contained a row of doorless toilet stalls against one of the walls. Showerheads protruded from the tile on an adjacent wall, a drain set into the flooring beneath each shower. There was a counter in which four sinks were set, a drawer beneath each sink. Fluffy white towels of varying sizes were stacked beside each basin. There was a large sunken tub in one corner of the room. Above the standard faucets at the head of the tub, there hung a long, detachable showerhead with a spray nozzle at its end.

"Bend over here," Katie said, moving toward the sinks. She turned on a faucet in the basin at the far end of the counter. "This last sink is for cleaning equipment and toys." She picked up a small bottle of dishwashing liquid and squeezed a stream of it into the water. "I'll just drop your plug in there. You can take care of it after you clean yourself."

She spoke so matter-of-factly Jaime almost forgot to be embarrassed as she leaned over the counter, legs spread, bottom out. She was just glad the thing would be removed. Katie reached bare-handed for the base of the plug and gave it a firm tug. After a bit of initial resistance, it slid easily out of Jaime's bottom. She stood abruptly and closed her legs.

Katie dropped the plug into the water and then turned off the faucet. She moved to another sink to soap and rinse her hands. She gestured with her head toward the toilets. "The end one is a bidet. You can wash yourself there."

"A what?" Jaime looked down at the last toilet, which did look different from the others, its shape more elongated. It had no seat. There was a set of faucets at the back.

"A bidet," Katie repeated. "You know, like in Europe? It's like a mini bathtub for your privates." She giggled. "I'd never seen one either when I got here, but they're very handy for quick cleanups. You just crouch over it facing the faucets and turn them on. You can adjust the temperature just like you would a bath. It fills really fast, and there's an automatic dispenser in there that adds soap to the bowl as it fills. You can use one of those washcloths there to clean yourself." Jaime saw the small stack of white washcloths neatly folded on a wide shelf above the bidet. A larger stack of hand towels rested neatly beside the washcloths.

Intrigued, Jaime crouched as directed, facing backward on the porcelain. She turned on the faucets, causing two jets of water to spray into the bowl, one cold, the other first warm and then quite hot. Purple liquid also seeped into the bowl, the smell of fresh lavender and lemon wafting up from the now bubbling water. After a moment, Jaime turned off the faucets, the bowl now filled. She reached for a washcloth. "Wow, this is really cool," she enthused as she washed herself with the warm, scented water.

"Yeah," Katie agreed. "I love it. But you better hurry up. I still need to inspect you and show you your room."

"Inspect me?" Jaime asked, confused.

"Yes. We have to make sure you're properly groomed before your training session this afternoon. Lucia handles daily grooming first thing in the mornings, but she's not available right now."

"Lucia?"

"Yes, another of the staff slaves. You'll meet everyone who's on the grounds at lunch."

Jaime toweled herself dry and dropped both the wet and the dry towels into the small hamper beside the bidet. Katie led her to the center of the bathroom. She tilted her head as she eyed Jaime's naked body with a critical expression. "Put your arms up, hands behind your head and spread your legs. I'm going to do a check to feel for any stubble. It's kind of, um, personal." She flashed another shy smile.

Jaime assumed the position, silently marveling how quickly she'd become accustomed to being naked. It helped that both Katie and Hans were naked—it wasn't like she was being singled out or anything. Katie moved to stand behind her. She jerked away involuntarily as Katie's fingers trailed along her underarms. "That tickles!"

"Get used to it," Katie replied tersely. "You move around like that when a Master is inspecting you and you'll be sorry."

"I can't help it!" Jaime protested.

"You better learn to, then," Katie said ominously. "Let me try again, and this time concentrate on holding your position." She ran her fingers lightly along Jaime's armpits. It tickled just as much, but she was more prepared and managed to stay still.

"See?" Katie said from behind her. "That wasn't so hard, right? And your underarms are nice and smooth, good job. Staff slaves are to be smooth at all times, unless otherwise directed. It's a matter of accessibility and vulnerability."

Katie crouched behind her and ran her hands lightly up and down Jaime's legs, again tickling her, though it wasn't as bad as under her arms. "Okay," Katie said, standing. "You're good. Now your pussy and ass. I've found it's easiest to check when you're sitting down." She moved toward the tub. "Sit here on the edge so I have easy access. Spread your legs as wide as you can."

Jaime did as she was told, vaguely embarrassed by the position, in spite of the fact she'd licked this girl's pussy just a while before, with much the same view she was now offering Katie. Though she didn't relish the idea of Katie inspecting her pussy and ass for errant hairs, if she'd missed a spot, it was far better for a staff slave to discover the problem than anyone upstairs.

Katie crouched before her, a look of concentration on her face as she ran her fingers lightly over Jaime's mons and labia. She ran a finger down to Katie's nether entrance and rimmed it lightly. Jaime was about to close her legs, when Katie said, "Uh oh. You missed a spot right here." She stroked the skin between Jaime's two holes. "We better fix it real quick. You just stay right there."

Katie jumped up and rushed over to the sinks. She opened a drawer and pulled out a fresh disposable razor and a small tube of something. She turned on the faucet and reached for a fresh washcloth from the stack. While she was doing this, Jaime reached down to touch the area in question. Sure enough, she could feel a small, soft patch of fine pubic hairs. How had she missed that? She'd been so careful that morning, or so she'd believed.

Katie returned to her with the items in hand and crouched once more. "Lucia will groom you in the tub every morning, but we don't have time for that right now." She uncapped the tube and squeezed a small amount onto her fingers, which she smeared onto Jaime's perineum. She then sat beside Jaime on the sill of the tub. "Okay, hold still." She placed one hand on Jaime's thigh, and used the other to gently glide the razor along Jaime's skin. She followed up with her finger. "Perfect," she announced.

She jumped up and handed Jaime the washcloth. "Wipe off the shaving cream and let's get a move on." She returned to the sink and put away the items. "You can drop the washcloth in with your plug. Go ahead and rinse it off now. It's soaked long enough."

Jaime wiped off the remnant of shaving cream with the damp cloth and stood. She moved toward the last sink and pushed down the lever to release the sink plug. Ignoring her distaste for the task, she picked up the anal plug by its base and ran clear water over it as the sink emptied. She reached for another clean washcloth and set the plug on it while she rinsed the damp cloth and wrung it out.

"Good," Katie said, moving to stand beside her. "Dry off the plug and then just drop the used washcloths in the hamper there." She pointed to another hamper, this one to the left of the sink. "That plug belongs to you now. There's a container for it in your bureau. Come on"—she glanced at the wall over the tub, and Jaime, following her gaze, saw the clock affixed there—"we just have time for me to show you your room and then we have to get back upstairs."

Holding the plug gingerly between thumb and forefinger, Jaime followed Katie out of the bathroom. "Do all the staff slaves sleep down here?"

"No," Katie said. "Only those who are not specifically owned. That would include Lucia, Danielle, and now you." She smiled brightly at Jaime. They stopped at the door on the left closest to the bathroom. The room was identical to the others, the bed inviting with its pale blue coverlet and plump pillows, except for one thing.

Above the bed affixed to a large eyebolt embedded in the wall, hung a long chain, a pair of wrist cuffs secured at the ends of the chain. At the base of the mattress lay a long metal bar with cuffs on either end. Jaime drew in a breath and took an involuntary step back, bumping into Katie, who stood just behind her.

Katie put a comforting arm on her shoulder. "Those chains?" Jaime squeaked. "Those cuffs? Do I have to sleep in those?"

"It's just for two weeks," Katie said, her tone sympathetic. "And, yes, you will sleep chained during the two-week training. I admit it takes a little getting used to, but just focus on the erotic aspect of it. Didn't you always dream of being a naked slave girl chained to her bed, just waiting to do her Master's bidding?"

Jaime had to admit that, yes, she'd had that precise fantasy. But fantasy, she was quickly coming to realize, was a lot easier to handle than the real thing. "What if there's, I don't know, a fire or something? Isn't this dangerous?"

Katie pointed to a small black webcam discreetly mounted high in one corner. "That surveillance camera has a microphone in it too, so they can hear if you call out or anything like that. The Masters never leave us unattended, so even if you're bound and gagged and left alone for hours on end, you're not really alone."

"Bound and gagged and left alone for hours on end…" Jaime repeated faintly, her heart jolting into an unpleasant rhythm. "They do that?"

"Only if you misbehave, silly," Katie said with a laugh. "Just be a good girl, and you have nothing to worry about."

~*~

Lunch consisted of tomato soup and grilled cheese, but not the canned, reconstituted soup and processed cheese food on white bread of Jaime's youth. Instead, the obviously homemade soup contained fresh tomatoes and basil, and the sandwiches were made from thick slices of cheddar cheese perfectly melted on buttery, toasted sourdough. Brewed iced tea and lemonade were set in large glass pitchers along the table.

Jaime hadn't been sure what to expect as far as a seating arrangement, having read novels where the slaves were expected to kneel beside their Masters and be handfed, or were forced to kneel in rows, eating with their mouths directly from bowls set on the ground. Instead, the subs entered the dining room first, waiting quietly behind their chairs as the Doms entered and took their seats around a long, rectangular table.

Jaime was delighted when Anthony came into the room, though she was reintroduced to him now as Master Anthony. He welcomed her warmly to The Enclave, and for the first time that day, she relaxed, at least a little. Master Brandon sat to Anthony's left, Katie tucked between him and Mistress Marjorie. Master Julian was seated beside Mistress Marjorie, Hans to his left.

Master Mason, a big, burly man with a shaved head and tattoos, sat at the other end of the table, closest to the kitchen. To Master Mason's right was an empty chair, eventually occupied by Ashley, a staff slave who worked in the kitchen and had prepared the lunch that day, which she served with the help of another staff slave named Lucia, who sat on Master Mason's left.

Ashley, who appeared to be in her mid to late twenties, had pixyish features and very closely cropped hair, really little more than a crew cut. She was petite with small, high breasts, multiple piercings along both ears and in both nipples as well as her eyebrow and lower lip. She, like Master Mason, had multiple tattoos along her arms and on her back.

Lucia was in her early forties with lovely coppery skin and black hair that framed a face with eyes so darkly brown there was almost no demarcation between the iris and pupil. After serving, she slid silently into a chair beside Master Lawrence, who sat on Master Anthony's left.

Between Master Lawrence and Master Mark sat slave Danielle, who Jaime guessed to be in her mid twenties. She was lovely to look at, with a sheet of very straight, very blond hair hanging in a shiny curtain down her long, slender back. She had large dark blue eyes, a pert nose and a bee-bitten mouth. While the others subs had smiled at Jaime, Danielle's plump lips had lifted into a curve that was more sneer than smile, her expression at once haughty and dismissive. Something about the girl's demeanor threatened to cast Jaime instantly back into middle school, until she came to her senses and realized she had nothing to fear from, or to prove to, this person. She was there to train and learn, not to compete in a popularity contest.

The two seats to Jaime's right were empty, and she deduced they must be for Mistress Aubrey and Gene, who probably remained in town during the workday. Master Mark was on her left. Her skin actually tingled when his hand lightly brushed her arm at one point when he reached for something on the table.

The Doms talked among themselves as they ate, making small talk about local politics, the Asheville food scene and the weather. When everyone was finished eating, Master Anthony asked, "So, what are everyone's plans for the afternoon?"

Master Mason said, "Ashley and Lucia are with me. We're going to work in the vegetable garden and then they're both going to work on their cock sucking skills, isn't that right, slave girls?"

"Yes, Sir," the pair answered in unison, Ashley's tone strident, Lucia's barely a whisper.

"We have plans for Katie involving trust and water play," Master Brandon volunteered, his eyes flashing as he fixed his gaze on Katie, who kept her eyes on the table. Mistress Marjorie nodded, placing her hand lightly over Katie's.

"Anthony, I need to talk to you about some financial issues this afternoon, if you have the time," Master Lawrence said.

"Not a problem," Master Anthony replied. "I do want to connect with slave Jaime, but that can wait until later." Jaime smiled gratefully at him, also eager to reconnect with the man who had brought her here in the first place.

"It's such a lovely summer day," Master Julian said, fixing his eye on Jaime. "I think Hans and I will take the newbie out and put her through a few, uh, exercises." His eyes twinkled evilly, and Jaime had a sudden fantasy of him twirling his mustache like a villain in a silent film, though he was clean-shaven. Her stomach, meanwhile, dropped like an ancient elevator lurching to life, and she wished she hadn't eaten quite so much of the delicious food.

"Great idea," enthused Master Mark. He turned to his right, placing his hand on Danielle's bare shoulder. "Take Jaime back to the mudroom and fit her out with some hiking gear and supplies while we decide on a game plan for the two of you."

"Yes, Master Mark," Danielle said in a thick Southern drawl, batting long, perfect lashes in his direction and swishing her shiny blond hair. "Right away, Sir." She pushed back her chair and stood, not even glancing in Jaime's direction.

Jaime, uncertain, glanced across the table toward Katie, who mouthed silently, "Go."

Jaime rose to her feet as well, wondering if she was supposed to take her plate to the kitchen. Danielle was already disappearing through the swinging kitchen doors, her plate left on the table. Taking Danielle's lead, Jaime hurried to the doors and pushed through.

The kitchen was huge, with top-of-the-line stainless steel appliances, granite-topped counters and hanging pots and pans, everything gleaming and in its place. She caught sight of Danielle's retreating back as she moved through a doorway.

Following, Jaime entered what must be the mudroom, though it looked nothing like her parents' mudroom back in Vermont, which had been filled year-round with boots, umbrellas, jackets, parkas, sweaters, scarves, gloves and mittens, much of it piled in corners, some of it undisturbed probably since Jaime had been in the third grade.

This mudroom also contained jackets, coats and boots, but everything was neatly arranged and stowed. There were cabinets hung all around the walls, some of them extending to the ground. Danielle stopped in front of one of these and pulled open the doors. Without looking at Jaime, she said, "What size are your feet? Nine? Ten?"

"Uh, eight, actually." Jaime moved beside Danielle, who was eyeing a neat stack of shoe boxes.

Danielle shifted as she approached, obscuring Jaime's view of the boxes. "Too bad," she announced, reaching for a box and then slamming the cabinet closed. "The smallest size here is a nine. But no biggie"—she yanked open a drawer and pulled out two pairs of thick socks, which she tossed in Jaime's direction—"you can just double up on the socks. You'll be fine." Her drawl, Jaime couldn't help but observe, was much less noticeable.

Jaime automatically caught the socks, though just barely. She wasn't thrilled about the idea of hiking in new shoes that were a size too big. "Are you sure?" she asked. "Can I just check if—"

"No," Danielle said forcefully. "I told you that's all there is. You better move your ass and get those socks and boots on. We're going on a hike, girl. Didn't you hear the Masters?" Danielle reached for a pair of boots from a neat row and sat on the floor, pulling out the socks stowed inside her boots.

They put on their footwear in silence. Jaime had a lot of questions, but didn't feel comfortable asking Danielle. She was confused by Danielle's cold, even hostile reception, especially after Katie's warm welcome. Had she done something wrong? She almost opened her mouth to ask, but the sound of footsteps approaching silenced her.

Hans appeared and also moved toward the wall along which the boots were aligned, reaching for a large pair. More comfortable with him, Jaime asked, "What about clothing? We aren't going out hiking naked, are we, Hans?"

"Of course we are. We're slaves," he replied as if the question were absurd. Then, his tone softer, he added, "If you are worried about being observed, don't. The Enclave is in a secluded area and the land is private. It's only occasionally that hikers stray onto our land, and if they do"—he shrugged elaborately—"it's their problem, isn't it?"

"You have an issue with being naked, newbie?" Danielle asked, her face once more twisted into a sneer. "It's a little late for that, isn't it? I thought you were a sub?"

"It's her first day, Danielle," Hans interjected. "Cut her some slack."

"Oh, I can cut her all the slack in the world, but that's not going to help her when her training really starts." Danielle fixed her large, beautiful eyes on Jaime and flashed a dazzling smile that came nowhere near her eyes. "You think you can just waltz in here with those fake tits and that spray-on tan and have your pick of the single Masters, but you got another think coming. Don't get too comfortable, is all I've got to say."

Jaime stared, dumbstruck, her mouth falling open. *Fake tits? Spray-on tan? What the fuck?* "I don't—" she began indignantly.

"Shh," Hans interrupted. "The Masters."

Jaime bit back her retort as they listened to the masculine rumble of voices and the clomping of boots along the kitchen floor. Hans and Danielle both shifted quickly so they were kneeling up, their arms behind their backs, their eyes down. Jaime struggled to follow suit, though her bootlaces were not yet tied.

She could see the Doms' boots appear in her line of vision, Master Mark standing in front of Danielle, Master Julian in front of Hans. As if it had been choreographed, each slave leaned gracefully down and brushed the top of their Master's boot with their lips. Jaime glanced sidelong at them, biting back a sigh of envy as Master Mark stroked Danielle's pretty head.

At a tap on the shoulder, both slaves rose back to a kneeling position. Master Mark's boots appeared in front of Jaime and his hand rested lightly on her head. "Stand up, Jaime."

Jaime rose to her feet, her heart beating rapidly. The too-big shoes felt clunky on her feet. It was odd to be wearing hiking boots and nothing else. Master Mark pointed at the boots. "Make sure and tie those laces securely." As Jaime crouched down to obey, Master Mark set down a large backpack. "You'll be carrying this pack on the trails."

Jaime looked at the canvas backpack and nodded. "Yes, Sir." When her shoes were tied, she stood once more. Danielle and Hans were standing at attention. They, too, were now wearing backpacks on their shoulders, though their packs were smaller than Jaime's.

Hans stood erect as a soldier, his body smooth, muscular and tan. Danielle stood proudly as well, her high, round breasts thrust forward, the pretty, dark pink nipples erect at their tips. Her rude, unfounded jibes still rankled, but Jaime made a conscious effort to let it go. Somehow they had got off on the wrong foot, but she would do her best to make it right. She would need to get along with this girl, at least for the next two weeks.

Taking her cue from the others, Jaime hoisted her pack onto her shoulders. It was surprisingly heavy, which made her wonder what was inside, not that she dared to look without permission.

Both Masters had changed into jeans and T-shirts. Master Julian opened the back door of the mudroom, and they filed out into the afternoon sunlight. They stopped just outside the door. To their left was a large vegetable garden with vines laden with tomatoes, some small and green, some plump, red and ready for picking. There were neat rows of basil, dill, rosemary, fennel and other herbs Jaime didn't immediately recognize. The air was fresh and cool, a slight breeze offsetting the warmth of the sun.

"Oh," she breathed, taking in the spectacular view. Beyond several flower beds filled with blooms stood a placid lake glittering in the dappled sunlight, ducks and geese paddling on the water. Beside the lake was a wooded forest, and beyond that, a breathtaking view of mountain vistas, purplish blue in the distance. The place really was a paradise.

Both Danielle and Hans removed their backpacks and set them on the ground. After a quick nod from Hans, Jaime did the same.

"Sunscreen," Master Julian said. Danielle opened her backpack and produced two containers of spray-on sunscreen. The three slaves were directed to spread their arms and turn slowly as Master Mark and Master Julian covered their exposed skin with the spray. When they were done, Master Mark handed baseball caps to each of them, and Jaime pulled hers down over her ears, thinking what a peculiar picture the three of them made, naked in boots and caps. Finally ready, they hoisted their packs into place once more.

"Okay, then, kids," Master Julian said with a broad smile as he cupped Hans' smooth balls in one large hand. "Let's take a hike."

CHAPTER 6

Jaime couldn't help but glance continually around for any trespassers as they moved through the open space behind the house. She saw no one, but was relieved nonetheless when they entered the cover of the trees. Their boots crunched softly along paths carpeted with dried pine needles and dead leaves. Birds warbled and small animals darted in the foliage around them. Otherwise all was silent as they walked.

The trail steepened once they cleared the copse of trees, and the sun was warm on Jaime's shoulders. She was glad of the sunscreen, but annoyed she'd been forced to wear shoes that didn't quite fit. The boots lifted and rubbed against her heels with each step she took, and she predicted blisters in her future. She would have liked to stop and retie them a little tighter, but didn't have the nerve to make the request.

A hike seemed like a strange sort of slave training, but clearly it was something they all did with some regularity, and she decided to suspend her questions and just go with the flow. Her job, as Katie had reminded her, was to listen and obey. So far, hopefully, she'd been doing that to everyone's satisfaction.

They had been climbing steadily for perhaps twenty minutes. Jaime, while fit, was a bit winded, not yet used to the higher altitude, she supposed. She was glad when Master Mark halted the procession as they came to a broad, flat rock at a fork that diverged into two paths. One of the paths was marked by a small reflective sign tacked to a tree trunk, a white circle painted at its center. The other path had a red circle painted on its sign.

"Let's take a little break and have some water," Master Mark said. He nodded toward Danielle and Hans. "You both have water in your packs. Let's sit down a few minutes and rest before we continue." Turning to Jaime, he asked solicitously, "How are you holding up? You do much hiking?"

Flustered but pleased by the sudden attention, Jaime stammered, "I'm fine, Sir, thank you. I did a lot of hiking back in Vermont, where I'm from."

"Far from home," Master Julian commented.

"Yes, Sir," Jaime agreed, thinking he, a Brit, was farther still, though she refrained from comment, since this wasn't, after all, just a hike among friends.

They settled on the smooth, warm rock ledge. It was a relief to remove the heavy backpack from her shoulders and, again, Jaime resisted the impulse to open it and peek inside. Instead, she used the opportunity to reach for her bootlaces, which she tightened and retied. Danielle and Hans each retrieved a bottle of water from an insulated sack inside their packs. They unscrewed the lids of their bottles and handed them to the Masters, Danielle to Master Mark, Hans to Master Julian.

After the men had drunk their fills, they gave the bottles back to their slaves. Danielle and Hans each took a long drink. Without a glance toward Jaime, Danielle placed her bottle back into her backpack. Hans handed his bottle to Jaime, and she gratefully drank the few ounces that remained.

"I think this is a good time to split up for our training sessions," Master Julian said.

"Why don't I take Jaime," Master Mark said, and Jaime's heart leapt with excitement.

"Sorry to pull rank, old boy," Master Julian said in his polished accent, "but I have a rather delicious training plan in mind for the newbie. I do hope you don't mind?"

Master Mark didn't respond immediately, and Jaime held her breath, wondering if he would protest. "Not at all. That's fine. No problem."

Jaime glanced from Master Julian to Master Mark, her heart now down in her too-big boots. She could feel Danielle smirking beside her.

Master Mark glanced at Jaime, and for just a second she thought she saw something in his eyes—regret? Desire? She looked down, aware she was probably projecting her own feelings onto him. *Stop it,* Jaime reminded herself. *You're not here to find a boyfriend. You're here to learn.*

Master Julian stood. "Let's go, kids," he said with a wolfish smile.

Adjusting her backpack on her bare shoulders, Jaime scrambled from the rock after Master Julian and Hans, not allowing herself to glance back at Master Mark and Danielle. She kept her focus instead on her feet in their increasingly uncomfortable boots, carefully stepping over stones and protruding tree roots as they ascended along the mountain path.

The three of them stopped after another twenty minutes or so at another stone outcropping, this one set between two large oaks with arching branches that met in the middle, creating a natural canopy of pleasant shade. Hans opened his pack and removed a folded blanket, which he spread on the ground beneath the trees.

"Take off your pack," Master Julian said to Jaime. "Open it and remove the items inside. Line them up neatly on that corner of the blanket. Take off your cap and socks and boots, too."

Jaime shuffled off the pack, glad to shuck it from her shoulders. She removed the baseball cap and shook her hair back, tucking it behind her ears. Sitting on her butt, she stretched out her legs and untied her bootlaces. It was a huge relief to pull off the heavy boots and sweaty socks, though as soon as she did, she regretted it. There were, indeed, blisters on each heel, white and throbbing in the cool air. It would be a bitch to get the boots back on. Ah well, for now, at least, she was grateful for the reprieve.

Focusing on her task, she opened the flap of the backpack and reached inside. The first item she withdrew was a coil of bright red cotton rope. A pleasant shiver of anticipation moved through her as she set it down. Next she pulled out two smaller hanks of neatly wound white rope with metal clips attached, along with a pair of nylon wrist cuffs with Velcro closures. She extracted a short-handled cane, its bamboo rod thin and wicked. She set it down carefully, the skin on her still tender ass suddenly tingling.

Next came a large tube of lubricant and a small cardboard box of disposable gloves. Finally she pulled out a large metal briefcase, which explained why the pack had been so heavy. She was dying to open it, but decided to wait for further direction. Master Julian sat on the blanket, his back against one of the trees, his long, muscular legs stretched out in front of him. He regarded Jaime. "Do you know what's in that case?"

"No, Sir."

"Open it."

Jaime did as she was bidden, unlatching the clasps and lifting the lid. Inside was a kit of some kind, compartmentalized into many pockets and slots cut into foam rubber. At the center was what looked like a handheld generator, shaped like a fat black plastic pencil with an electric cord at one end. All around it, each in its own separate cushioned slot, was an array of glistening glass tubes and balls of various shapes and diameters, as well as several metal pinwheels with sharp-looking teeth.

She looked up at Master Julian, whose lips had curled into a slow, cruel smile on his handsome face. "You know what you're looking at?"

"I think so, Sir. It's a violet wand kit." Jaime had seen the devices used at various clubs and BDSM conventions over the years. As she recalled, the globes at the end of the wands came alive with color—lightning bolts of amethyst, magenta, plum and royal blue sparking as the electricity danced through the glass. The effect was beautiful, but not something she'd ever wanted to experience herself.

"It is," Master Julian agreed. "Since we don't have an outlet handy, we'll use the portable wand for today. It's that one, there." He pointed, adding, "Lift it out, if you please, then close the case and place the wand on top it."

Jaime lifted out the delicate glass rod tipped with a glass orb the size of a ping pong ball by its plastic handle, pulling it free of its spongy bed. She closed the lid of the case and set the wand carefully on top of it. "I don't like to break up the kit," Master Julian continued, "which is one reason why I had you tote the whole thing. That"—his evil grin widened—"and because it's good to build up your stamina by carrying heavy loads. If we weren't bringing the kit, I would have put a few bricks in your pack. Builds muscles, and character, too. Isn't that right, slave Hans?"

"Yes, Master Julian." Hans, standing at attention on the edge of the blanket, said in a strident, military tone.

"That red rope," Master Julian continued, "isn't just any ordinary bondage rope. It's called conductive rope, and it's got metal filaments woven all through the cotton fibers. We're going to tie you up today between these two trees"—he waved languidly toward the tree trunk opposite him—"and give your bondage a special, added zing. A zap on any part of the rope will travel along its length, sometimes in unexpected ways you should find quite, uh, thrilling." Master Julian's gaze shifted to Hans, where it lingered, his tongue moving slowly and sensually over his lower lip as he stared.

"Oh!" Jaime exclaimed, the word slipping out before she could stop it.

"Yes?" Master Julian said, lifting his eyebrows in query as he returned his gaze to her. "Do you have something to say on the subject?"

"I, um, it's just, that rope sounds kind of, I don't know, dangerous, Sir?"

"No danger of electrocution, if that's what you're worried about. Sometimes there can be small burns left on the skin, if the user isn't careful and knowledgeable about what he's doing." He shrugged. "Happily for you, dear girl, that isn't the case here. You're perfectly safe. I might hurt you—no, let me amend that, I'm definitely going to hurt you, but I would never harm you."

Jaime swallowed hard, willing herself to stay calm. She trusted Master Anthony absolutely, and therefore, by extension, she would trust Master Julian. She understood the distinction between erotic pain and suffering versus actual bodily harm, and even as her mind rejected the concept of electric shock play, she couldn't deny the hot stirring of lust and longing rising from deep in her psyche.

"Yes, Sir," she murmured. "Thank you, Sir."

"You're welcome, slave girl," he replied with a chuckle. "Now, stand up just about there"—he pointed toward the center of the blanket—"in an at-ease position."

As Jaime moved to obey, Master Julian turned his focus to Hans. "Cuff her to the trees and then bind her body using the *Shibari* knots Master Anthony taught you."

"Yes, Sir," Hans said. He moved quickly, taking two hanks of rope and the wrist cuffs. He attached the cuffs, one to the end of each rope, and then wrapped the cuffs around Jaime's wrists, pressing the Velcro snugly closed. He then tied the other end of each rope to a low hanging branch on either tree. As he pulled the rope taut, Jaime's arms were raised. He adjusted each rope until her arms were stretched into a Y over her head, and then knotted them into place around the branches.

Jaime had been so focused on what Hans was doing, she was now startled to see Master Julian had removed both his boots and his jeans. He leaned against the tree trunk, naked from the waist down, his rapidly rising cock fisted in his right hand, his eyes fixed, not on Jaime, but on his naked slave boy.

Hans had retrieved the coil of conductive rope, which he began to wind and knot around Jaime's body, looping it in a figure eight over and around her breasts, and drawing a length up between her labia, managing it in such a way he was able to wind each end around her upper thighs. Jaime could feel the heat of her arousal between her legs as the rope slid and tightened against her throbbing clit.

Master Julian appeared suddenly in her line of vision. He had pulled off his T-shirt as well, and was now completely naked, save for the cover of dark curls on his chest, which trailed down his flat belly to his pubic hair and framed his large and fully erect penis.

"Please me, boy," he said to Hans, pointing to the ground in front of him.

Hans sank at once to his knees. He placed his hands behind his back and leaned forward, his lips parting, his tongue appearing. Master Julian gripped the back of Hans' head and pulled him forward onto his shaft, not stopping until Hans' nose touched his pubic bone.

Hans' eyes had closed, and he seemed completely relaxed and receptive, despite the huge cock down his throat. He didn't even appear to be breathing. Jaime watched, fascinated and in awe. She held her breath as she watched, wondering how long Master Julian would keep

Hans in that difficult position. She could see the latticework of welts on Hans' back and ass, some in faded browns and purples, some fresh and still ridged as his skin struggled to heal itself.

Finally, after at least a minute and a half, during which she'd already reached the point of failure and gasped for air, Master Julian released his hold on Hans' head and stepped slowly back, his erect cock bobbing parallel to the ground. As Hans took in a deep breath, he looked up at his Master with what could only be described as adoration.

"You may," Master Julian said softly, replying to some telepathic communication between them.

Hans dipped his head and took Master Julian's shaft once more into his mouth, this time with no assistance or direction. He worshipped Master Julian's cock and balls for several delicious minutes while Jaime enviously watched the erotic scene, the rope at her crotch moistening with her juices.

Finally, Master Julian pulled away. "Enough." He laughed. "You don't want to make me come before I'm ready, do you, boy? What happened the last time you did that, hmm?"

"You whipped me until I bled, Sir," Hans said quietly.

"And did you deserve that?"

"Yes, Sir. Thank you, Sir," Hans replied.

Jaime couldn't stop the shiver of erotic fear that rippled through her at this exchange. Her eyes flickered involuntarily to the short, whippy cane beside the silver briefcase.

"You're welcome, boy. Now, get the violet wand and we'll give the trainee a little sample of its power, shall we?"

"Yes, Sir." Hans took a few steps and bent down to retrieve the wand. He knelt in front of his Master like a knight before a king, the wand balanced on his upturned palms like an offering.

Master Julian took the wand. "Kneel up, chest forward," he ordered.

Hans straightened his back and arched forward. His nipple jewelry glinted in the dappled light. Master Julian held the tip of the wand against the tiny barbell at Hans' left nipple. There was a small crackling sound as bolts of color shattered inside the tiny glass globe, followed by Hans' muted gasp. His cock, however, had begun to rise like a balloon filling with air.

"Metal attracts and concentrates the charge," Master Julian explained in a calm voice as he touched the ball of the wand to Hans' other nipple. Again Hans gasped and winced, though his cock now jutted out in full erection.

Jaime hadn't seen it before, but now noticed the metal cock ring at the base of Hans' shaft. "Hans has a very high tolerance for pain, but this gets him every time." Master Julian touched the tip of the wand to the cock ring, and this time Hans cried out, his face twisted in a rictus of pain. Sweat had broken out over his upper lip and along the line of his sternum.

Jaime drew in a sharp breath and bit her own lip to keep from protesting in Hans' defense.

"Your turn," Master Julian said, turning his cruel, sensual smile on her. Jaime shrank involuntarily back, though bound as she was, she couldn't move far.

"Please," she blurted. "I'm afraid."

"Oh dear," Master Julian said. "I thought Hans taught you on your ride here—you don't address a Master or Mistress directly without express permission. I guess you didn't learn that lesson yet. You will, naturally, have to be punished for that." Jaime closed her eyes, silently cursing herself. Master Julian continued, "But not now. I'll leave that to Master Lawrence. He's our resident disciplinarian. Meanwhile, let's review what you should have done." He glanced toward Hans. "Tell her, Hans, how you approach a Master when you have an urgent need to speak."

"Yes, Sir." Still kneeling, Hans looked at Jaime. "When you have a compelling need to speak, something that absolutely can't wait until you are invited, you may say, 'Excuse me, Master, may I have permission to speak?' Then, you wait for them to grant permission. Sometimes you don't really need to speak, and you are just being lazy or cowardly. If that is determined, they might refuse. Then you just keep your mouth shut. They know what is best for you. If, however, they grant you the right to speak, you may then ask your question, or say whatever it is you need to say. This is understood, yes?"

"Yes," Jaime whispered. Had she been lazy or cowardly in blurting out her fear? Was it a pressing matter of great urgency that required she be heard? No. She had to admit, it was not. She was being a coward. If Master Julian thought she could handle the wand, then she could handle the wand.

"Now," Master Julian continued. "Is there something you need to say, slave Jaime?"

Jaime shook her head, her eyes down. "No, Sir."

"Excellent. I thought not." He moved closer and ran the ball of the wand along the curve of her right breast. To her surprise, there was no powerful, jolting shock, but only a gentle, fizzing sensation, almost like bubbles popping against her skin. "Not so bad, eh?" Master Julian said. "Though that was at the lowest setting." He adjusted something at the base of the wand and rolled the globe over her right nipple. The sensation was definitely more intense, though not painful—it was more of a buzzing tickle. He moved the wand, touching the ball to the conductive rope, and this time the shock traveled in a sizzling path around her breasts.

"Ah," she breathed, her head falling back.

The sudden stinging shock at her cunt caused her head to whip upright again. "Ow!" she cried involuntarily.

"The rope's wet with your cunt juices, you slut," Master Julian laughed. "That dramatically increases the conductivity of the wand." He zapped her again, and she squealed. He slid the ball of the wand over and around the rope at her crotch, shocking her over and over again. As she adjusted to the sensation, it became more tolerable, almost pleasurable. As if sensing this, Master Julian stopped and stepped back.

"Play time's over," he said, reaching for his cock with his free hand. "Now I want to fuck you in the ass." Turning to Hans, he said, "Get the stool, slave."

"Yes, Sir!"

Hans moved toward his backpack and withdrew a folding stool, which he opened and placed just behind Jaime's knees. Standing behind her, he lifted her into the air and set her down so her knees rested on the high stool. "Go on," he added, giving her ass a light slap, "stick it out more. Master wants to fuck you. You should be honored."

Gripping the rope above her cuffs for added stability, Jaime tried to do as she was told.

"Let's gag her, too," Master Julian said from somewhere behind Jaime. "In case anyone is hiking nearby. We don't want them to hear her scream."

As he said this, Jaime realized they'd never discussed her safeword, not once since she'd arrived at The Enclave. Had they just forgotten? And if they gagged her, what was her hand signal? Would it be the universal clenching and unclenching of her fist? But what if it was something different at The Enclave? Why hadn't anyone told her? Why hadn't she thought to ask?

"Please," she said urgently. "Permission to speak."

"Oh god," Master Julian said, his tone weary. "Okay, okay. Only because it's your first day. What is it, slave Jaime? What now?"

"My safeword," she said hurriedly. "We forgot to discuss my safeword. And if I'm gagged, what gesture do I use?"

There was dead silence for several long beats while Jaime waited for his reply. Then both Master Julian and Hans began to laugh. Jaime was at once alarmed and a little annoyed by their response.

Finally Master Julian said, "Where do you think you are, girlie? This isn't some amateur scene at a BDSM club. There's no negotiation. There's no *safeword*. You signed that away, sweetheart. For the next two weeks, and longer if you're lucky, we *own* you, heart, body and soul."

Turning to Hans, he said, "Get her ass ready for me. Don't use too much lube. I want to really feel the clench. Oh," he added in what seemed like an afterthought. "And while I fuck this girl, cane her breasts. Let's add some stripes to match the new ones she's going to get from Master Lawrence when we get home."

There was the snap of rubber gloves behind Jaime and then the cold goo of lubricant between her ass cheeks. "Relax," Hans ordered as he pressed a thick finger into her nether hole. Jaime wished it were that easy. He moved his finger slowly inside her, pushing it deeper, his other hand gripping her shoulder to hold her in place on the stool. Jaime closed her eyes and took in a deep breath of the cool, pine-scented mountain air. She let it out slowly, willing herself to relax her muscles as best she could.

"Better," he finally said, withdrawing his finger.

Master Julian appeared in her line of vision, holding something between thumb and forefinger. Hans walked around her and knelt in front of his Master so the two of them were in profile in front of her.

"Watch and learn," Master Julian said to Jaime. He tore open the packet of what Jaime now saw was a condom. Hans opened his mouth and Master Julian placed the flat rolled ring of latex upright between Hans' lips. Hans leaned forward on his haunches, his mouth a perfect O, the condom delicately balanced.

He placed his hands at the base of Master Julian's penis as he slid his mouth over the head. He moved slowly forward and then pulled back, the condom now in place on Master Julian's erect cock, the whole process occurring in a matter of seconds. Jaime, who had once tried a similar maneuver with much less successful results, was suitably impressed.

Master Julian stepped behind her and she felt his hands on her ass. In spite of her resolve to stay relaxed, she tensed, her breath shallow and rapid in her throat.

"Shh," Master Julian murmured, his voice low and soothing. "You're actually doing very well, Jaime." He stroked the back of her neck and then her cheek with unexpected tenderness. "I know this is all quite overwhelming. Since we only have you for two weeks, we want to give you the full immersion experience. Having no safeword is really very freeing. You have no decision to make, no guard to keep up. You simply let go. Give yourself over completely to the experience, and let it take you where you need to be."

His hands moved to her shoulders, his fingers kneading the flesh in a relaxing massage. "Slow your breathing. Open yourself fully to me."

Jaime leaned gratefully into Master Julian's soothing touch. "Yes, Sir," she whispered.

"Good girl. Now I'm going to fuck you." His hands fell away from her shoulders. "Hans, get the wand, the cane and the ball gag. You know what to do."

"Right away, Sir," Hans replied, and Jaime immediately forgot the soothing words and touch of a moment before, her muscles rigid with fearful anticipation.

"Open," Hans commanded. Reluctantly, Jaime opened her mouth. He pressed the hard rubber ball between her teeth. Master Julian buckled the headgear into place at the back of her head.

Hans stepped back, the cane in one hand, the violet wand in the other. Jaime tried to swallow the saliva already pooling in her mouth, but her tongue was pressed too far back by the gag. She was distracted by the sudden press of what must be Master Julian's cock head between her ass cheeks.

"Relax," Master Julian murmured against her ear. "You're holding yourself back from me. That is not submissive behavior."

As much as she wanted to obey, Jaime was strung taut as a bow, as if she might snap in half if pulled too hard. Nevertheless, she willed her muscles to ease their clench. She must have succeeded, at least a little, because Master Julian said, "Better," as he pressed into her tiny, tight hole.

"Almost as good as a boy," he murmured. His fingers were digging into her hips, his cock stretching her wide. "Hans, you may give her five strokes to each breast. Use the wand however you wish, with a focus on the ropes at her cunt. Jaime, your only job right now is to accept what is given to you."

He jerked her back against his body and she felt like she was being split suddenly in two. She grunted with the shock of it. Master Julian sighed contentedly and began to move, pulling her back and then pushing her forward. She gurgled against the gag as he swiveled and thrust, the pain easing almost into pleasure, her clit pulsing against the damp, tight rope lodged firmly between her labia.

The first cut of the cane sliced along the top of her right breast. She bit down on the rubber ball as pain exploded like stars in front of her eyes. Hans delivered the second stroke to her left breast, at the same time using his other hand to send a thrilling shock to her cunt. The third stroke landed on the underside of her right breast, the fourth on her left. As Master Julian pummeled her from behind, the wand globe skittered along the conductive rope, sending shockwaves of stimulation over Jaime's skin.

The fifth and sixth cuts of the cane were delivered in rapid succession, one across each nipple. Jaime screamed against the gag, the sound muted and burbling against the rubber filling her mouth. Master Julian continued in a steady, pumping rhythm behind her, slamming like a piston against her.

A bead of sweat rolled into Jaime's eye and she tried to blink it away. She was gripping hard on the ropes above her cuffs and snorting like a racehorse through her nostrils. Again the wand touched the ropes that snuggled against her clit, and this time Hans held it there as he caned her stinging, welted breasts. Master Julian's cock filled her completely, and a dark, sensual pleasure welled from somewhere deep in her core, as if he were stroking her clit from the inside out. The cut of the cane, the surge of the violet wand, the cock buried to the hilt inside her, the ropes and cuffs, the two handsome men using her for their pleasure—it all coalesced into powerful, sensual overload. Jaime, to her astonishment and absolutely beyond her control, began to climax, wave after powerful wave of orgasm sweeping through her as she trembled in her bonds and moaned helplessly against her gag.

As if taking his cue from her, Master Julian stiffened suddenly and then thrust hard and deep inside her, his body hot and sweaty against her back, his breath a heaving rasp in her ear. He remained that way for several long moments, and she could feel his heart beating against her back.

His cock dislodged from her ass as he pulled away from her. Still shuddering from the aftershocks of her orgasm, Jaime was left kneeling on the stool, her arms extended, her asshole gaping.

Master Julian appeared in front of her, a lock of his hair fallen over his high forehead, the spent condom dangling from his still erect cock. "What. Just. Happened." His eyes were glinting with steel, no trace of a smile on his handsome face.

Jaime, her mouth still plugged, couldn't reply, nor did she want to. Hans spoke for her. "I do believe the slave girl has come without permission, Sir," he said, frowning with disapproval.

"Is that right, Jaime?" Master Julian said as Hans knelt before him and quickly stripped off the used condom, dropping it into a small plastic bag he had at the ready.

Humiliated, Jaime could only nod, the drool hanging from her chin, sweat stinging the angry red welts on her breasts. Her arms ached and she longed to hide her face from Master Julian's stern, probing gaze. She waited miserably for his rebuke.

Instead, to her astonishment, he began to laugh. "You really are an incorrigible little slut girl, aren't you? I have to admit, your sexual responsiveness is really quite appealing. I don't generally like working with girls, but I might just volunteer for your orgasm control training. I do love a challenge."

Still chuckling, he reached around her head and unbuckled the ball gag, which he pulled gently from her aching jaws. She longed to wipe away the spit on her chin and chest, but was grateful at least for the removal of the gag. She flexed her fingers over the cuffs, drawing Master Julian's gaze upward. "You want to be released, don't you?"

"Yes, please, Sir," Jaime replied timidly, still not sure how much trouble she was in.

Master Julian shook his head. "Not yet, dear girl. Or rather, we're going to let you off the stool, but before we untie your wrists, you're going to practice your oral skills, such as they are, on slave Hans. It's his lucky day. You're going to get the chance to make him come for the second time today. You will do it without the use of your hands, and you will do it in under five minutes." He shifted his gaze to Hans, who was standing nearby, his cock at half-mast. "Lower the ropes so we can get her into position."

"Yes, Master Julian." Hans reached up to one of the branches where the rope was secured and worked at the looped knots. The tension on the rope holding up Jaime's right arm slackened, and her arm dropped down suddenly, nearly causing her to fall off the stool. Master Julian, however, reached out a steadying hand and firmly clasped her shoulder to keep her in place while Hans readjusted the second rope.

Master Julian stepped back as Hans moved behind Jaime and wrapped one strong arm around her waist. The stool was pulled from beneath her and she was lowered to the blanket, still on her knees. He reappeared in front of her.

No doubt the idea of being sucked off by a girl for the second time that day was less than exciting to him, but hey, Jaime told herself, it's better than nothing, surely? And if his Master wanted it, Hans should want it too, as should she. She was here to serve, obey and please this man to whom she'd promised her complete and unconditional obedience for the next two weeks, whether he was gay or straight or pansexual. This wasn't about her titillation, or Hans' for that matter. They were both there for Master Julian.

He had settled back once more against the tree, his jeans pulled on but not yet zipped, his broad, muscular chest bare. He pulled his cell phone from his pocket and touched its screen. "Okay, I'm setting the timer for five minutes. Ready, set, go!"

Startled, Jaime strained forward, opening her mouth and sticking out her tongue. She silently cursed the fact she couldn't use her hands.

Thankfully, Hans moved closer, allowing her to take his cock into her mouth. He smelled of sweat and musk, his cock salty against her tongue.

She sucked at the shaft, willing it to elongate, relieved when it began to inflate in her mouth. She moved her head back and forth as best as she could in her bound position, running her tongue along the smooth, silky skin and using her lips to create what she hoped was a pleasing suction. She put everything she had into it, and though Hans' cock had hardened to full erection, he stood stoic and still. She thought about earlier that morning on the ride to The Enclave. He had basically fucked her face then, using her mouth to masturbate.

Do it again, she silently begged, keenly aware of the passage of time. *Please, Hans, just fuck my face like before. He didn't say you couldn't help out.* Her stomach sank as she realized that Master Julian hadn't given Hans any sort of directive. She glanced up at the slave. He was staring into the middle distance, a bored look on his face, his hands clasped behind his back.

Shit!

She redoubled her efforts, bringing all her skills to bear, tickling, teasing, kissing and sucking for all she was worth. If only she could use her damn hands! Finally Hans moaned softly, his cock pulsing against her tongue. Hope leaped to life in Jaime's chest, and she took his shaft as far back in her throat as she could, milking its length with her lips and tongue.

She became aware of a chiming sound. It took a few seconds to process what she was hearing. Master Julian confirmed it by saying, "Time's up. Looks like slave Jaime needs a lot of work in a whole lot of areas. Ah well, if she came to us perfectly formed, where would the fun be in that?"

Hans stepped back, his erect cock falling from Jaime's mouth as he moved. Jaime, defeated, let her head hang down. "We need to be getting back," Master Julian continued cheerfully. "Hans, untie the girl and put away the things."

Hans released the wrist cuffs and Jaime's arms fell heavily to her sides. His cock flaccid once more, he pulled her to her feet and made quick work of the conductive rope, expertly undoing the knots and winding the rope back into a neat coil. She rubbed her arms, which tingled back to life as the blood rushed through her muscles.

Master Julian handed her a bottle of water, from which Jaime gratefully drank. "Get your boots back on," he said, "and we'll head back."

Jaime sat on the blanket near her socks and boots. The welts on her breasts were stinging, her bottom was a little sore from the anal sex, and she was exhausted. Worst of all, she had no idea what was going to happen to her now. The anticipation was almost worse than the inevitable punishment to come.

She winced slightly as she drew the double pair of socks as carefully as she could over her right foot. "What's the matter?" Master Julian asked.

"Oh," she replied, momentarily confused, wondering how he could have gotten inside her head like that. Then she realized he was looking at her feet. "Blisters," she explained. "My boots are too big."

"What size are you?"

"Size eight, Sir."

"What size are the boots?"

"Size nine."

Master Julian lifted his eyebrows. "Why are you wearing the wrong size boots?"

"Danielle said that's all there was, Sir."

"I just stocked those shelves myself yesterday," Master Julian said, rubbing his chin, a quizzical look on his face. "I'm certain there was a woman's size eight there. How strange." He shrugged. "Ah well, can't be helped now. Just be careful. When we get back to the house, we'll have Dr. Aubrey take a look. She should be home by now."

Jaime remained mute, though inside she was seething, her suspicions now confirmed. For whatever reason, Danielle seemed to have it out for her. She realized she would need to be on high alert around the beautiful blonde. She would be damned if a woman with the apparent maturity and viciousness of an eighth grade girl was going to get the best of her.

She was distracted from her musings by Master Julian's pronouncement. "And then, if there's time before supper, Master Lawrence can administer your punishments. Let's tally up the transgressions as we hike back, shall we?"

CHAPTER 7

Jaime shivered under the spray, soaping up and rinsing off as fast as she could, careful when washing her still-tender breasts. The shower stall was little more than a curtained-off corner of the laundry room with only one spigot—cold. While the other slaves from the hike had gone down to their quarters for a shower and rest, she had been relegated there to clean up, informed slaves awaiting punishment were not permitted to use hot water.

She dried herself quickly and hung the towel over the shower curtain rod. She wished she had a blow dryer, hairbrush and some makeup. She reached for her collar, which she buckled back into place. She thought about the beautiful, obviously hand-crafted collars the staff slaves wore and wondered as she stroked the soft leather of her simple black band if she, too, would one day wear something as beautiful.

As she was running her fingers through her hair, Mistress Aubrey appeared in the doorway dressed in a blue blazer, white blouse and paisley skirt, sensible pumps on her feet, every bit the professional returning from a day's work. "Hello, Jaime. I just got in, and I understand your feet need a little attention." As she spoke, her eyes moved over Jaime's bare body, settling on her breasts, where the welts from the caning were still visible.

She moved closer until she stood directly in front of Jaime and ran a finger over one of the welts. "Nice," she pronounced. "Earning your stripes, I see." She smiled, a dimple appearing in her right cheek. Jaime smiled uncertainly back. "Come sit over here. I have my bag with me." Mistress Aubrey gestured toward a wide, low stool set against the wall near the shower stall. She was carrying a burgundy leather case, a sleeker, more updated version of a traditional doctor's kit.

Jaime tried not to limp as she walked, the blister on her left heel tight and inflamed. She perched on the stool, and Mistress Aubrey crouched in front of her. Placing the case on the ground, the doctor unsnapped the closures on the top and opened it. Turning her attention back to Jaime, she lifted Jaime's right foot in her cool, slender fingers and examined it.

"Not too bad," she said, lightly touching the tender sac of liquid just above the heel. "The skin's not broken and it doesn't look too irritated. I think we'll just cover this one with a little ointment and an adhesive bandage. The skin will provide a natural barrier to bacteria." She reached into the bag and retrieved a large bandage in a paper wrapper, dabbed a little ointment over the blister, tore off the bandage wrapper and gently applied it over Jaime's heel.

She picked up Jaime's left foot, her brow furrowing. "Oh, now this one, it hurts, doesn't it?" She touched the puffy, throbbing blob with her fingertip and Jaime winced with pain.

"Yes, Mistress," she breathed.

"We'll just take care of this one real quick." Mistress Aubrey rose to her feet. She moved toward the sink beside the washing machine and washed her hands with soap and water. She dried them on a towel and returned to crouch once more in front of Jaime.

Reaching into the bag, she pulled out a pair of disposable gloves and snapped them expertly into place. "I'll just swab the blister with a little iodine first," she said, removing a small plastic bottle and a cotton ball from her bag. She lightly touched the blister with the cool, wet cotton and set it aside. Next she took a small plastic pouch from the bag and carefully tore it open. Inside was a long, thin needle. Jaime turned her head and closed her eyes.

Mistress Aubrey laughed. "Oh, come on now, you aren't scared of needles, are you?"

"Um, a little, Mistress," Jaime admitted. *A lot,* she thought.

"Oh dear, that's going to be a problem for Master Mason." She chuckled. "Or rather, the problem will be yours when you go for training with him. Needles are his specialty, and no Enclave slave escapes unscathed."

As she spoke, Mistress Aubrey slipped the tip of the needle just under the edge of the blister. Jaime steeled herself for the pain, but was surprised when she barely felt the prick. Turning back to see, Jaime watched as the clear liquid drained from the blister, the skin over it deflating. Mistress Aubrey used a square of gauze to wipe away the seepage.

"There," she said with a bright smile. "All done. See, that wasn't so bad. We'll just cover this with some antibiotic ointment and a nonstick gauze bandage, and you'll be right as rain in a day or so." Mistress Aubrey stood and patted Jaime's head. "I'll give some bandages and ointment to Lucia—she can change the dressing in the morning."

"Thank you, Mistress Aubrey."

"You're welcome. Now, I understand you're due for a punishment." Mistress Aubrey's words sent the momentary sense of well-being Jaime had experienced at the doctor's capable hands skittering away like a mouse streaking for its hole.

"Yes, Mistress," she admitted, looking down. Master Julian had made her list her transgressions as they hiked back to the house— speaking out of turn, coming without permission, and failing to make Hans orgasm within the prescribed time limit.

"We'll save that for after dinner." The sound of the clock chiming in the foyer made Mistress Aubrey glance at her watch. "Let's see. It's five thirty. Free time for non-kitchen staff is from five to six so you still have about thirty minutes to relax. Maybe you'd like to sit on the veranda and watch the sunset? That door there leads outside. You'll see the veranda on your right." She pointed toward a door at the back of the room. "Or you could go take a rest in your room in the slave quarters. It's entirely up to you. At six you are to report to the kitchen to help with any last minute prep work." She bent down and retrieved her doctor's kit. "See you at dinner." She swept out of the room.

Jaime stood and took a few tentative steps. The doctor had worked a miracle—Jaime no longer limped and, while the blisters were still tender, it wasn't anything she couldn't easily tolerate.

She fingered one of the O rings on her collar. She thought about going to lie down in the room that would be hers for the next two weeks, deciding instead to get some fresh air. Going out the door that led outside, she stepped onto the wide stone path and walked between rows of leafy vegetables and herbs that had been enclosed in chicken wire, no doubt in an effort to keep deer and rabbits from sneaking a midnight snack.

The veranda was paved in the same smooth stone as the path and swept spotlessly clean. No one was outside, and Jaime welcomed the chance for a little solitude before her next adventure. There were several tables made of wicker and topped with glass, each with chairs placed around it and shaded by a wide canvas umbrella. Black metal and mesh portable fire pits were placed strategically near each table.

There was a separate area to the side of the veranda, topped with a trellis of bare wooden beams. Chains hung at intervals from the beams, and the stone flooring had been covered with what appeared to be padded tatami mats. The space must have been set up for outdoor BDSM play, and Jaime wondered when she would get a chance for an experience there. She knew she should be careful what she wished for, and a shiver of edgy anticipation moved through her.

She sat gingerly on one of the chairs, her ass still tender from the caning that morning. There was a cool breeze, and soon it would be too chilly to remain outside naked. For the moment, however, it was perfect. The air had a lovely, blue tinge to it as twilight settled over the mountainside. Jaime leaned back in her seat and closed her eyes, drawing in a deep breath and letting it out in a long sigh.

"You look very relaxed."

Startled, Jaime jerked upright, her eyes flying open. She started to stand, not sure of the proper protocol. "Oh! Sir. I didn't realize there was anyone—"

"Calm down. It's fine. Don't get up. This is free time." Master Mark sat down beside her at the small table. He smiled at her, and again she was assailed with a sense of recognition.

Without thinking, she blurted, "Do I know you from somewhere? I'm sorry, but you just seem so familiar."

He regarded her silently a moment, as if weighing something in his mind, and then said, "No. I don't think so. I would remember if I'd met you." Something in the way he said it made Jaime warm inside. She had spoken without first asking permission, but he hadn't seemed to notice or mind.

Still, she needed to be more careful. She was exhausted, not only physically but mentally, and this was only the first day. She had already been punished once today, and the dreaded anticipation of more punishment after dinner was suddenly more than she could bear. How could she possibly get through two weeks of this?

"Hey," Master Mark said softly. "What's going on right now? Your whole demeanor just changed. Are you okay?"

His kind concern tore the flimsy vestige of control she was clinging to into shreds, and tears sprang to her eyes. One rolled down her cheek and she wiped it away. She closed her eyes and wrapped her arms protectively around herself, trying desperately to keep it together. Her entire body was rigid with the effort, and she began to tremble.

"I know it's hard, Jaime." His voice was soothing. She felt his hand on her arm. His fingers moved in gentle circles over her skin. "This training process is not easy, and a lot has been thrown at you. Expectations are very high here at The Enclave. For what it's worth, I think you're doing exceptionally well."

The tears rolled faster and she silently cursed herself, but his soft touch, his gentle voice and his encouragement opened the floodgates on her self-control, and, to her horror, Jaime began to cry.

Through her tears, she looked over at him with a pleading expression. "I'm sorry. I'm so sorry. I'm not really crying. I mean, I don't know why I'm crying. It's just— I just—"

"Hush now, shh." Mark stood and reached for Jaime, pulling her up into his arms. "It's okay. It's okay to cry. It's a good release."

He stroked her back while she sobbed into his chest, her tears wetting his shirt. "I'm sorry—" she began again, and again he shushed her.

"Stop it, slave Jaime. Stop trying to control the process. Don't try to hold anything back. Let it go."

His tone had become more commanding, as had his words, and the effect was centering. Though she continued to cry, the desperation had gone from her sobs. She relaxed against his strong body and just let herself feel what she was feeling. After a few minutes, the tears stopped. Still he held her. They stayed that way, slowly rocking, for a long time, and a deep sense of peace settled over Jaime. She could have remained there forever.

The sudden commotion of footsteps on the stone made them both look up, and Master Mark's arms fell away from her. He stepped back as they both turned toward the sound.

Master Brandon and Mistress Marjorie appeared, each with a wineglass in hand. "Oh, we didn't realize anyone was out here," Master Brandon said.

Mistress Marjorie moved toward them. "Why, Jaime," she said as she got closer. "Have you been crying?"

"It's okay," Master Mark interjected. "Jaime just needed to release some tension. It's been a long first day."

"And it's not over yet," Master Brandon added with an evil grin. "I understand a punishment is in order for this young lady."

Mistress Marjorie's smile was sympathetic. "Don't worry, Jaime. You'll be fine. Punishment is just part of the process. Go on into the kitchen and get a glass of water, honey. I think you're due there in a few minutes, is that correct?"

Jaime wiped her eyes and swallowed. "Yes, Mistress Marjorie."

She glanced back at Master Mark. He smiled at her. "You'll be fine," he said. "Better than fine, I promise."

"Thank you, Sir." Jaime wanted nothing so much as to return to those strong arms and let him hold her for the next decade or two. But she knew he was right. She *was* fine. The tears had definitely helped. She could still feel the warmth from his embrace. She was ready to face whatever lay ahead.

As directed by Mistress Marjorie, Jaime walked around the side of the house to the mudroom, which led directly to the kitchen. She entered the warm, inviting space, the smell of roasting meat assailing her nostrils and stimulating her appetite.

Master Mason stood at the butcher block in the center of the work area, whisking something in a bowl. He wore a full-length black bib apron over his clothing, and his shaved head gleamed in the overhead fluorescent light. The girl Jaime recognized as Ashley stood beside him, chopping vegetables on a cutting board, an identical apron covering her small frame. Ashley's hair was little more than fuzz on her head, recalling a baby chick's down. Her head, Jaime suddenly realized, must have been shaved not that long ago. Lucia, also aproned, was stacking dishes and silverware onto a large tray at a nearby counter.

Master Mason looked up as she entered and flashed a grin. "There she is. The newbie." If he noticed she'd been crying, he didn't comment, for which Jaime was grateful. He gestured with his head toward a set of hooks just inside the door where Jaime stood. "Grab yourself a fresh apron and we'll put you to work." As Jaime reached for an apron and tied it around her naked body, Master Mason continued, "Go to the sink and finish up what's in there. Get those pans scrubbed and loaded in the dishwasher so we'll have room for dishes after dinner. You can go ahead and run the pots and pans cycle once you've scrubbed off the gunk."

Jaime moved as directed toward a large double sink. One side was filled with sudsy water, a number of pots and pans soaking within. There was a pair of rubber gloves beside the sink, along with dishwashing soap, sponges, brushes and cleaning pads.

She turned on the cold tap and splashed some water on her face. Cupping her hands, she let them fill with water and drank deeply. Reaching for a nearby dishtowel, she wiped her face and hands and then pulled on the rubber gloves, ready to work.

When she was done, she removed the gloves and set them neatly where she'd found them. She turned to face the room. Her hair was still damp from her cold shower, long, curling tendrils falling forward into her face. She tucked the tangled mess behind her ears as best she could, not sure what to do next.

Master Mason was bent over the open door of the bottom of the double ovens. He stood and turned, a large roasting pan in his hands with a huge pot roast on the rack. He set it down and turned back toward the ovens, closing the bottom door and opening the top. The smell of freshly baked bread wafted tantalizingly into the room.

Master Mason looked over at her with a nod. "All done? Good. Hang your apron on that hook by the door and then go out to the dining room and see if Lucia needs any help with the table settings. You may then wait behind your chair for dinner, which is in"—he glanced up at the wall clock that hung above the double ovens—"six minutes." Ashley, who was now tossing a salad in a huge wooden bowl, kept her eyes on her task.

Jaime hung her damp apron on its hook and pushed through the swinging doors into the dining room. The long table was beautifully set with china, silverware and crystal. Uncorked bottles of red wine and glass pitchers of ice water were placed at intervals along the table. Fresh flowers were artfully arranged in a large vase at the center. Lucia was pouring water into the glasses.

"Hi," Jaime said shyly. "Can I help?"

Lucia looked up and smiled back. "I'm just about done, thank you." She set the pitcher on the table. "I have to go back into the kitchen in a second. You can just wait behind your chair until all the Masters and Mistresses arrive." But instead of heading back to the kitchen, Lucia regarded Jaime with an appraising gaze. "You know what? I have a minute. Let me see if I can do something with your hair."

Jaime touched her head self-consciously. "Thanks," she said gratefully. "Whatever you can do is great."

Lucia stepped behind Jaime. She stroked Jaime's hair smooth with her fingers and began to deftly weave large strands together, pulling them back in what Jaime realized must be a French braid.

"Your hair is like my daughter's—it has a mind of its own," Lucia said.

"Your daughter?" Jaime was startled to think of this woman having a daughter. Somehow she had just assumed all the subs at The Enclave were single and unattached. Did a daughter mean a husband? How old was this daughter? Did they live nearby?

As if reading her mind, Lucia offered, "She's grown now. Lives in California. Has a daughter of her own with the same unruly hair." She laughed softly. "My husband was the same, though he let me cut it short for him." She sighed a little, adding in a quiet voice. "I'm a widow."

"Oh," Jaime said, touched and saddened by Lucia's revelation. "I'm so sorry."

"Thank you. He was the love of my life, but I'm coming to realize, slowly, that the world goes on, even when someone you love leaves it. This place—The Enclave—saved my life. It's given me direction and happiness. Love will come again, in its time."

Jaime pondered these wise words, curious to know more, but sensing now wasn't the time to ask. Lucia patted her shoulder and stepped back. "There," she said. "All done."

The hair was pulled neatly back from Jaime's face, the end of the damp braid hanging between her shoulder blades. She wished she could see the overall effect—she'd never managed to master a French braid on her own—but knew it was better than the tangled mess Lucia had had to work with. She imagined a younger Lucia kneeling behind a little girl, fingers moving rapidly as the child shuffled impatiently. The image made her smile.

"Thank you, Lucia," she said to the already retreating woman.

"*De nada*," Lucia replied with a smile before she disappeared behind the swinging doors.

A moment later Gene, Danielle and Katie entered the room. They took their places behind their chairs, both Gene and Katie flashing Jaime a smile, Danielle behaving as if she didn't exist, which suited Jaime just fine.

A silent minute passed as they stood waiting, and then the Dominants entered, preceded by footsteps and the rumble of their voices. Master Brandon and Mistress Marjorie appeared first. Master Lawrence entered next, Master Mark a moment later. Jaime's heart leapt when he smiled at her. "Everything good?" he queried.

It is now, she wanted to quip, but resisted the urge. "Yes, Sir. Thank you, Sir." He took his seat. Jaime, like the other subs, remained standing behind her chair. Finally Master Anthony arrived, along with Mistress Aubrey. Master Mason entered from the kitchen, the roast, now sliced and on a serving platter, in his large hands. Lucia and Ashley followed, carrying trays loaded with baskets of bread, salad and roasted vegetables. Once the Masters and Mistresses were seated, the slaves, save for Lucia, sat as well.

As platters of food were passed around the table, Lucia poured wine for those who wanted it. Jaime, her nerves becoming increasingly jangled at the thought of her impending punishment, gratefully accepted a glass of wine from the naked woman with a whisper of thanks.

She sipped the wine and nibbled at the delicious food, aware she needed to keep up her strength. The Doms laughed and talked, sometimes engaging the subs, all of whom seemed relaxed and happy. Jaime was startled by Master Mark's hand on her thigh. "You're jumpy. Calm down," he said quietly.

Jaime realized she'd been jiggling her leg nervously up and down, something she used to do as a child when anxious. Her father had put his hand on her thigh in just that manner, admonishing her with a smile to "stop being a jitterbug."

She stilled her leg at once, embarrassment making her face heat. "I'm sorry, Sir." At the same time, his hand on her thigh sent a thrill zinging down her spine. She closed her eyes, recalling the warm, calming embrace of his strong arms wrapped around her, and she relaxed.

You'll be fine. I promise.

She opened her eyes. Master Mark was watching her, and he smiled and nodded, as if he'd been reading her mind. She smiled back. Then she noticed Danielle watching them from Master Mark's other side, her eyes narrowed, her lips pressed tightly together. As Master Mark turned back toward his plate, Danielle's sullen expression instantly morphed into placid serenity.

Dinner finally came to an end, after a dessert of fresh raspberries and white chocolate gelato. The Doms began to rise, and the subs all jumped to their feet, moving quickly to stand behind their chairs, once more at attention. Jaime followed suit, her heart thumping in unpleasant anticipation.

"Slave Jaime," Master Lawrence said, fixing his gaze on her. "Come here." A spurt of adrenaline zipped through Jaime's veins. She moved down the table past Master Mark and Danielle. Master Lawrence held out a leash. "Come closer so I can clip your collar." Jaime imagined she could feel Danielle's triumphant stare as she was led from the dining room.

Stop giving her free rent in your head, Jaime admonished herself. *She isn't worth it.* She focused instead on recalling the feel of Master Mark's arms around her. Thus fortified, she followed Master Lawrence into the living room.

He walked her to the large fireplace. A small wooden platform raised about two feet from the ground with posts rising from each corner had been set on the floor in front of the huge, flat stone hearth. Eyebolts were embedded at the tops and along the sides of each post.

Several blocks of wood of varying sizes had been placed beneath the platform. A gear bag rested nearby.

"You will spend the evening on the punishment platform," Master Lawrence said. He unclipped the leash from her collar. Enclave members had begun drifting into the living room and were taking seats in various parts of the large room. Jaime did her best to keep her focus on Master Lawrence. "You will be punished for each of your transgressions. When the punishment is over, the slate is wiped clean. You will start fresh in the morning. You will handle your punishment with stoic grace and acceptance, understood?"

"Yes, Master Lawrence." Jaime silently prayed she would manage to do so.

Bending down, he pulled out one of the wooden blocks from beneath the platform to use as a stair. "Climb up here. Get on your knees and face the room."

Jaime stepped onto the block and settled onto the platform as directed, her back to the fireplace, her bottom resting on her heels.

"Lift your ass up and spread your knees wider," Master Lawrence said.

Jaime obeyed, gripping the posts for purchase.

Master Lawrence reached for the gear bag and unzipped it. He pulled out a bundle of nylon cuffs with clips at the ends. Teasing them apart, he wrapped cuffs around her wrists and clipped them to the eyebolts near the top of each post so her arms were extended, but bent at the elbow. Moving behind her, he wrapped the cuffs around each ankle, and clipped these in place against the back posts.

He stepped in front of her and regarded her critically for a moment. She couldn't help but notice the marked bulge at his crotch. Despite his stern countenance and forbidding demeanor, he clearly got off on what he was doing.

He bent down and brought up a smaller wooden block. This he placed beneath Jaime's lifted bottom. "You can rest your ass on this as you need it. You're going to be here a while." Jaime settled gratefully against the support.

Master Lawrence stepped back and turned to face the room. "This trainee is being punished tonight for a number of transgressions," he said in a loud voice. "Her first transgression is continually speaking out of turn."

He reached for the gear bag and unzipped it. He withdrew something and held it up so Jaime could see. She bit her lower lip as she regarded the object with instant and deep dismay. It was a stainless steel contraption, the front part coated in black rubber. Though she'd never personally experienced one, Jaime knew what it was—a dental gag, the kind that fit in your mouth like a horse's bit. It was just as bad, if not worse, than a ball gag, since your mouth was held open, making it impossible to swallow. There was a leather strap on the back to keep it in place.

Master Lawrence moved to Jaime's side. "This gag will serve as a reminder that slave girls don't speak until they are spoken to. Open wide." He tapped her cheek with his finger. Jaime didn't dare disobey.

She forced open jaws she hadn't realized she'd been clenching. Master Lawrence placed the hinged, rubber-coated metal into her mouth, positioning it until he was satisfied. Reaching back, he secured the thing around her head, and then adjusted the hinges, forcing her jaws to widen.

Jaime's mouth instantly pooled with saliva. She tried, and failed, to swallow, her throat muscles clenching ineffectively with the effort. She blinked back tears of humiliation and reminded herself this punishment was finite. Soon it would be over, and her slate would be wiped clean.

"Second transgression: coming without permission." He reached into the gear bag and pulled out a small butterfly-shaped item made of soft, purple plastic, elastic straps hanging from its four wings. He pressed what she recognized as a Venus butterfly against her spread pussy and snapped the elastic straps around her thighs to hold it in place. He turned on a small remote, causing the masturbatory device to buzz into life against her clit. "You will *not* come for the duration of this punishment, unless or until directed. You will exercise self-control. Are we one hundred percent crystal clear on this directive, slave Jaime?"

Unable to reply, Jaime could only nod her agreement. She could do this! She'd never particularly liked or responded to the insistent, almost annoying tickle of this kind of toy. She would just ignore it. Mind over matter. She would not come. She would not.

"Third," Master Lawrence announced in a voice designed to carry, "You failed to make slave Hans come within the prescribed time limit. We will be working on your oral skills, or rather, your lack thereof, throughout your stay here." There were a few chuckles from the room. "Meanwhile, tonight, you will observe a typical evening here at The Enclave from the punishment platform until it pleases us to let you down. All staff slaves are experts at pleasing both men and women in the oral arts. Pay attention. Maybe you'll learn something."

He stepped away, giving Jaime a view of the room. Everyone was assembled—Master Brandon and Mistress Marjorie with Katie, Gene and Mistress Aubrey with Master Julian and Hans, Master Anthony and Master Mark with Lucia and Danielle, Master Mason with Ashley. Without another glance at her, Master Lawrence walked toward Master Mason and Ashley.

Master Anthony and Master Mark, who were seated side-by-side on a large sofa in the furniture grouping closest to Jaime, both stood and casually unzipped and lowered their pants before sitting back down. Lucia and Danielle, each kneeling in attendance, began to stroke and fondle the men's cock and balls. The men, engaged in conversation, appeared to ignore the ministrations of the girls, though their rising cocks belied their seeming lack of attention.

Danielle glanced sidelong toward Jaime as she kissed and licked along Mark's shaft, her fingers lightly cradling his balls, and jealousy slithered through Jaime's gut like curdled milk. If only she were the one kneeling there before Master Mark with his cock deep in her throat, instead of bound to the punishment platform, drool sliding out of her gaping mouth.

She shifted slightly on the hard wood in an effort to move the butterfly's direct focus on her clit. Her effort was unsuccessful, and the thing continued to buzz steadily, if ineffectively, against her.

She looked away from the cock worshipping and saw that Master Brandon, too, had taken down his pants, which he'd removed altogether. He was standing near the windows, naked from the waist down. Though she'd noticed Mistress Marjorie's slave collar earlier that day, it was still something of a shock to see her on her knees. Master Brandon's cock was in her mouth, her hands lovingly cradling his balls, her eyes focused upward in adoration. Katie was behind him, also on her knees, her face pressed between his ass cheeks, her head moving up and down in tandem with her Mistress.

Master Julian and Mistress Aubrey were in the process of yet another scene, this one involving their slave boys, Hans and Gene. Clamps had been attached to both slaves' nipples, the chains of the clamps clipped together as they stood facing one another. Focusing her attention in their direction, she could hear Mistress Aubrey outlining the scene. "I'm going to stand behind you, Hans, and fondle your cock, while Master Julian does the same for my boy. When you are given the command, you will come. Make sure you both keep those nipple clamps in place. Careful about jerking each other's chain."

Master Julian chuckled, adding, "Don't either of you dare come before you are told. Got it, boys?"

"Yes, Master Julian," the slaves replied in unison. Jaime thought the setup unfair, since Hans was going to be stroked by a woman, not his gender of choice. Maybe, she realized suddenly, that was irrelevant. This wasn't about his getting off—it was about pleasing his Doms.

She watched, her own discomfort momentarily forgotten. Mistress Aubrey stood behind Hans, Master Julian behind Gene. Master Julian placed his hands on Gene's shoulders and pulled him back a little, which caused the chains linking the two slaves to tauten. Gene, whose face Jaime could see, winced as the clamps tightened on his nipples. His cock, she observed, was fully erect as Master Julian reached around to circle the base of it with his hand.

Mistress Aubrey, her back to Jaime as she pressed against Hans, who was easily a foot taller than she, said, "Good luck, boys. Make us proud."

Despite her self-assurance that she was immune to the limited charms of the Venus butterfly, Jaime's clit throbbed against its steady thrum as she watched Master Julian pulling at Gene's hard cock. Gene's eyes had closed, his face a study in concentration. His neck was flushed red, his chest rising and falling. Jaime wondered how long he'd be able to hold on before he was given permission to come.

She thought about orgasming on command. How was that even possible? You came when your body was ready to come, not when someone else told you to. And yet, this was apparently expected behavior here at The Enclave, and presumably something she would learn if she managed to hang on for the duration of the training.

She was already expected *not* to come until given permission. Yet, that was just as elusive a concept to her. How, again, did one control one's body in that way? If the nerve endings were stimulated to a certain point, you climaxed. End of story. Even as she thought this, she rejected it. Master Lawrence had told her not to come, as if this were a choice. He was confident she could master control over her body and her reactions. Who was she to refuse at least to try?

Unable to resist, she looked again at Master Mark and Master Anthony. The girls were still worshipping their cocks. Both men were leaning back against the couch, their eyes closed. The naked, kneeling girls bobbed over their Masters' laps with undivided attention.

The sound of approaching footsteps drew Jaime's attention from the scene. Master Lawrence stood in front of her once more, Master Mason now beside him, along with Ashley. She had a tattoo of a rose on one hip, a knife with a drop of blood at its tip on the other.

Master Mason unfolded a large, thick towel on the floor in front of the platform and directed Ashley to step onto it. He turned his attention to Jaime. "Mistress Aubrey mentioned you have a bit of an issue with needles," he said in his deep, rumbly voice. "We'll have to work on that, young lady. Meanwhile, I thought you might enjoy a demonstration with a properly trained slave girl. Ashley can handle quite a bit of intensive needle and blood play, isn't that right, sweetest girl?"

"Yes, Sir," Ashley said softly. Jaime noticed then the myriad tiny scars that covered the young woman's breasts and shaven pubic mons.

Master Lawrence stepped behind the diminutive Ashley and reached beneath her arms, bending his arms up at the elbows to catch her in a hold against his chest. "I'm going to support slave Ashley while Master Mason engages in a little needle and blood sport for your viewing pleasure." His pale blue eyes gleamed sadistically.

Jaime would have swallowed hard, if she could have swallowed. She wanted nothing more than to close her eyes and turn her head away. While she'd knowingly and somewhat willingly agreed, per the terms of the contract, to engage in needle play, watching it was almost worse than enduring it. She could handle the pricking pain of a needle's jab, but the sight of anyone's blood, hers especially, was enough to make her pass out.

Mind over matter. You can do this. It's safe and consensual. You're here because you want to be. So is Ashley. These thoughts helped to steady her nerves as Master Mason produced a packet of thinly gauged needles and began to stick them one-by-one in a circular pattern around each of Ashley's pencil-eraser pink nipples. Jaime glanced repeatedly at Ashley's face as the needles pierced her flesh. Throughout, Ashley kept her eyes on Master Mason, her expression serene and accepting.

On the plus side, the buzzing at Jaime's cunt had been reduced to a merely irritating buzz, her arousal from watching the oral sex scenes obliterated by what was going on in front of her. She was just congratulating herself on getting through the needle play without embarrassing herself, when Master Mason produced a small, glinting rectangle of steel. It was a single razor blade, the kind used in old-fashioned razors.

"Oh god," she moaned, though the sound that emerged was just a garbled, guttural grunt.

"Steady," Master Lawrence, who was watching her with a hawk's gaze, said. "You are only a witness tonight, slave Jaime." His voice, for the first time since she'd met him, was gentle. "This is not happening to you. This is happening to slave Ashley, and it's what she craves. It pleases both her and her Master. Not all satisfaction is sexual, and not all pain is suffering."

Jaime nodded. She would have thanked him for the advice, had she been able to speak. Instead, she could only drool. "Don't look away," he continued, his tone a little more strident. "Watch and learn."

A wave of dizziness assailed Jaime as Master Mason slid the sharp edge of the razor in a line along Ashley's mons. A moment later the line turned bright red. The cut was only about an inch long and presumably not deep, but within seconds droplets of blood began to ooze from the wound.

"Gungghhh," Jaime moaned incoherently, her eyes fluttering shut of their own accord. A wave of nausea threatened to engulf her.

"Stop it!" Master Lawrence admonished sharply. "Open your eyes. Stay in the moment."

Jaime forced her eyelids to lift and ordered her eyes to focus on the people in front of her. Master Mason was kissing his slave girl with the passion of a lover. She could see their tongues entwining as he gently stroked her cheek, his other hand cupping her mons. When he finally let her go and stepped back, he said, "Make yourself come for us, Ashley. Show this trainee your gratitude."

"Yes, Master Mason. Thank you, Sir," Ashley said, her eyes fixed on his. Master Lawrence was still behind her, still supporting her against his body. She reached with her left hand for her now bloodied pussy and began to rub. As her fingers moved, a few drops of the impossibly red blood splashed to the towel beneath her feet. Jaime watched, at once horrified and transfixed, as Ashley masturbated.

After only two minutes or so, Master Mason said, "Come for me, sweet slave."

Ashley shuddered and jerked forward, her mouth open, her face twisted in what could be pleasure or pain, or both. Master Lawrence let go of her and she fell slowly to her knees, her hand still buried between her legs.

Jaime noticed a sudden jolting tingle at her clit. Master Lawrence's hand was in his pocket. She realized he must have turned up the intensity of the butterfly with his remote. Her clit was throbbing and she longed for the feel of a hard, perfect cock to fill the emptiness aching inside her. In spite of her intense physical discomfort, her knees aching on the hard wood, her jaw muscles rigid, drool spilling down her chin and chest, and in spite of the bizarre, bloody scene before her, or perhaps partially because of it, she realized she was on the verge of a climax.

No. No, no, no, you will not come. You will not come.

"Come for me, slave Jaime." Master Lawrence's voice cut across her frantic inward directive.

Jaime's eyes flew open, her gaze turning involuntarily toward Master Mark. He was looking directly at her, directly into her soul. She shuddered and jerked, letting the climax she'd managed to keep at bay sweep over her. She'd just come, not for Master Lawrence, but for Master Mark.

CHAPTER 8

Mark strummed his guitar, humming the tune that had awoken him before dawn. No one else was out on the deck, save for a pair of hummingbirds zipping and diving at one of the several red birdfeeders that hung from the rafters. Mark savored the utter peace that surrounded him.

The sky was pink and gold, a silver glaze washing the sides of the mountains as the sun worked its way upward. The air was crisp and cool in the early morning light. It was Mark's favorite time of day, and his most creative. He closed his eyes as he hummed, breathing in the scent of jasmine and pine.

"Mind if I join you?"

Mark turned to the sound of Anthony's voice. "Oh, hey. Please do."

"Thought you might like a cup." Anthony held out one of the two coffee mugs he had brought with him.

Mark placed his guitar carefully against the wall and reached gratefully for the steaming mug. "Thanks, yes." He sipped at the hot brew while Anthony took a seat beside him. Anthony had thoughtfully prepared the coffee just as Mark liked it, with just a little cream, no sugar.

"That was pretty, what you were playing. Kind of haunting. Something of yours?"

"A tune that was in my head this morning when I woke up. I was just fooling around with it."

"Such a talent, Mark. You think you might go back to it someday? Get a new band going? Try again?"

"I honestly don't know," he replied, rolling the idea around in his head, and then letting it slip away. "We were on the road for five years straight, pretty much. We were all heading for a brick wall, not just Jake." He shook his head sadly. "You know what they say…but for the grace of God…"

"That had to be very hard, watching him self-destruct like that," Anthony replied quietly. "I can understand why you need a break from that whole scene, at least for a while." He smiled thoughtfully. "You're still so young. Plenty of time to figure out what's next, when you're ready. I'm glad you're here now, with us. I hope, whatever you ultimately decide, that you continue to make this your home. You're an excellent addition to The Enclave." They both sipped their coffee. "By the way, I think your training is coming along very well."

Mark's smile was easier this time. "Thanks. Though I'm not sure Lawrence would agree with you."

"Oh, I think you're wrong about that. Lawrence is just very—exacting. He's old school, doesn't believe in any overt display of affection during the training process. Don't get me wrong. He's very, very good at what he does, but he can be a little, uh, rigid."

Anthony took a long drink of his coffee. "You, on the other hand, are a romantic. Just be mindful of setting limits and sticking with them. You need to be firm and consistent, yes, but don't think you have to lose your humanity or compassion in order to achieve that. You're finding and developing your own style, what works for you as a Dom. Just follow your instincts. You'll be fine."

Mark was silent as he thought about this, his mind instantly veering to the scene on the veranda with the trainee. It was true Jaime's tears had momentarily circumvented his mind and gone straight to his heart. Had he done the wrong thing, offering her gentle encouragement, and then taking her into his arms? Had he behaved, not like a Dom, but like a potential lover?

There was something about the girl, something that spoke directly to him. From the moment he'd first seen Jaime, he'd sensed a spark of passion and strength in her, something that went beyond her obvious physical beauty and desire to submit. When the tears had spilled down those soft cheeks, it had been the most natural thing in the world to take her into his arms.

But had he done her, and himself, a disservice in the process?

He was almost certain Lawrence would say that he had. But then, as Anthony had pointed out, Lawrence and he had very different styles. Mark understood a Dom needed to bend his sub, but not break them. And Jaime, he'd sensed at that moment, was near the breaking point.

Just follow your instincts, and you'll be fine.

Yes, in his heart of hearts, Mark felt he had done the right thing in offering her the comfort he had. If holding her so close had resulted in a raging erection, that was beside the point. He was human, after all.

He looked up from his coffee cup musings and smiled. "Thank you for the advice and encouragement, Master Anthony. I do believe coming here was one of the best decisions I've ever made."

"I'm glad you feel that way, Mark. We'll do some more work this morning on Shibari bondage. We need to get a better sense of Jaime's endurance and comfort level with extreme bondage. We'll use Danielle as well—she's very limber and compliant. She's also due for a bit of a punishment. Did you hear what happened with the hiking boots?"

"The hiking boots?" Mark echoed, shaking his head. "What happened?"

"Apparently, Danielle was careless when giving Jaime her boots. She gave her the wrong size. Jaime got blisters as a result. Aubrey took care of it—no big deal—but that sort of behavior needs to be addressed and dealt with."

"Agreed," Mark replied. Switching gears, he asked, "Did you find Jaime at The Garden?"

Anthony smiled. "Yes. Just like I found you at Lair Sade."

"And I was definitely lost." Mark laughed, but then sobered. Lair Sade, a private, members-only BDSM club in Charlotte, had been a haven for Mark after the band's breakup and his return to his hometown to lie low and lick his psychic wounds. It was a chance to rediscover a part of himself that had lain dormant for far too long, his life consumed with music, touring and all the attendant insanity that had accompanied it. Though he hadn't yet shaved off his signature beard or cut off his dreadlocks, members at Lair Sade were used to discretion in all things dealing with the outside world, and no one had hassled him or even let on they knew who he was, which had been just what he'd needed at the time.

"You weren't lost, Mark," Anthony said with a kind smile. "You just needed time to heal, to rediscover. I'm glad you were willing to take the leap from casual scening to a real exploration into D/s as a lifestyle. You've got what it takes, Mark. You're not afraid to put your heart and soul into the process. You're willing to give as much as you demand of your subs, and that's key. Without that, it's just a game."

Pleased but mildly embarrassed at the praise, Mark deflected, "I'm looking forward to working with Jaime. What's her experience in the scene?"

"Jaime's never been formally trained," Anthony replied, "but she's got a lot of potential. Master Julian was quite enthusiastic about his session with her yesterday. He's going to continue to work with her on anal comfort and acceptance—one of her weak areas. From what I can glean so far, she's a true submissive with a fairly high tolerance for erotic pain. She's inexperienced but eager."

"Like me." Mark laughed.

"Don't sell yourself short, Mark. You've already mastered many of the key training techniques and skills. More importantly, you have a natural penchant for erotic dominance without the attendant ego that sometimes gets in the way."

Mark wondered if Anthony was making an oblique reference to someone else, but he didn't pursue that. "Breakfast should be ready by now," Anthony said, rising from his chair. "The girls picked fresh blackberries and raspberries yesterday, and Mason was just taking out some muffins when I went in for coffee. I'm going to go snag a few before they disappear."

Mark stood as well and picked up his guitar. Breakfast was the only informal, self-serve meal at The Enclave, with fresh fruit, yogurt and cereal always available, along with whatever biscuits, muffins or egg dish Mason was in the mood to prepare. Though Mark ate sparingly in the mornings, when he entered the house from the deck, the aroma of the fresh muffins, along with the mouth-watering smell of frying bacon and brewed coffee drew him toward the kitchen as surely as if he'd been on a leash.

Aubrey and Gene were at the dining room table eating their breakfast, professionally dressed for their workday. Not for the first time, Mark wondered what it must be like, working together by day as doctor and nurse, the consummate professionals, and living together in the evenings as Mistress and slave. However the relationship worked, it was clear the pair was in love.

Love. He'd written enough lyrics about it, but did he really have any idea what it meant?

A muffin in hand, Mark loped up the stairs to his bedroom to put away his guitar, his mind turning to bondage rope and lovely, naked slave girls.

~*~

Chains clanked against the edges of Jaime's dream. She opened her eyes, instantly awake. The soft, warm glow of the night-light bathed the room. She lay curled on her side, her hands folded beneath her cheek.

The cuffs and chain had made it difficult to get comfortable at first, but oddly enough, or maybe not so oddly, given how she was hardwired, she'd been incredibly aroused by her predicament. Once left alone, she'd lifted her hands in front of her face, turning her arms this way and that as she admired the leather and chain that held her captive. There was enough give in the chain to allow her to touch herself despite her wrists being cuffed together, and the thought of the cold metal links moving over her body as she stroked herself had been tempting in the extreme.

She'd resisted, not only because she was exhausted from her very long and very intense first day, but because the tiny red light of the webcam aimed directly at her bed reminded her she was being watched. Who was watching her? Was Master Mark watching her?

Though she doubted there was someone actively monitoring her at all times, she didn't dare take the risk. There had been a very specific clause in the contract about never touching herself in a sexual way when alone, unless expressly directed to do so. She wasn't about to fuck things up by taking such a stupid chance.

There was a light knock at the ajar door. "*Buenas dias,* sleepyhead." Lucia stepped into the room. "Time to get up."

Jaime struggled into a sitting position, holding her cuffed wrists in front of her. "What time is it?"

"It's nearly seven o'clock. You are to report for an outside training session at the dungeon beside the veranda at eight. Master Lawrence permitted you to sleep a little later than usual your first night here. But you need to move now so you won't make either of us late. I'll see you in the bathroom."

"Wait," Jaime called to Lucia's back. "What about these?" She held out her wrists, the chain clanking between her breasts.

Lucia turned back to face her. "You can undo the cuffs yourself. Just release the clips. It's a little awkward, but you'll get used to it soon enough."

"I can?" Jaime stared down at her wrists, stunned.

"Sure. Didn't you realize that? There's no padlock or anything. The chains are more, what's the word, symbolic, than anything. It's a mindset—it helps get you in the right headspace, you know?"

Jaime nodded. If that was its purpose, it had been right on the mark. She focused on her bonds, twisting her right hand to get at the clip holding the left wrist cuff in place. When she'd freed herself, she looked up, but Lucia had gone.

Fully awake and eager for whatever the day held, Jaime climbed out of the bed. She hung the chain with its cuffs on the eyebolt in the wall, running her fingers lightly over the links. She had done it! She'd made it through her first day and night at The Enclave. She pulled the quilt into place and neatly arranged the pillows at the head of the bed.

Padding on bare feet, she walked to the bathroom and headed directly for one of the toilets. Though not particularly keen to use the toilet in front of others, she realized that was kind of silly, given the fact they were all kept naked 24/7. Modesty had no place in a sub's repertoire.

When Jaime came out of the stall, she saw Danielle standing in front of the mirror, a blusher brush and compact case in her hand. "I didn't realize we could use makeup," Jaime blurted as she approached.

Danielle didn't even glance in her direction, but Lucia replied, "Staff slaves can. You can't, not while you're in training. Now hurry up and shower. You'll find a fresh toothbrush and a tube of paste there in the first stall." She pointed, adding, "Wash and condition your hair, too, but move as fast as you can. I'll groom you and fix your hair." She glanced pointedly at the clock, and Jaime hurried over to the shower stalls.

When she emerged from the shower, Lucia and she were the only ones left in the bathroom, which suited Jaime fine. She toweled herself dry and wrapped the damp towel in a turban around her head.

Lucia sat on the edge of the sunken bathtub, a tray containing a razor and various tubes and jars balanced by her side. There was a chair made of sturdy white plastic in the otherwise empty tub, its metal legs tipped with rubber caps. "Sit in there," Lucia directed as she turned on the tap and reached for the removable shower nozzle.

Jaime climbed into the tub and sat on the wide plastic seat. "I don't think she likes me very much."

"Who, Danielle?" Lucia shrugged. "She's had it tough. She didn't train here, you know. She came with someone, Master Alan, about four months ago. They were long-term guests, and she stayed with him in his room upstairs. Then something happened. I'm not sure what—she doesn't talk about it—but he took a job offer overseas and left her here. I'm not even sure he's coming back. Master Anthony gave her the opportunity to stay on as a staff slave, and she took it. But it had to be hard—being left behind like that. I feel sorry for her."

"Wow," Jaime replied, digesting this new information and the different light in which it cast Danielle in her mind. Though there was no getting around the fact that so far Danielle had acted like a bitch, Jaime couldn't help but feel sorry for her.

"Now," Lucia instructed. "Stop talking. I have to focus and I don't want to nick you."

"Yes, Mistress Lucia," Jaime teased, but she shut her mouth.

Lucia worked quickly, first shaving Jaime's armpits. Then she removed the bandages over Jaime's heels. "This one is barely noticeable," she said, nodding toward what little remained of the blister on Jaime's right heel. "We can leave the bandage off that one, I think." She quickly and expertly shaved Jaime's legs and then her pubic area. She rinsed away the cream and patted Jaime dry. Next she massaged a soothing lotion that smelled appealingly of fresh grass and lemon peel over Jaime's skin. Finally, she applied some ointment to an adhesive bandage and pressed it over the still-tender skin above Jaime's left heel.

"Now your hair. I'll do a French braid, like yesterday. You're to wear it up this morning for the rope work."

A thrill of nervous anticipation shot through Jaime's gut as she climbed out of the tub and moved toward the counter. She hung her towel and ran her fingers through her damp hair. Master Lawrence had informed her the first session of her morning would involve Shibari bondage training, and, while Jaime loved to be bound, she was aware Shibari could be a very intense sort of bondage, the kind that rendered you completely immobile in potentially painful positions.

Lucia appeared behind her a moment later. She brushed out Jaime's hair and plaited it deftly into a smooth braid. Jaime regarded herself in the mirror as Lucia worked. The welts on her breasts had faded to pale pink lines. Her face looked pale. She wished she were permitted the use of makeup. As it was, there was no way to compete with the model-perfect Danielle.

Stop it, she admonished herself. *There's no competition. That's not why you're here.*

The two girls went up the stairs to the kitchen. Master Mason sat at a small table, poring over what looked like a cookbook. He barely acknowledged them as they entered. Ashley was already in place at a counter with a peeler in hand, an apron covering most of her slight, naked form, a large bowl of potatoes in front of her.

Lucia pointed toward a huge, stainless steel coffeemaker that contained a large carafe. "Coffee. Muffins. Bacon. Fruit." Beside the coffeepot there was a large basket with a gingham dishtowel over it. Next to that was a platter of fried bacon, and beside that a big ceramic bowl filled with plump, fresh berries. "Juice and yogurt are in the refrigerator. There's bread for toast, if you want it. We get our own breakfast in the mornings. Get what you want, and you can eat there." Lucia pointed toward the table where Master Mason sat. "Or you can take it outside to the veranda, if you want." Lucia glanced at the clock. "You have fifteen minutes."

Jaime nodded and smiled her thanks. She poured herself a cup of coffee, adding cream and sugar. She selected one of the still-warm muffins from the basket, and added a few fresh berries to her plate. She stood uncertainly a moment, wondering if she should venture out to the veranda or sit at the small table where Lucia now sat eating a cup of yogurt and fruit beside the still engrossed Master Mason.

Who was she kidding? There was no contest. The last time she'd been on that veranda, a gorgeous Dom had held her in his arms. She moved through the spotless mudroom and managed to open and then close the back door while juggling her plate and coffee mug.

Her heart leaped with excitement when she saw Master Mark's mop of curly hair and broad back at one of the tables. *Down,* girl, she admonished herself. Master Anthony was also seated at the table, facing her direction. As she approached, he looked up and smiled. Lifting his hand, he beckoned her forward. "Good morning, slave Jaime. How was your first night?"

"Good morning, Sir," Jaime said, approaching their table with her breakfast. It still felt strange to be naked in front of these fully clothed men. "I slept well, thank you."

Master Mark turned as she walked toward them, his gaze sweeping in a slow, sensual caress over her body that made her feel flushed.

"Good morning, Master Mark," she managed, hoping her voice didn't betray her nerves, or her desire.

"Good morning, Jaime. Sit down and join us. Once you've eaten, we're ready to begin the morning session."

Excited at the prospect of training directly with Master Anthony and Master Mark, Jaime sat at the table, wondering if she'd be able to get down a bite of food.

A swish of shiny blond hair in her peripheral vision made her turn. Danielle was in the outdoor dungeon, balanced astride a wooden sawhorse. Her arms were bound together at the wrist and suspended from one of the beams in the overhead awning. She was blindfolded, her face a grimace of pain, her slim, muscular legs trembling from the effort of holding herself in place. In spite of her dislike for the girl, Jaime's fists clenched and she couldn't suppress the gasp of sympathy. All Danielle's weight must be focused on her cunt, and it must hurt like hell.

Following her gaze, Master Anthony said calmly, "Slave Danielle is being punished for a transgression. The punishment will be over soon. As soon as you finish your breakfast, in fact. Then we will begin the session."

Jaime looked away. She forced herself to take several bites of the muffin and to eat the berries, chewing as quickly as she could to end Danielle's obvious torment. She slurped her coffee and set down the mug. "Finished, Sir," she said breathlessly.

Master Mark laughed and shook his head. "Maybe we need to work on remembering to chew next time. Are you that eager to be bound, slave Jaime?"

"Or is it that you find it difficult to watch another sub being punished?" Master Anthony asked, fixing her with his discerning gaze.

Jaime nodded. "It does look very painful, Sir."

"That's the point," Master Anthony replied. "From now on slave Danielle will think twice, I hope, before handing out the wrong size hiking boots."

His words hit Jaime like a blow to the gut. Danielle was being punished because of *her*.

Master Mark touched her shoulder. "It's time for a lesson in Shibari."

The two men stood, and Jaime rose as well. She glanced at her plate. "Leave everything on the table," Master Anthony said. "It will be cleared away during chores. Come over to the dungeon and kneel quietly while we take Danielle off the horse."

Jaime followed the men to the space. She knelt to one side, noting the dozen or so coils of red and white rope set along the perimeter of the mat. She watched as the two men removed Danielle's blindfold, released her arms and lifted her from the sawhorse.

Once she was settled on the mat, Master Mark rubbed salve onto the girl's mons and labia, and Danielle moaned softly, whether from pain or lust, it wasn't clear. Jaime's pussy tingled as she imagined his touch. It would almost have been worth it to feel the cut of hard wood between her labia, if she got to feel his soothing, sensual touch afterward.

Danielle seemed to agree. "Thank you, Sir. Thank you, Master Mark," she murmured breathlessly, batting her big blue eyes. Jaime tried to push her uncharitable thoughts aside. After all, Danielle's Master had abandoned her. That had to be horribly humiliating. Beyond that, the poor girl might have had her heart broken.

Finally Danielle was settled in position beside Jaime. As the men moved the sawhorse out of the way, Danielle shot Jaime a venomous look. "Bitch," she hissed in a whisper. "Tattletale."

No! I didn't—" Jaime began, but was silenced by Master Anthony's stern look. Slaves did not speak unless spoken to. She pressed her lips together, her sympathy for Danielle's suffering and situation obliterated by the unjust accusation.

The two men returned to stand in front of the kneeling slave girls. "Slave Jaime," Master Anthony said, "what do you know about Shibari?"

"I know it's a kind of very intense bondage, Sir, and that it originated in Japan."

"That's correct. It literally means *to bind.* There's another term, *Kinbaku,* a term used interchangeably, that means tight binding. The emphasis isn't on the binding itself, the bondage, but more on the relationship between the one binding and the one being bound. It's a path, if you will, an extension between the two, that creates a special kind of intimacy."

Master Mark had picked up one of the coils and let it unwind. He ran his fingers sensually along the rope. "When practiced correctly," Master Anthony continued, "it's not just about techniques and knots. It's a full involvement of the spirit, the mind and the heart. All the senses are engaged."

Master Mark lifted the rope to his face and inhaled deeply, his eyes closing. "Yes," Master Anthony continued softly, watching the other man, "in this silken rope you can smell the heady scent of bondage, of submission, of suffering, of ecstasy." Jaime stared, mesmerized by the sensuality of Master Mark's actions.

Master Anthony finally broke the mood as he bent and retrieved a second coil of rope. "Mark, do you wish to work with slave Danielle or slave Jaime?"

"Since slave Danielle already has experience with Shibari, I'll work with the trainee this morning," Master Mark replied.

It took every ounce of willpower not to flash a satisfied smirk in Danielle's direction. Instead, Jaime fixed her gaze on the tatami, though she couldn't completely control the smile that played on her lips.

"As we move through this exercise," Master Mark said, "it's important to stay very aware and connected, because this type of bondage can trigger powerful emotional reactions. The positions and pressure inflicted by the ropes are not always easy to manage or endure and are sometimes quite painful. What I want you to do is focus on eroticizing the sensations. Use your breathing to flow with the pain. Embrace the loss of control, let the bondage empower you. Let it set you free."

"Beautifully said, Mark," Master Anthony said quietly, voicing Jaime's unspoken thought.

Master Mark turned his gaze to her. "Do you have any questions before we begin?"

"No, Sir," Jaime replied, her heart's tempo increasing.

"And you, slave Danielle," Master Anthony said. "Are you ready?"

"Oh, yes, Sir. Always, Sir," Danielle breathed, her expression the very picture of earnest, eager submission.

"Okay," Master Mark said. "We'll start by binding your arms behind your back. Remember, this isn't just about bondage. Let all your senses engage. Give yourself fully to the process. "

The two men moved behind them. Jaime focused on the sensation of the strong, silky rope being wrapped and looped around her upper arms. As it tightened against her skin, she could feel Master Mark's warm breath on the back of her neck. The second rope crossed her upper torso and back. As he worked, his strong hands stroked her body with a sure, sensual touch. Waves of pleasure rolled in a shiver of sensation over her skin.

The men moved around them, crouching, reaching, shifting, bending, Master Anthony murmuring softly to Master Mark as they worked. Master Mark wrapped Jaime's breasts in beautiful but painful patterns, the bonds cutting into her flesh and turning it purple.

As she was increasingly immobilized in her bonds, Jaime began to slip into that dark, delicious subspace where she could and would take whatever her Dom cared to give her. She was poised, ready to soar on powerful wings of pure release.

"Open your eyes," Master Mark commanded. Jaime forced herself to obey. She inhaled but forgot to exhale as she stared into his fathomless gaze.

He reached suddenly, grasping her by the throat, his face inches from hers. "Breathe," he murmured, his voice throaty. "You belong to me now. The ropes are an extension of my hands, and of your grace. Prepare to offer yourself fully now, heart, body and spirit."

A long, deep shudder moved through Jaime's core. She sighed her agreement, letting the stale air at last escape from her lungs. He let her go.

She became aware of more ropes being attached to the bonds that crisscrossed her upper body. The ropes were pulled taut, forcing her upward until only her knees were touching the tatami. Danielle was being tethered in kind. The men worked in tandem, standing on stepstools to secure the ropes to the wooden beams overhead.

All at once she was hoisted into the air and then, before she could think or react in any way, her legs were pulled from beneath her, her equilibrium turned topsy-turvy, everything happening so quickly she didn't even have time to gasp. She was upside down, the blood rushing to her head. Every muscle, every joint, every fiber of her being was alive and screaming. The tension of the ropes tight against her skin took her breath away. She felt hands moving over her, stroking, touching, soothing, igniting.

"Beautiful. She is a natural." It was a man's voice, but she could no longer tell who was speaking. She drifted in the deep, utter purity of subspace, the pain still very much there, but welcome. She opened the arms of her heart to embrace it, the knees of her soul bowing in pure submission.

When next she opened her eyes, she was sitting on the tatami mat, leaning back into a strong, safe embrace. A profound peace pervaded her being; a serenity the likes of which she'd never experienced in her life. As she became more fully conscious, she strived to hold the feeling, to keep it close, to imprint it in her mind and heart so she could take it out later and relive it, treasure it, breathe it, keep it safe and secret somewhere deep inside.

CHAPTER 9

Jaime felt the push of Master Mark's hard cock and then the flood of warmth and welcome as he entered her. She moaned her approval. He pressed her against the mattress as he moved inside her. His fingers tightened on her wrists as he stretched her arms over her head. "You're mine, Jaime. You've always been mine. You were born with my name under your tongue. Say it. Say my name."

"Master Mark," she murmured dreamily, arching up to take him deeper. "Master Mark, Master Mark, Master Mark." He moved inside her, bringing her close, closer—

"Rise and shine, sleepyhead."

The light burned through Jaime's eyelids. *No. No. Not yet. Please. Don't go.*

Master Mark slid from her, his image turning filmy and ghostlike, his face dissolving beneath the glare of the overhead light. Jaime opened her eyes.

Katie was smiling at her from the doorway. The smile edged into a frown as her gaze moved down Jaime's body. "What are you doing there?"

Jaime jolted fully awake. Her cuffed hands were wedged between her legs, two fingers still pressed into the stickiness of her wet dream. Luckily, the coverlet was over her body, hiding, or at least obscuring, what she'd been doing in her sleep. Heat warming her cheeks, she jerked her hands away. "Oh! I didn't mean—"

"Never mind that," Katie interrupted. Her eyes darted from Jaime to the webcam and back to Jaime, and Jaime understood. She flashed Katie a grateful look as she sat up. She worked the clips on her cuffs as

Katie continued, "It's Monday, and Monday is our heavy duty cleaning day. You'll be on bathroom patrol, lucky you." She flashed a sympathetic grin. "The silver lining is you get to work with Master Anthony this afternoon."

Jaime very nearly clapped her hands in childish excitement at the prospect. After hanging her cuffs and chain in their place on the wall, she made her bed. She thought back on the day before. Sunday she had spent a difficult but rewarding morning working with Mistress Marjorie on positions training in the second floor dungeon, really more of an exercise room, complete with mirrored walls and ballet bars.

"You have natural grace," Mistress Marjorie had encouraged her as she struggled to master the various standing, kneeling, sexual and punishment positions required of all staff slaves at The Enclave. "You'll need to memorize these positions quickly. Practice is the best way. I'll make sure you get in at least an hour a day." At the end of the session, she gave Jaime a laminated chart outlining ten basic slave positions, along with several variations on each. Jaime had taped it to her bedroom wall, and she glanced at it now, promising herself to work on them during free time.

Jaime was intrigued by Mistress Marjorie's ability to submit to her husband, and then to so effortlessly segue into her dominant persona when dealing with the slave staff. Jaime had never known a true switch before, but for Mistress Marjorie it seemed as natural as breathing.

The session after lunch on Sunday had been less appealing, and a lot more exhausting. Master Brandon had overseen stamina training on the side lawn. Katie and Jaime were paired against Hans and Lucia in a tortuous relay race. Teammates had to run back and forth carrying a heavy concrete brick, which they would hand off to their partner, who would then sprint back and forth across the lawn cradling the rough, scratchy weight as best they could, before handing it off once again.

The teams had been unfairly matched, with Hans and Lucia barely breaking a sweat as they sprinted like athletes and effortlessly handed off their brick to each other. While Jaime was slender, she well knew that thin did not equal fit, and it had been a long time since she'd done much exercise beyond window shopping and walking from her office to her car. Poor Katie huffed and puffed as she stumbled forward, her face red, the sweat streaming. Thank goodness Master Brandon finally called a halt to the exercise before Katie had a heart attack.

"You did very well," Jaime heard Master Brandon tell Katie as he led her away, his arm around her shoulders. "Much improved since you first arrived, hmm?" Jaime could only wonder what it must have been like before.

Now Lucia was waiting for her in the bathroom and, though it had only been a few days, Jaime had quickly become accustomed to the washing and grooming routine. It was surprising, too, how easily she'd adjusted to being totally naked, save for her collar. Within a few minutes she was showered, smoothed of any stubble and ready to face whatever awaited her.

It looked like another perfect summer day had dawned as Jaime took her breakfast to the veranda. She sat with Mistress Aubrey and Gene, who kept their clinic open on Saturdays, and thus took their weekend on Sundays and Mondays.

"I've volunteered Gene for your session this afternoon," Mistress Aubrey announced. Jaime, who had been lost in a daydream, snapped to immediate attention at these words. She looked at Gene, who grinned and cocked one eyebrow. She was dying to ask what the session would involve, but held her tongue.

When breakfast was over, Jaime reported to the laundry room, which was where all the cleaning supplies were kept. Katie, Lucia and Ashley were already there, standing at attention, arms behind their heads, eyes straight ahead. Jaime took her place in the row and stood likewise. Danielle, Hans and Gene appeared a few seconds later and took their places silently, forming a second row behind the first.

Master Lawrence came in and stood in front of them, his arms behind his back, his posture military-straight. On the edge of her vision, Jaime could see him examine each slave with a critical eye. When he got to her, she stood as straight as an arrow, breasts thrust forward, feet precisely shoulder-width apart, fingers laced firmly behind her head. When he drew his fingers lightly over her armpits, she managed to stay stock-still, though it tickled like crazy.

"Chin up," he snapped, pushing at her chin with his index finger. Master Lawrence would have made a good army drill sergeant. She imagined all of them shouting out, "Sir-yes-sir!" after he barked out an order.

"Is something amusing, slave Jaime?" Master Lawrence's cold voice sliced through her.

"No, Sir!" she replied, thankful he couldn't penetrate her thoughts. "Pardon me, Sir."

After a moment during which he stripped her flesh from her bones with his gaze, he finally looked away. Jaime sighed inwardly with relief.

"Slave Danielle," he said, fixing his eyes on the back row. "You will set out the shoes and hobble chains. Hopefully you won't end up on the punishment pony this time."

"Yes, Sir. Thank you, Master Lawrence," Danielle replied. Jaime felt the freeze of Danielle's silent fury directed toward her as Danielle moved forward to get the high heels for the female slaves and the heavy work boots for the males.

She'd tried to talk to Danielle, to tell her she didn't blame Danielle for what was surely an honest mistake, even though she suspected it probably wasn't. Whatever Danielle's motivation had been in giving her boots a size too big, Jaime had been willing to let bygones be bygones.

She'd further tried to assure Danielle she hadn't been the one to say anything about it to the Masters, but her words fell on deaf ears. Danielle simply walked away each time Jaime began to speak.

Danielle set the pairs of shoes down in front of each slave, along with a pair of ankle cuffs attached to either end of a small hobble chain. At a signal from Master Lawrence, Jaime and the other slaves bent down to slip on the shoes and attach the ankle cuffs. While the visual effect was erotic—naked slave girls working in high heels and chains—it definitely made cleaning more challenging.

"It keeps you focused," Hans had explained, when she'd wondered out loud about the training aspect. "And it eroticizes the experience. Something as menial as cleaning out a toilet becomes sensual when you think about the submissive aspect of what you are doing."

Easy for him to say—he got to wear the boots, not the heels.

It was amazing how many toilets there were in that huge house. In addition to the four in the slave quarters, there were three on the first floor, eight on the second and four on the third. Jaime needed every minute of the morning to clean the toilets and wash all the bathroom floors, along with wiping down the counters, cleaning the sinks and shower stalls, and polishing the mirrors. By the time lunch rolled around, she was more ready for a hot shower and a nap than a meal, but there was no time.

The afternoon session was to take place in the main dungeon, and Jaime was both nervous and excited at the prospect of working directly with Master Anthony. She was sure whatever was in store for her, it would stretch her limits and push her boundaries. In a way, she wished the training didn't include a second sub, but no one had consulted her on the matter.

Happily, she had just enough time to take a quick shower in the slave quarters before the session. As she brushed out her hair in front of the mirror, she stared at her image. Though she was only in her fourth day of the two-week stint, the face that looked back at her was different than the nervous, uncertain girl she'd seen upon arrival.

Even without makeup, her cheeks were rosy and her eyes had a sparkle to them, as if she carried a bright, warm secret deep inside. She smiled. For the first time in her life, she felt as if she were being true to her inner self—to that part of her that contained her essence. Her previous life as a ski instructor in Vermont and then as a clerk and paralegal in Asheville seemed almost like a dream. Or no, not a dream precisely, but a different life, one lived in black and white, while The Enclave was a burst of vibrant color.

She knew she was in the throes of a crush, if not necessarily on a particular person, then on the whole place that was The Enclave. Yes, the training was difficult and exacting. It required more of her than she'd ever given to anything else in her life. And yet, it was precisely because of that, because she was asked every day, every hour, to give all she had to give, that it was so worthwhile and so fulfilling.

"I want to be here," she announced to the mirror. Then she caught sight of the reverse image of the clock behind her, and she scurried out. Fortunately, she was the first to arrive in the main dungeon. She knelt quickly on one of the yoga mats, assuming a kneeling, at-ease position, her back straight, upward palms resting lightly on her knees. As she waited, she looked around the room, drinking it all in.

The space was huge, nearly as big as the main dungeon at The Garden. It was outfitted with beautifully crafted, high quality BDSM equipment, including three X crosses, two spanking benches, two bondage chairs, a cock and ball torture chair, stocks, several cages and a suspension swing. There were racks of whips, canes and paddles, coils of rope and chain, counters neatly lined with gags, cuffs, blindfolds, dildos, plugs, pots of wax and candles, along with trays of needles and metal implements that made Jaime shudder just to look at.

Turning to face the open double doors of the dungeon, Jaime drew in a deep breath and let it slowly out. In addition to positions training, Mistress Marjorie had worked with her on breathing, on letting submissive peace move through her being. "Eventually," Mistress Marjorie had assured her, "you will find that your nervous anticipation no longer serves you. You will let it go. You will stop trying to control the moment, and that is when you will achieve true submissive serenity."

Jaime closed her eyes and focused on calming her mind and body. Though she remained jittery with anticipation, some of the clatter quieted in her head, and the butterflies, while still batting around in her belly, weren't quite so insistent.

She kept her eyes down as Master Anthony entered the dungeon. His black, polished boots appeared in her line of vision. She could see Gene's bare feet behind him. Master Anthony touched the top of her head and stroked her hair.

"Stand up, slave Jaime. Hands behind your back, legs spread wide." Jaime rose, trying for the fluid, graceful movement she'd practiced with Mistress Marjorie the day before, not sure she succeeded.

Master Anthony was dressed in black leather pants and an open black leather vest, no shirt beneath. His chest hair was silver against tan skin, his muscles every bit as ripped as a man half his age. He moved close and reached for her throat. He gripped her hard just beneath the jawline and she gasped, her nipples instantly erect. With his other hand, he reached between her legs and cupped her already throbbing, wet cunt. His palm rubbed against her vulva. She moaned, her hips arching forward of their own accord.

"Stay still," he ordered, his tone quiet but firm. A shudder moved through her loins as he pushed a single finger into the grip of her wetness, and she blew out a ragged breath. He increased the pressure under her jaw, blocking her ability to breathe. She felt her face tighten, her heart beating overly fast. Master Anthony stared deep into her eyes and she felt as if she were balanced on a cliff—the slightest puff of air would send her flying.

All at once he let her go and stepped back. Somehow Jaime managed to keep her position as she bit back a whimper of frustrated desire. It wasn't the man, necessarily, but his sheer mastery that held her in such thrall. She struggled to control herself as he began to speak. "Today we will work on focus during distraction and on orgasm control," he said. "Slave Gene will assist me in the exercise. Your task during the session, slave Jaime, is to follow my instructions, no matter what else is happening at the time, and that includes holding back from orgasm when so ordered, and then coming when I command it."

"Yes, Sir," Jaime managed, though his words created a sudden, anxious tightness in her chest. Most of her intensive training to this point had been passive—taking a whipping, enduring caning or anal penetration, suffering through difficult bondage sessions. Today's assignment would require her active participation and control of what she still considered automatic, physiological responses to stimulation. Master Anthony had already reduced her to a sopping wet, trembling puddle of submissive desire within thirty seconds of entering the room. How the hell was she going to get through this training? She knew it was possible in theory to control one's orgasm and to come on command, but she had no idea if she would be able to accomplish these goals. Or no, strike that—she was pretty sure she was going to fuck this up.

"During the first part of this exercise," Master Anthony continued, "you will be secured in a bondage chair. Gene will play with your cunt while I torture your breasts. You will focus on achieving orgasm, and not letting the erotic pain get in the way. Your ultimate goal is to use that pain to help propel you to your climax. The challenge is to balance on the tightrope between pleasure and pain, between release and control, until I give you permission to let go. Do you understand the assignment?"

"I-I think so, Master Anthony."

He led her toward the bondage chairs. There were two types. The first chair was made of stainless steel. There was an adjustable steel collar at the top center of the chair, as well as steel cuffs on the armrests and the front legs for full restraint. This chair brought medieval torture scenes to Jaime's mind.

The second chair had a wooden frame, the seat and back made of red, padded leather. The top half of the chair formed a T cross, and the seat was shaped like an inverted V. Master Anthony led her to this chair and directed her to sit, her bottom resting on the point of the V, her thighs along either side, her back against the T cross.

He strapped her wrists into leather cuffs that hung from eyehooks at the top ends of the T and then cuffed her ankles to the chair legs. Turning a lever on the side of the chair, he widened the V until her thighs were spread, her cunt fully exposed and accessible. He stood back and regarded her appraisingly, his gaze moving like fingers over her skin.

After a moment he turned toward the entrance of the dungeon, where Gene knelt quietly on a yoga mat. "Slave Gene. Come over here and kneel between slave Jaime's legs. You will focus on oral pleasure. You may use your hands as well."

Gene stood and walked quickly toward them, his pierced cock already rising to the task. He licked his lips and flashed a grin at Jaime as he knelt before her. She was far too nervous to smile back.

The sudden, unmistakable sonic snap of a whip startled her. Master Anthony was holding a short-handled single tail whip. "Repeat your assignment to me, slave Jaime, and then we begin."

Being bound as she was, arms and legs spread wide, cunt on full display, Jaime had a hard time concentrating. Her mouth was dry, her heart fluttering wildly in her chest. "You're going to torture my breasts"—she stared at the single tail whip as she spoke—"while slave Gene makes me come."

"Be more precise. What is this exercise about?"

Jaime tore her gaze from the whip and looked directly at Master Anthony as she struggled to compose her thoughts. "Um, it's about control and focus. Focus on my orgasm while you, um, distract me with breast torture." His nod gave her more confidence, and she continued, "I am to get myself to the edge of a climax, but then wait until you give me permission to come, Sir."

And I have no idea if I can do this. She sent a brief, heartfelt prayer to the BDSM gods, wherever they might be.

"That is correct, slave Jaime." Master Anthony snapped the whip once more in the air, and Jaime's breasts tingled, her nerve endings alive with expectation. He looked down at Gene, who waited patiently between Jaime's spread thighs. "You may begin, boy. Do your best, as I know you will."

Gene placed his hands on Jaime's thighs as he leaned forward. His tongue appeared between parted lips. He drew a long, wet, sensual line over the folds of Jaime's vulva. Already deeply aroused, she shuddered with pleasure. He licked and kissed her sex with the ardor and passion of a skilled lover and she moaned her approval.

A sudden, sharp line of fire snapped across her left breast and she cried out. Ignoring everything but his task, Gene licked in a teasing circle around her throbbing clit as the second stroke of the whip left its mark on her right breast. Instinctively she tried to close her legs and her arms, but she was unable to move. The whip struck again, its tip finding her nipple. The pain obliterated everything else. Jaime screamed.

"Focus," Master Anthony said calmly. "Accept with grace and joy what both slave Gene and I are giving you."

The next stroke hit her other nipple.

Jaime screamed again, her only focus on the pain.

Gene pushed a finger inside her, and her vaginal muscles clamped down hard around it. His tongue soothed away the pain in her nipples, moving in fluttery strokes over and around her hard, aching clit.

The whip struck in rapid, stinging strokes on the undersides of Jaime's breasts as Gene continued his sweet attention at her cunt. "Focus. Control. Grace," Master Anthony intoned. The whip continued to sting, but the pain was bearable now, almost welcome. The pleasure mounted, moving through her like a rising tide. Gene did something amazing with his tongue and Jaime knew it was a matter of seconds before she lost it.

Oh god, oh god, let me come. Please. Say it.

The whip continued to caress her with its now delicious sting. She managed to open eyes she didn't realize she'd closed. Master Anthony was watching her face as he flicked the whip in perfect precision. He was so masterful, with his dark eyes, intense expression and complete control of the situation. Gene's tongue, lips and fingers were driving her wild.

Please, please, please, oh fuck. "Oh, ooooo..." Without her permission, or anyone else's, Jaime orgasmed, the climax dragging her under and spinning her in its wake. Even as she shuddered and bucked in her restraints, she knew she'd fucked up—she'd failed at focus and control.

Remorse quickly overtook the raw, animal pleasure of the climax. When she could get her breath, she gasped, "I'm sorry. I'm so sorry, Sir, I—"

"Silence," Master Anthony interrupted sharply. "You did not ask for permission to speak."

Jaime snapped her mouth closed, her face hot with embarrassment and shame. Of all people, Master Anthony was the one she wanted most to impress, and she'd failed him. Gene, witness to her shame, was still kneeling between her legs, but he was sitting back on his haunches, his hands in his lap, his gaze downward.

"We begin again," Master Anthony continued, his voice once again soft, his expression kind. "This time, work on harnessing the pain, rather than fighting it. Work on reining in the pleasure, rather than giving in to it. Before you can truly submit, you must learn to control your reactions, your responses, your desires and your needs. Before you give yourself fully to another, you must first become the master of yourself."

He gave a small nod to Gene, who resumed his sensual, singular attention to Jaime's now-sensitized sex. The whip flicked down in a snapping arc on tender breasts. Sweat trickled down Jaime's back and prickled at her armpits. She clenched her hands into fists, determined this time to succeed, to become her own master.

She felt dizzy. Her cunt throbbed, pleasure rising in her core, as the whip snapped and cut across her flesh. The tip found her nipples once more, pain exploding like firecrackers at her nerve endings.

"Now," Master Anthony said, his voice strong. "Come for me, slave Jaime. Give me your submission."

At that precise moment, Gene slipped his fingers inside her, twisting them in a way that connected perfectly with whatever he was doing with his tongue. The whip continued to snap and bite at her breasts but she now welcomed its relentless sting. She actually visualized herself walking that narrow tightrope between pleasure and pain, high above the world, lifted by her Master's command.

She came, the orgasm ten times—a hundred times—more powerful than the first stolen climax, its onrush blinding in its impact, its perfection, its grace.

When she finally opened her eyes, it took her several seconds to focus and reorient herself. She felt as if she'd run a marathon, and won. She had done it! She'd focused, worked through the pain, staved off her orgasm, and then come on command. She flashed a grateful glance and smile at Gene, who, it seemed to her, had worked some kind of magic to send her over the edge at just the right moment. He, however, was not looking at her, his gaze fixed instead on Master Anthony.

Some of Jaime's pleasure ebbed. She flexed her fingers, which tingled uncomfortably from lack of blood flow. Her breasts stung. She was sweaty, thirsty and exhausted. The exercise seemed to be over. She wanted to be let out of the cuffs. She needed to pee.

Master Anthony was watching her, and she had the uncomfortable feeling he was reading her less than obedient, less than submissive thoughts. She looked away and drew in a deep, cleansing breath, trying to refocus on acceptance.

Master Anthony touched her cheek. "You did well, slave Jaime. We'll continue to work on your control skills, and also on acceptance and the need to stop anticipating."

So he *had* read her mind. She nearly smiled in her chagrin and silently promised herself to do better.

Master Anthony glanced down at Gene. "How long has it been since you orgasmed, boy?"

"Three days, Sir," Gene replied promptly.

"Your Mistress has given permission for you to come today, if I agreed you earned it. You did. So stand up and take your pleasure. I will direct you."

Gene jumped eagerly to his feet, a wide grin on his face. "Yes, Sir. Thank you, Sir," he said enthusiastically. His cock was fully erect, the golden hoop of his Prince Albert piercing glinting at the base of the head.

Master Anthony leaned close to Jaime's chair and adjusted its legs until her knees were touching. He released a lever on the chair's side, which caused the top half to ease back until she was lying flat. He stood over her and unzipped his leather pants. Without taking them down, he reached into the open fly and pulled out his cock, which, even in its semi-erect state, appeared to be quite large.

He wrapped his hand around the base and shifted until he was standing just over her head. With his other hand, he gestured to Gene. "Stand on her other side. We're going to ejaculate at the same time, on my command." Gene scooted quickly to Jaime's other side, his expression puppy-dog eager.

The two men began to masturbate, their cocks poised over Jaime's upturned face. She lay, still bound, arms spread wide, as they pulled and tugged at their shafts. Gene's gaze was fixed intently on her welted breasts. Master Anthony was watching her face. After only a few minutes, he said, "Open your mouth, slave Jaime, and accept our gifts. Keep your focus on me."

To Gene, he commanded in a slightly breathless voice, "Come for me, slave Gene. Now."

On cue, the perfectly trained slave boy began to spurt, his jism splattering Jaime's cheeks and chin. Unable to control her reflexes, Jaime's eyes squeezed shut, though she managed to keep her mouth open. Recalling Master Anthony's admonition, she quickly opened her eyes. Master Anthony, his gaze still fixed on hers, shot a ribbon of ejaculate directly into Jaime's open mouth. She sputtered and swallowed, struggling for some modicum of grace as she tried not to choke.

Recovering, she drew her tongue over her lips. Master Anthony's come was salty-sweet. His cock still erect and dripping, he reached down and pushed his hand between Jaime's legs. A few well-directed strokes of his fingers against her cunt had her instantly pulsing with need. He rubbed her for perhaps thirty seconds and the wave of a climax began to roll toward her.

"Are you ready to come again, slave Jaime?"

"Yes, Sir," she gasped, the wave rising.

"Well, don't." His fingers kept moving. "You are on the edge. Learn to balance there."

Jaime stiffened, her fists clenching above the cuffs, her heart thudding, her breath rasping. It felt good. Oh god, too, too, too good.

Fuck, oh fuck, fuck, fuck, fuck.

The wave crashed over her.

The fingers were withdrawn. The room was deadly silent, save the thudding of Jaime's heart in her ears.

Finally Master Anthony spoke. "Ah well. You know what they say. Progress, not perfection. That's why it's called training. Shall we begin again?"

Chapter 10

"That's it," Mason said as he watched Mark push yet another needle through the skin of the orange. "Your technique is excellent. You're ready to work with a live subject. My girl will be happy to volunteer." They were in Mason's suite on the second floor of The Enclave where the Dominants and their personal slaves slept. Mason's space consisted of an L-shaped room, one part containing the bedroom, the other his private playroom/dungeon.

"Let's move on to knives."

Mark glanced up quickly. "Knives?" An involuntary shudder moved through him. "Sorry. I know it's a major rush for you and Ashley, but blood, all that"—he shook his head adamantly—"I'm just not into it."

Mason smiled, shaking his own head. "Don't be so quick to dismiss something, just because it takes you out of your comfort zone, Mark. Think if we let the subs do that—we'd only have floggers and Hitachi wands in the dungeons."

Mark laughed. "Okay, okay. You're right. I'll try to keep an open mind."

"Good." Mason stood from the worktable at which they'd been practicing and turned toward a freestanding wardrobe. He opened the doors and selected a large, flat wooden box from a shelf. He returned to the table with it, along with a tissue-box-type plastic container of pre-moistened anti-bacterial wipes.

"This is my knife play collection, carefully honed, pun intended," Mason said with a grin, "over my twenty-plus years in the scene." He set down the box and opened the lid. Beneath a folded piece of black cotton he revealed half a dozen black velvet bags, each set into its own molded partition. There was also a packet of small plastic cards with a rubber band wrapped around them, as well as a large box of various types of adhesive bandages and a tube of antibiotic cream.

"Those look like credit cards," Mark remarked, pointing toward the stack.

"They are." Mason picked up the packet and tossed it toward Mark, who automatically caught it. "Edge play isn't just about cutting and drawing blood—the core of the experience is mental. It's a mind fuck in the best sense of the word." As Mark stared down at the expired gasoline card on top of the packet, Mason continued, "One very effective technique during knife play is to blindfold your sub. She doesn't know what to expect. That's when the plastic cards can come into play. Her brain will have been geared by you to expect a knife's edge. You can use the edge of the credit card and really bear down on the skin without risk of cutting. You know it's perfectly safe, but she doesn't. Hence the mind fuck."

Mark nodded, his imagination rippling with the possibilities. "That makes sense. It sounds hot."

"Smokin'," Mason concurred. He reached for one of the velvet bags and pulled a knife out by its handle. He set the knife down on the unfolded cotton fabric. "When choosing knives for play, just as when choosing them for cooking, you want to focus on functionality, not fashion." He selected a second knife and slid it from its velvet sheath. He handed it to Mark. "This is a good starter knife. The length of the blade is approximately the width of your hand, for easier control. The weight, size and balance are important. You don't want something with too long a blade, especially when starting out, since they can be unwieldy and hard to balance."

Mark lifted the knife and shifted it from hand to hand, imagining the blade sliding along bare, smooth skin. "That's right," Mason encouraged. "The handle should feel comfortable at all angles in your hand so you have full control and can properly judge how much pressure you're putting on the blade. Remember, even here at The Enclave, rack is the name of the game."

"Rack?"

"You know, R-A-C-K," Mason spelled out. "Risk-aware, consensual kink. It's a level beyond S-S-C."

"Safe, sane and consensual," Mark replied, glad he at least knew that one, and feeling foolish that he hadn't heard of RACK before, though he understood and practiced the concept behind it.

"Yep." Mason nodded. "It's all part and parcel of our core principals of consent, communication, responsible play and risk mitigation. With something like knife play, it's especially important that everyone is made completely aware of the potential risks and complications of what they are doing. The first step is making sure you, as the Top, do, in fact, know what the hell you're doing. We'll go over the basics, and you can use these knives to work with on your own before we actually scene this afternoon."

"This afternoon?" Mark queried, surprised. "Isn't that a little quick?"

Mason shook his head. "Nah. I've watched you in action, Mark. You're a natural. You already have the whole mind fuck concept down, and you have the passion and intuition to make any scene a success." Mark warmed beneath this praise. "Skill with the blade isn't that crucial yet. I mean, yeah, you'll be using a real knife, but I'll handle any actual cutting. We'll never move out of your comfort zone during the actual scene."

Mark liked and trusted Mason, whom he regarded not only as a teacher, but as a friend. "Okay," he said. "I'm willing to give it a try."

"Good man." Mason selected another knife and pulled off its velvet cover. "Some people use fruit and paper and stuff to practice, but I believe the best dummy to use is yourself. You need to know, up front and personal, exactly what that blade feels like on your own skin before you get anywhere near your sub."

"But you said you don't have to cut yourself?"

"No. Not talking about an actual cut. Knife play isn't about cutting, in general, unless that's your particular kink. It's about the sensation of the blade grazing your skin, the potential, the *possibility* that it might happen—that it *could* happen. That's the mind fuck, see?"

Mark nodded.

Mason set down the knife and pushed up the sleeve of his knit black top, revealing his hairy, muscular forearm. "Now, if you're kinked like me"—Mason turned his arm over and drew the tip of his blade in a small line along his inner arm. Mark watched, both horrified and fascinated as a thin line of blood beaded in its wake—"you get off on the blood and the pain, and the endorphin rush it brings."

He looked up at Mark and smiled a sadist's smile. "I know, I know," he said as Mark opened his mouth to protest, "it's not your thing. I get that." He reached for the box of Band-Aids and pulled one out, quickly tearing off its paper covering and applying it to the tiny, self-inflicted wound on his arm, which, Mark now noticed, was covered in myriad tiny scars.

"Like I said, you don't have to actually cut yourself to learn to do this properly," Mason continued calmly as he pulled down his sleeve. "It's all a matter of technique, and of paying attention, close attention, to your sub's reactions." He popped open the plastic tissue box and plucked a pre-moistened wipe from it.

Picking up the knife, he wiped its blade and then looked over at Mark. "Now let's practice some technique. Use your knife and copy what I'm doing on your own arm, to get a feel for what I'm talking about."

Mark, wearing a button-down shirt already rolled to the elbow, didn't need to push up his sleeve. His heart beating a little too fast, he tentatively touched the edge of the cold blade to his bare skin. "That's right." Mason nodded encouragingly. "Now, pull the knife toward you—never push it. You want to hold your blade the way an artist holds and controls a paintbrush. You have to anticipate a sudden flinch, jerk or quiver so that any cut is intentional, never accidental. Your sub is your precious canvas, and you want to be creative while always maintaining full control."

Mark watched carefully, copying Mason's movements with his own knife, a surge of adrenaline kicking through his gut at the thought of doing this to someone else, to a naked, vulnerable sub girl who trusted him completely. The erotic power was a natural aphrodisiac, and he suddenly understood what a rush edge play could be.

The image of Jaime bound to a bondage table, blindfolded and at his mercy, tried to push its way into his consciousness, but he managed to shake it away. He focused instead on the knives and what his friend was teaching him. As with any BDSM scene, he instinctively understood it wasn't necessarily about the tools you were using, but the whole setup and execution—placing the submissive in the proper mindset and giving her, and in the process yourself, what she needed and craved.

Mason brought out a bucket of ice from a small refrigerator he kept in the corner of the room, along with a candle and a lighter, and a violet wand kit. They experimented with chilling and heating the blades, as well as adding an electric thrill to the experience with the violet wand. They worked steadily for over an hour, discussing technique and nuance as Mark gained comfort and experience handling the knives.

Finally Mason set down his blade. "Take the kit," he said. "Keep working. I've got a scene scheduled with the trainee this afternoon. I want you to join us and put your practice to the test."

Before Mark's brain processed Mason's words, his cock sprang to attention, his earlier fantasy leaping flow-blown back into his consciousness.

He could no longer deny it—it was becoming increasingly hard to keep his growing feelings for the girl at bay. In the two months since he'd been at The Enclave, he'd worked intimately with all the staff slaves, as well as two other trainees, neither of whom had been invited to join The Enclave community, though both had been worthy subs— just not the right fit. While he'd grown and developed as a Dom with each experience, and had genuine fun and sexual thrills with some of the female subs, no one had gotten under his skin the way Jaime had over the past few days.

He'd been trying to put his feelings aside, to dismiss them as casual attraction to a beautiful woman. After years of fortune and fame, he'd had his fill and then some of beautiful women eager to be with him, not because of who he was—but because of what he represented as a rock star, with all the glitter and fame that went with it. It was that same fame and its attendant pressures that sapped both his energy and time, making a love connection virtually impossible.

Love!

Who said anything about love?

Jaime was there for another week or so. Then the odds were good she'd disappear, the same as the others. The Enclave was a special place but an exacting one, and the commitment, especially for staff slaves, was intense and all-consuming. It was foolish to allow oneself to become emotionally connected to the trainees, especially for someone who hadn't fully committed to the place himself.

Annoyed with himself for brooding, Mark pushed away his thoughts and went in search of his guitar. He would refocus with his music, and then practice with the knife kit for the afternoon's session.

~*~

I can't do it. No way. No fucking way. Jaime clenched her hands into fists against her thighs, her muscles rigid with anxiety. Ashley and she knelt together on the mat in the main dungeon waiting for Master Mason to arrive and begin the scene. Ever since Master Lawrence had informed Jaime she was to report to the main dungeon after lunch for knife and needle training with Master Mason, Jaime's mind had been in turmoil. She was grateful Ashley was going to be there with her, but also knew Ashley was totally into the extreme play that made Jaime sick to her stomach just to think about.

Ashley turned to regard her. "What's wrong with you? You're all tensed up."

"I can't do it," Jaime blurted, voicing her silent fears. "I'm terrified of needles and knife play. I thought I could handle this, but I can't. I just can't."

Ashley was silent for several long beats. Eventually she shrugged. "So go, then. Leave. Quit."

"What?" Jaime was confused.

"It's not like you're here as a prisoner, Jaime. If you don't want to continue your training, you can just walk out. No one's going to beg you to stay."

Avoiding the real issue for a moment, Jaime blurted, "But what about the money? I already spent it."

Ashley blew out a dismissive breath. "Master Anthony won't care. In case you hadn't noticed, money's not exactly an issue around here. It's not about the money—or it shouldn't be. If you're here because you got paid, then this definitely isn't the place for you." She stared hard at Jaime. "You wouldn't be the first trainee to fail, you know. You won't be the last, either. It takes real courage to submit."

Ashley's words stung. "It's not about the money for me either," she retorted hotly. "I do have submissive courage, I do! But I have limits, too. Hard limits. Everyone does."

Ashley shook her head. "Not here, they don't. At least, you don't get to decide what they are. The Masters decide for us." Her voice softened as she continued, "They're highly skilled at what they do, Jaime. If Master Anthony thought enough of you to invite you here, then he trusts that you're willing and able to undergo the training process in its entirety. If he hadn't thought so, you wouldn't be here."

Jaime nodded, mollified. "I get that. And I want to succeed. I've never felt so alive as since I got here. I've never felt so worthwhile or vital. But"—she struggled to articulate her thoughts—"I'm afraid of some things, you know? I'm afraid of confined spaces and I'm afraid of needles and seeing my own blood. I'm afraid I'll pass out. I'm not like you—this kind of edge play isn't a turn on for me—it freaks me out."

"That's a good thing, Jaime."

"What?" Again Jaime was confused.

"Look," Ashley explained, "everyone is scared sometimes to do something. They don't think they can do it. They don't want to fail. They don't want to make a fool of themselves. That's when the courage really kicks in. For me, believe it or not, it's about cooking. About becoming a real chef, not just some sous chef in a second-rate restaurant, which is what I was when Master Mason found me."

She angled her body slightly toward Jaime and laid her hand on Jaime's arm. "Let me see if I can explain this to you. I get off on pressure—you have to if you're in the restaurant business. That pressure is like fuel. Master Mason's been giving me more and more responsibility in the kitchen lately, and, to quote you, it's been freaking me out. But it's also the best thing in the world for me, and I know it."

Her pretty, pixie face became more animated. "Whenever I think, *uh-oh, I don't feel ready, this is going to come out bad, I'm going to fail*, then I get this *physical* feeling, like a hand has reached into my gut and twisted it. I don't like that feeling, but I like the whole arc of it. I *need* the whole arc for it to be good. You're scared shitless right now because you're facing a scene that doesn't get you all hot and excited. It's not a sexual turn-on for you, like whipping or bondage. But the Masters obviously believe it's necessary for you, if you want to achieve true submission, that is. If you want to move beyond scratching your particular kink itch."

"Okay," Jaime acquiesced, chagrined to hear herself described in this way, but equally aware Ashley was pretty much on the mark. "I get that, but can't I achieve true submission, as you call it, without having my hard limits violated?"

"Don't think of them as limits. There are no limits, except the ones you erect in your head. Achieving submission is like any other worthy but difficult goal. The people who succeed are the ones who think through what they really want from the experience and then work incredibly hard, day after day, to attain their goals. They don't just flop around like fish out of water. They have a vision, and they work their asses off to make it a reality. Whether it's becoming a top-notch chef or becoming the best sub you can be, one worthy of becoming an Enclave staff slave, it's all the same thing."

"But what if I fail?" Jaime asked in a small voice.

Ashley shrugged. "Then you fail. And you try again. You keep at it, despite failing, or *because* of failing, if that makes sense. It's like creating that perfect recipe. You rework and rework and rework it until you get it right. The bar is definitely high here at The Enclave, but that's what makes it so exhilarating, don't you see? Yeah, you have to struggle, and yeah, sometimes you fail, but how you react to that failure is where the choice comes in. You can either get pissed and give up, or you can ask yourself, 'How can I make it better? What can I do to be a better sub, not for Master X, but for myself?'"

Ashley turned toward the entrance of the dungeon at the sound of approaching footsteps. Her countenance smoothed into serenity, her body arched into statuesque perfection. "You can do it, Jaime," she whispered as Jaime, too, struggled to assume the at-ease, kneeling-up position. "Have faith in yourself."

Two sets of boots appeared in front of their lowered eyes. At a tap to her shoulder, Jaime looked up, not into the face of Master Mason, as she'd expected, but into Master Mark's lively eyes. "Oh," she blurted in happy surprise before realizing she'd made a sound. She pressed her lips together and looked down, wondering if he'd seen the blush rising on her cheeks.

"Good afternoon, girls," Master Mason growled in his deep bass. "Today's session will involve needle and knife play." He turned to Master Mark. "I understand Jaime has issues, difficulties, with this kind of edge play. What do you think about securing her in one of the St. Andrew's crosses to keep her from fidgeting or turning away while she watches the demonstration?"

"I think it's an excellent idea," Master Mark said. He tapped her shoulder again. "Get up, slave girl. I'll strap you in while Master Mason and slave Ashley prepare for the demonstration."

Relief flooded through Jaime as she followed Master Mark through the dungeon toward one of the X crosses that stood near the back of the large space. She was going to be an observer; that was all!

Yet, at the same time, she found herself oddly disappointed. Ashley's words had made a strong impression on her, giving her resolve she hadn't had previously. She had almost looked forward to the chance to prove, both to herself and to her Masters, she had the courage and determination to handle whatever they deemed was right for her. Still, the relief was greater than the need to prove herself. There would be other times for that during her training, she was pretty sure.

She resisted the strong urge to lean into Master Mark's touch as he cuffed her into the cross. He added a leather restraint across her forehead that made it impossible for her to turn away. When he was done, he ran his fingers lightly over her nipples, trailing his hand down her abdomen to between her spread legs.

She nearly moaned aloud, only barely catching herself in time. As it was, her perking nipples and instantly sopping pussy had to be obvious testament to her desire for the man. She had to bite her lips to keep from groaning with frustration when he dropped his hand from her body and stepped away. Her clit throbbed in protest and her nipples ached.

Still, she had to admit, having him around made the prospect of what she knew was going to be a boundary-pushing scene a lot easier to bear. She watched as the two men dragged a second cross into position so it was directly in her line of vision. The diminutive Ashley stepped up onto a platform, her back to Jaime. She spread herself into an X on the cross and the Masters cuffed her wrists and ankles into place.

"Slave Ashley is fully trained in edge play," Master Mason said as he worked. "But we always use restraints during knife and needle play, just as a precaution. A securely bound sub can't move unexpectedly if they, for example, sneeze or something. Any cutting or piercing I do will be on purpose, not because of a slip of the knife or unexpected jab of the needle."

Master Mason brought over a tray laden with supplies and set it on the bondage table near Ashley's cross. On it, Jaime could see dozens of single-use hypodermic needles tipped with black plastic hubs, each individually wrapped in clear plastic. Beside the heap of needles, there was a small red plastic container with a white lid, the words *Danger – Destroy by Incineration* printed on its label. There was a small cardboard box stuffed with medical procedural gloves, one of them protruding from the opening, along with a box of skin cleansing wipes. Finally, and rather mysteriously, there was a spool of red satin ribbon and a pair of scissors.

Master Mason pulled two gloves from the box and slipped them over his large hands. He picked up one of the needles and tore off its plastic wrapping. "We're going to enjoy a little piercing play today, nothing permanent. When we're done, the needles will be removed, and the tiny puncture wounds caused by the superficial piercing will be healed within a few days."

He asked Master Mark to come closer for observation and began to talk about things like nerve endings, and the dermal layer of skin through which he would be drawing the needle, and how to do it so there was both an entry and exit point. "Like this, see?"

The point of the first needle disappeared into the skin on Ashley's upper back, and Jaime felt a wave of nausea move through her. She closed her eyes. "You don't want to go into the subcutaneous layer or down into the muscle," Master Mason continued, his deep voice rumbling in Jaime's ears. "Not for this kind of play."

Not for any *kind of play—not with me.*

"Slave Jaime." Master Mark's voice penetrated Jaime's thoughts and for a moment she feared she might have spoken out loud. "Open your eyes. You do not have permission to close them."

Jaime blew out a breath and forced herself to obey. The nausea had subsided, and she reminded herself that what was going on in front of her was fully consensual and pleasurable to both the giver and the receiver.

"To make it more fun," Master Mason was saying, "you can pierce a pattern into the skin. See if you can tell what I'm doing here." He had already placed several needles in a vertical line down Ashley's back. Jaime was relieved there was no blood in evidence. Ashley hadn't moved a muscle.

He worked methodically, reaching for one needle at a time, ripping the wrapper and sliding the sharp point home. Jaime saw that the line of needles was edging closer toward the spine as it moved down Ashley's tattooed back. Jaime forced herself to watch, telling herself the exposure would help inure her to the whole thing, and actually finding it to be true.

When he was done, Master Mason stepped back, and Jaime could see the line had flared out slightly for the last several needles at the bottom of Ashley's back. "There," he said, running his gloved finger lightly over the horizontal needles. He looked at Master Mark, who stood on Ashley's other side. "Now it's your turn. You do the other side, and follow my pattern, only in mirror image."

Jaime sensed his hesitancy. Was this a training session for him, too? And was he, like she, struggling to find his courage? The thought both comforted and intrigued her. She watched intently as he gloved his hands and reached for the first needle. He moved with less assurance and speed than Master Mason, but the first needle slid in with apparent ease on the opposite side of Ashley's spine.

Master Mark seemed to find his stride as he moved down her back, pushing sharp needle after needle into the tattooed flesh until there were two matching lines of needles, like the rungs of curving ladders that narrowed and then widened down her back.

"Excellent job," Master Mason boomed. "Like I said, Mark, you're a natural."

Master Mark looked pleased, and Jaime found herself pleased for him. She flexed her hands over her cuffs, wishing she had the right to put her arms around the man and smother him in congratulatory kisses.

Master Mason put his face close to Ashley's and murmured something Jaime couldn't hear. Ashley turned her head toward her Master, and Jaime could see the beatific smile on her face. Jaime imagined she could feel the other woman's radiant serenity emanating from her like a force field and her heart ached with longing.

Master Mason stepped back. "Now for the pièce de la résistance," he said with a grin. He reached for the ribbon and the scissors, quickly cutting two long strips of ribbon from the spool. Jaime's view of whatever Mason was doing was blocked by the big man as he stood directly behind Ashley.

When he finally stepped aside, Jaime drew in a breath of awed admiration. By lacing the satin ribbon in a crisscross pattern around the hubs of the needles, he'd created a ribbon and needle corset on Ashley's back.

"Beautiful," Master Mark, apparently equally awed, breathed.

"Yes," Master Mason said, beaming. "Normally I'd leave that in for a while just to enjoy the effect, but for now we need to finish the process." He tugged gently at the ribbon, unwinding it carefully from the needles still piercing Ashley's flesh. Popping the lid of the sharps bin, he dropped the ribbon inside it.

"Remember," he continued, "the piercing stimulates the nerve endings and draws your sub toward her limit of sensation. When you run the scene yourself, especially the first time with a new sub, you have to carefully monitor her reactions and limits because you eventually have to take out the needles you put in, and that stimulates the nerve endings all over again. The goal, you see, is to take your sub to her personal limit, but not send her too far over it. As with any scene, you want to leave them wanting more."

Jaime couldn't imagine ever wanting *more* needle play, but of course she held her tongue on the matter.

Gripping the plastic hub of the top needle on his side, Master Mason drew it slowly from Ashley's skin, leaving droplets of blood in its wake, which he quickly dabbed with a cleansing wipe. Jaime's eyes fluttered shut, but she quickly forced them open.

The next several needles came out clean—no blood. When he was done, he pushed the open sharps bin in Mark's direction. "Now you."

Master Mark plucked a wipe from the container and held it with one hand as he removed the first needle on his side. There was no blood. He worked carefully and methodically, and only the second to last needle resulted in droplets of red blood beading against Ashley's skin.

Master Mason dropped his gloves into the sharps bin and Master Mark followed suit. Master Mason carried the tray over to the sink set into a counter on the side of the dungeon and returned a moment later with a black briefcase in his hand.

Jaime was quite pleased with herself. She'd worked through the initial nausea and managed to keep her eyes open, except for that one, brief slip, through the whole process. She was a little apprehensive about the knife play to come, but reminded herself she'd gotten through it that first night when Ashley had been cut in front of her, and she could do it again.

Master Mason set the briefcase on the bondage table and clicked open the lid. He lifted out something wrapped in a black velvet bag. As he drew the object from the bag, Jaime saw the shiny blade of a knife. Her heart began to beat, quick and desperate, like a whispered prayer.

He turned to her with an evil smile. "Your turn."

CHAPTER 11

Mason sat on one of the recovery sofas, Ashley nestled on his lap, his arms loosely around her. She had her cheek cradled against his chest.

Mark was reassured by Mason's presence for his first knife play scene, but also a little self-conscious. Funny, he had no trouble performing in front of thousands on a music stage, but this was different. Jaime was placing her trust in his hands, in spite of her obviously very real fear. While he felt confident of his skills, he took his responsibility to her seriously. He wanted the scene to be a success for them both, whether or not they had an audience.

He released Jaime from the cross and placed his arm around her shoulders. He could feel the tension radiating from her. As he led her to the bondage table, he murmured into her hair, "Relax, slave Jaime. Show your courage. Show your grace. You can do this. I know you can."

He helped her onto the bondage table, his cock nudging to attention from their direct physical contact. It was odd how quickly one adjusted to the staff slaves always being naked. While he admired the hard bodies of the male slaves, and enjoyed the sight of so much lovely female flesh, he'd become used to it, his cock no longer springing awake every time he saw bare breasts or a shaved pussy. But with Jaime it was different. With Jaime, his body reacted as if he were still seventeen.

He worked quickly, stretching her arms overhead and securing them in leather cuffs positioned at the top corners of the table. A plump cushion slid beneath her ass raised her hips and pelvis. "Spread your legs," he commanded. He placed his hand briefly over her mons, savoring the moist heat against his palm. Once her ankles were cuffed to the bottom corners of the table, he stepped back to admire the deliciously erotic presentation.

"You're going to need to stay very, very still during the knife play, slave Jaime. Any sudden movement when sharp blades are involved is never a good idea."

"Oh," Jaime gasped softly, her eyes flitting toward the nearby table where the knife kit waited, lid open, the long, dangerous blade Mason had removed gleaming on the velvet.

"I'll help you with that," Mark said. "These leather restraints will prevent you from any sudden jerking or unintended movement." He secured wide strips of leather made just for the purpose above and beneath her breasts, across her waist and over each thigh and calf.

"Try to move," he ordered when he was done.

Jaime managed to twitch a little, but otherwise was still. She was able to lift her head, but he could always add a forehead strap later if he felt it was necessary. Satisfied, he nodded. "Good."

Mark had entered that dominant headspace where power thrummed through his veins like jet fuel, his engines revved and ready to take off. He recalled a girlfriend from his college days. "What do you get out of this? It seems so unfair," she had said, after he'd spent a long time figuring out how to tie her down to the bed, and then had given her a butt blistering spanking, followed by several orgasms using his hand while she remained tethered, facedown on the bed. "You do all the work, and I get all the fun!"

He had just laughed and shrugged. Back then he didn't have the words to express the unparalleled thrill of pure erotic power and control he experienced when in the throes of a good scene. He would have described the deep intangible bond between Dom and sub when the connection was there—the way he experienced each stroke of the whip, each stinging kiss of the cane, each shudder of erotic pleasure, with as much intensity and passion as his sub. There was nothing like it—not even when he was making his music—nothing to compare in terms of pure, actualized and deep satisfaction.

With this trainee, with this girl he wanted to know better, the connection had been immediate and sure. Something in her drove him to be his very best self, both as a Dom and as a man. Though he had to keep his feelings in check for the duration of her training, he wasn't going to deny them, at least not to himself.

He moved around the table and stood beside her, looking down into her eyes. "Are you ready, slave Jaime? We're going to explore edge play now. There is no safeword, but I'll be here with you every step of the way." He placed his hand flat on her breastbone. He could feel the rapid beat of her heart against his palm. "Slow your breathing," he reminded her. "Deep, calming breaths."

He waited a moment as she drew in a breath and let it out slowly. "Again," he urged, his hand still over her heart. "Again."

When he was satisfied she had calmed enough to continue, he turned back toward the table and picked up the long, shiny blade Mason had selected. He held it so Jaime could see.

She drew in a sharp breath, and he was aware the heart he'd just helped to slow had kick-started back into a pounding tempo. How he loved this process of guiding a slave through a scene, of taking her to the edge of submission and then bringing her back into the safety of his dominant but loving control. He was the one who was making her heart pound with fear and desire. He was the one who would then calm her fears, only to kindle them again with a whisper, a touch, the stroke of a whip, the blade of a knife.

He set the knife down once more and returned to the bound, naked girl. He placed his hand on her throat and gripped in a light but unmistakable gesture of control just beneath her jawline. She began to tremble, and he could feel both her fear and her desire as if they were his own. He leaned close to her ear and murmured, "Remember, I am your Master during this session, and as your Master, I will always keep you safe. The journey of a submissive is not an easy one, but you are strong and courageous, and I know you can do this. I want you to do this, for me, and for yourself. Are you ready, slave Jaime? Are you ready and willing to submit to me, to place your trust in me as I guide you through this scene?"

"Yes, Sir," she whispered.

"Louder," he commanded. "Say it louder, slave."

"Yes, Sir," she said throatily, and he saw the resolve beneath the fear in her face.

He nodded, satisfied, his cock twitching with anticipation. "We begin," he said. Turning again toward the equipment table, he surveyed the gear Mason and he had set there for this session. Next to the knife kit was an ice bucket, a black satin sleep mask and a large, red candle in a glass container, along with a small box of matches. Mark picked up the box and removed a wooden match. He struck it on the side of the box and held the flame to the candle's wick until it sputtered to life.

He picked up the knife once again and turned back to Jaime. As he intended, her eyes fixed on the long, shiny blade, her lips lightly parted, her nipples engorged, round and red as ripe cherries. His mouth watered as he imagined suckling them.

He placed the knife carefully on Jaime's taut, flat stomach, balancing it so only the wooden handle actually made contact with her skin. Jaime gasped, and the knife shook slightly against her trembling muscles. Mark moved to the end of the table. In spite of her fear, or no doubt partially because of it, the pink folds of her pussy were swollen and moist with arousal.

Leaving the knife balanced between Jaime's hipbones, Mark turned back to the table and picked up the sleep mask. He placed it over Jaime's eyes and slid the elastic behind her head. Moving down along the table, he lifted the knife from her still-trembling body. "I want you to focus solely on the sensations produced by the sharp, seductive edge of the blade. Taking away your sight will heighten the sensation and help you stay focused on what you are feeling."

Mark glanced over at Master Mason. Ashley was now on her knees on the floor in front of her Master, her head bobbing on his cock, her back marked with two vertical rows of tiny red wounds that glistened with antibiotic ointment. Mason met his eye and flashed a grin.

For a moment, Mark wished he were alone with Jaime, the scene private and belonging only to the two of them. He knew even as the thought entered his mind that it was inappropriate. For now, at least, he was Jaime's trainer, nothing more. And this was his first real scene with knives—he needed Mason there as mentor and spotter in case anything went amiss.

Turning back toward the table, Mark put away the sharp knife he'd used to set the scene in Jaime's mind. He selected two more knives, one still in its metal sheath, the other in a velvet bag. He set the bag down beside her on the bondage table and moved close to her head, holding the sheathed knife near her ear.

"Prepare to suffer, slave Jaime," he whispered. He unsheathed the knife, and the unmistakable sound of the metal sliding against metal reverberated in the dungeon. The sound was primal and dangerous, designed to trigger Jaime's fight or flight response. She gasped. He lightly touched the sharp point of the blade to Jaime's right nipple.

With a cry, Jaime jerked her head, the only part of her body she could move.

"Stay still," Mark admonished, his heart beating hard along with hers. Satisfied the mind fuck was now in full swing, he set the sharp knife aside. He picked up the velvet bag and slid what Mason had referred to as the dead knife into his hand. This knife's blade had been purposely dulled using steel wool so that it wouldn't cut the skin, even if you tried.

But Jaime didn't know that.

"Stay very still," he warned again. "I don't want to cut you—at least not unintentionally." He glanced again at Mason, who lifted his right hand in a thumbs-up gesture of approval.

Turning back to Jaime, Mark held the dead knife at a forty-five degree angle against Jaime's arm and lightly scraped the blade along her skin. Jaime startled and gasped again, but was unable to flinch or jerk away. The bonds were doing their job.

"You belong to me, slave Jaime," Mark murmured as he drew the tip of the blade between her breasts. He touched the edge of the dull blade to her throat and dragged it along the pulse of her carotid artery. She shuddered. "A sudden move, a press of the blade, and you would feel the bite of steel and then the warm, wet ribbon of your life's blood…"

Jaime clenched her hands into fists over her head, her breath a shallow pant. Mark could feel the rise of her panic, which threatened to engulf her if he moved too far, too fast. He wanted her on the edge, yes, but he didn't want her to tumble over, to lose control, to forget her courage and her grace. It was his job to pay attention to her body and her cues, and to help her stay on the path of true submission.

Setting the knife aside a moment, Mark leaned over the blindfolded girl and spoke gently. "I need you to relax your body," he said. "I want your surrender, not your resistance." He cupped her hands with his and gently forced her fingers to uncurl. He stroked her cheek, his voice soothing. "I want you to breathe. Center yourself. Focus. Stop anticipating and just give yourself to the sensations. Hold nothing back."

He continued to stroke her soft skin until the coil of her tension eased a little more, and her breathing slowed to something approximating normal. He wanted to bend down and kiss her, but knew he mustn't. Instead, he moved his hand, trailing it along her throat and moving lower, drawing a circle around her distended nipple with his finger. He brought his thumb and finger together and squeezed the rigid nubbin, giving it a sudden, sharp twist.

Her cry of pain sent a jolt directly to his cock, and the power surged like an injection of pure heroin directly into his veins. He reached for the second nipple, twisting it until he drew another delicious cry of pain from the masochist bound, naked and spread before him. He cupped her smooth cunt, feeling the damp heat and Jaime moaned. However frightened she was of the knife play, the girl was sopping wet.

Unable to resist, he held his palm to his nose and inhaled the intoxicating scent of her musk. Tamping down his own immediate desires, Mark stepped away from the sexy girl. He selected a large knife and slid the blade into the ice bucket. Once satisfied it was fully chilled, he returned to Jaime. "Remember, stay perfectly still." He laid the flat of the icy blade across both nipples. Jaime stiffened and shuddered.

He returned to the table and grabbed several pieces of ice from the bucket. Leaving the knife balanced over her nipples, he moved to the end of the table. "Hold your breath," he ordered. "I don't want you to move a muscle." He waited a beat as he watched her comply. Then he pressed an ice cube into the heat between her spread legs. Jaime cried out, her brain no doubt trying to process the sensation at her cunt—was it a blade? Had he cut her?

He slid a second piece inside her and then gripped her warm thighs with his cold fingers. She shuddered and moaned. He moved back along the table and lifted the blade to reveal her reddened nipples, the areolas puckered from contact with cold metal.

Setting the blade aside, he stroked Jaime's cheek and saw she was clenching her jaw. He massaged her jawline with his thumbs for a few seconds. Not wanting her too relaxed, he slid his hand down to her throat, squeezing just hard enough to remind her who was in charge.

A deep, sensual shudder moved through Jaime's body and she shivered. Mark placed his hands over her breasts, cupping them. Her nipples jutted against his palms. "Poor baby," he crooned. "Are you cold?"

"Yes, Sir."

"I'll just have to warm you up then," he said with an evil grin she couldn't see. He brought over the candle and tipped the glass ever so slightly, letting just a few drops splash down to her breasts.

"Ah!" the blindfolded girl cried, straining helplessly in her bonds.

He let a few more drops land in a red pattern over her nipples. Jaime hissed with pain as Mark moved the candle slowly above her body, letting the wax splatter in a line down her stomach. He held the candle poised over her vulva and let several drops of hot wax fall.

As they made contact, Jaime whimpered. Mark glanced over at the pair on the recovery sofa. Both Mason and Ashley were watching now, Ashley once more perched on her Master's lap. Mason's eyes were glittering with intensity. *Yes,* he mouthed, nodding slowly. *Keep going.*

Mark set down the candle on the table and retrieved a small, narrow, rectangular spatula perfect for removing wax. The wax had cooled and hardened on Jaime's skin. Mark leaned close to Jaime's ear. "I'm going to use a very sharp knife to remove the wax," he said quietly. "You must stay perfectly still, slave girl, so I don't accidentally cut you. Understand?"

Jaime nodded, her lips pressed into a thin line. He didn't upbraid her for failing to answer a direct question with the proper title of respect. She was nearing sensory overload, he could see. Rather than distract her with protocol, he would give her just the push she needed to fly right over the edge.

He started with her chest, scraping the hardened wax from her engorged nipples and along the soft curve of her breasts. Jaime was trembling, a real knife's blade no doubt looming large in her mind's eye.

"You are doing so well, slave girl," Mark said, truly in awe of her courage and resolve. "You just need to slow your breathing. Embrace what is happening to you. Take it inside and use it to empower yourself." He put his other hand on her chest. Her heart was beating fast. "Breathe," he said again. "In...and out. In...and out. Yes."

Once she was calmer, he continued to drag the edge of the spatula along her abdomen, chipping away the bits of dried red wax as he moved down her body. Jaime, still believing a knife was at play, had begun to tremble again.

"Stay very still," he reminded her as he positioned himself at the end of the table. Carefully, gently, he scraped the bits of hardened wax from her spread cunt. This wax came off the most easily, aided no doubt by the slick lubricant of her arousal.

"Would you like to come, slave girl?"

"Oh god," Jaime moaned, arching her hips wantonly upward as best she was able in her bound position. "Yes, please, Sir. Please."

His cock and balls ached. Christ, he wanted to fuck her. Forcing his own selfish desires aside, he smiled cruelly, though Jaime couldn't see. "To earn that privilege," he said, "you will have to pay. I'm going to spank your cunt with the flat side of this knife. As long as you stay still, you won't be cut. If you can manage that, you will be rewarded with an orgasm."

Jaime inhaled in a sharp, quick gasp. If she refused or balked, he decided he wouldn't press the issue. He had given her a choice. Let her make it.

"Yes," she finally said, her voice low and throaty. "Yes, please, Sir. I want it."

"Then you shall have it. You will come on my command."

Mark touched the flat of the spatula against her spread vulva. Jaime tensed and gave a little whimper of fear, but stayed very, very still.

"Good girl," Mark encouraged. He began to tap lightly against the wet, pink folds of her cunt, gently at first, and then harder. Even though there was no danger of cutting her, the metal striking her delicate flesh had to sting. Taking careful aim, he caught her hooded clit with the square end of the spatula.

Jaime screamed, her hands clenching once more over her head, but her restraints and her sheer self-will kept her body still, save for the lingering tremble in her limbs. Mark continued to paddle Jaime's spread cunt until the folds were dark red. Jaime was breathing hard, her chest heaving. In spite of the erotic pain she was experiencing, he could see the glisten of her juices at her entrance.

Dropping the spatula, he stroked the slick, reddened folds with his fingertips. Using his other hand, he pushed two fingers into the tight, wet heat of her cunt. He could feel the vaginal muscles spasm against them. Jaime was panting, her whole body shaking with the strain of resisting what he was doing to her.

"Now," he said, thrusting his fingers like a cock moving in and out of her hot, sticky cunt. "Come for your Master."

Jaime groaned, the sound low and then rising up a feminine scale as she climaxed. Her body was sheened with sweat, her mouth a lovely O beneath the black satin of her blindfold. He continued to stroke and finger fuck her as she keened and shuddered, until finally she sagged back against the table, completely limp.

Mark moved quickly around to the head of the table and removed her blindfold. Jaime didn't open her eyes. She didn't move. There was no gentle rise and fall of her chest. Mark leaned closer, his fingers seeking the pulse at her neck. The beat was strong, her skin warm. Relieved, he stood again.

"Hey," he said softly, looking down at her with a smile as he stroked her cheek. The aching tenderness he felt at that moment made tears come into his eyes. Blinking them away, he queried, "You alive?"

After a few seconds, Jaime's eyes fluttered opened and she inhaled deeply, as if emerging from a trance. She blinked several times as she focused on his face. "No, Sir," she said, smiling the most beautiful smile he had ever seen. "I think I died and went straight to heaven."

CHAPTER 12

"Okay, girls. Let's see how your Dominatrix training is coming along since our last lesson." Mistress Marjorie stood in front of Jaime and the others—Katie, Lucia, Danielle and Ashley—who were all kneeling at-ease in front of her on yoga mats. Mistress Marjorie was beautifully dressed as always, today wearing a sheer burgundy silk blouse tucked into form-fitting black leather pants, her feet shod in high-heeled black leather mules. Her small, high breasts were clearly visible beneath the fabric, and the heart-shaped crystal padlock sparkled on her slave collar in the soft light of the dungeon.

"One thing I've learned over the years," she said as she looked from girl to girl, "is that in order to truly master something, first you listen and pay attention, then you practice, and finally, you teach. Ashley and Lucia, you will be the teachers during this first part of the session. Katie and Danielle, while you're both adept with the flogger, each of you could use more finesse and control with the cane." She turned at last to Jaime. "Jaime, with only one session under your belt, you've got a *lot* to learn."

"Yes, Mistress," Jaime agreed. While interested from an intellectual standpoint in the mechanics of wielding a whip and a cane, she was especially intrigued with what was planned for later that morning. Mistress Marjorie called it Sadie Hawkins Day at The Enclave, and while Jaime didn't know what that was, she'd gathered from the other female subs' excited discussion during grooming that morning that today was a day when things were turned on their heads, and subs became Dommes, at least for a few hours.

During a training session with Mistress Marjorie earlier in the week,

Jaime had been given a large flogger, a single tail and several canes of varying lengths and thicknesses. She'd worked on wrist and arm techniques, using the boxing bag that hung in the corner of the positions training room as her subject.

"Sometimes," Mistress Marjorie had explained when beginning the lesson, "as a trained slave, you might be called upon to dominate another sub for the pleasure and amusement of your Masters. As such, you'd better know what the hell you're doing. During these first two weeks, there isn't a lot of time to focus on this aspect of your training, but if you're invited to join The Enclave as a full-time staff slave, you'll be expected to become proficient with a flogger and a cane, along with basic bondage techniques and the proper use of sex toys on others."

Jaime tried to envision herself in full leather gear and stiletto heels, flicking a six-foot bull whip against the ass of a suspended slave boy, but she couldn't quite pull it off, even in her imagination. She had felt no particular thrill or rush of power when handling the flogger, nor did she seem to have much aptitude for the task, but she appreciated the importance of learning the basics. She wondered, as she watched Mistress Marjorie demonstrate with enthusiasm, what it must be like to be a true switch—as happy and actualized when using the whip as when on the receiving end of its delicious sting.

Mistress Marjorie clapped her hands, recalling Jaime back to the moment. "Okay, then. Let's begin! Katie, Jaime and Danielle, stand up and assume the corporal position while Mistress Ashley and Mistress Lucia select their canes for the training session. That is how you will address them for the duration of the session."

Turning to the two chosen teachers, she added, "Feel free to really use the cane, girls. I want to see some marks and welts, got it? Though no blood, please. That's beyond the scope of today's lesson."

Jaime's gut tightened. While she loved the cane, she also hated it. She forced herself to swallow her trepidation as she stood. Along with the other two, she turned around and bent forward to grab her ankles, bringing her head as close to her knees as possible as she thrust out her ass. Katie was struggling a little beside her to assume the position, while Danielle folded with the easy grace of a ballerina, her legs perfectly straight, her nose resting on her knees, her shiny blond hair falling in a sheet to the floor.

It's about doing your personal best. Jaime recalled a heartfelt conversation with Lucia when Jaime had been feeling down on herself after a particularly grueling session. *Focus on being the best sub you can be, not on how you compare to others.*

She felt a tap on her shoulder. "Stand up. You will have a lesson in using the cane first," Ashley said. As Jaime stood upright, Ashley continued, "Mistress Lucia and I will demonstrate, and then you'll give it a try, okay?"

Jaime nodded and then remembered to say, "Yes, Mistress Ashley." It was odd to address the naked, pierced and collared sub girl that way, until she whipped the cane suddenly through the air, and its whistling promise made Jaime, along with the still bent and waiting girls, flinch in anticipation.

Lucia and Ashley each had selected canes of medium thickness, and Jaime's skin prickled with sympathy and longing as she watched Lucia position herself behind Katie, Ashley behind Danielle.

"You start lightly," Lucia said, taking over the narrative by some silent or prearranged agreement. "A steady, easy tapping to get the skin acclimated and ready. You want to get the blood rising to the surface, you want to get the adrenaline flowing and the anticipation up."

They both tap-tap-tapped for a while, and then Ashley said, "You don't want them falling asleep, though." She struck suddenly, the cane thwacking against Danielle's right ass cheek. Danielle jerked but otherwise held her position. Ashley struck again, painting a matching line on the left side. Danielle yelped. Ashley struck her twice more, painting even, parallel lines above the first strokes. Danielle began to pant, and Jaime could see she was gripping her ankles hard, her legs trembling slightly from the effort.

"You've been practicing, I see, Ashley," said Mistress Marjorie, approval in her tone.

"Yes, Mistress," Ashley said, smiling sweetly up at Mistress Marjorie. "Master Mason recently discovered the purifying effects of the cut of the cane. It's his new favorite way to relax."

Mistress Marjorie nodded. "Perhaps we'll switch him yet," she said with a laugh.

"I don't think so, ma'am," Ashley said.

"No," Mistress Marjorie agreed, still grinning. "Mason is a Dom, through and through. Still, I had no idea you'd become so accomplished. Perhaps for your Sadie Hawkins switch with slave Julian, you'd like to try something different."

"Yes, ma'am," Ashley agreed with a grin. "I do have something else in mind, as a matter of fact. Hans and I have been talking."

"I bet you have," Mistress Marjorie said, laughing again. She looked at the bent-over girls. "I'm distracting you. Let's return the focus to the session."

"Yes, Mistress." Ashley turned to Jaime. "Here, you try now." Jaime took the offered cane and stepped hesitantly behind Danielle. "Watch what Lucia is doing."

Lucia was still tapping against Katie's ample bottom, which was turning a rosy pink. "Especially when you're just starting out," Lucia said, her eyes fixed on the movement of the cane as it made contact, "make sure to avoid the tailbone." She struck a little harder and a white line appeared against the pink flesh, which quickly darkened to red. Katie gasped but held her position. "When your sub is bent over, the muscles are pulled taut, making them more sensitive to impact," Lucia continued.

"That's right," Ashley chimed in, "so you don't want to strike as hard as if your subject is lying down. Go ahead," she urged. "You try it, Jaime."

"Copy what I'm doing," Lucia said. "Use a quick snapping motion of the wrist, and then let the cane bounce back as soon as it strikes, like this." The cane whistled through the air and connected with flesh. Katie gasped again and then whimpered.

"You can strike with the tip of the cane, which produces a sharp, concentrated sting, or you can use the side of the cane, aiming for contact about midway down its length, like this." Lucia shifted a little and the caned whipped through the air and landed with a crack against Katie's jiggling ass, leaving another welt in its wake.

"Oh!" Katie cried.

Ignoring her, Ashley continued, "As a novice, though, it's better to start with more carry-through." She placed her hand over Jaime's on the cane. "Like this, see." She guided Jaime's arm through the air, stopping just before making contact with Danielle's bottom. "This will produce a heavier feeling of impact that's not as sharp and stingy. It's less likely you'll inadvertently cut the skin this way. It's a safer stroke for a newbie. Go on, you try it."

Jaime drew in a breath and, concentrating fiercely, tried to mimic the movements of her teachers. She hesitated slightly at the moment of impact, and the cane glanced off Danielle's ass, the tip catching her hip and leaving an angry mark.

"Ow!" Danielle cried, outrage in the single syllable.

"Aim is important," Ashley said, winking at Jaime. "You don't want to hit bone like that, but that only happened because you didn't trust yourself. Follow through this time. Give her what she needs, and put your own fear aside."

Jaime wanted to apologize to Danielle, but knew that wouldn't be well received. Instead, she refocused on her task, ignoring the fear sweat pricking in her armpits.

She flicked her wrist, and the cane whistled and landed with a satisfying crack just where Danielle's ass met her right thigh.

"Yeah!" Ashley enthused. "That's it. That's the sweet spot. That's the best, right?"

Jaime's skin tingled with muscle memory of being caned just so. She nodded in agreement, and aimed again, catching Danielle in the same spot on her other thigh. They worked a while longer, and Jaime's confidence rose. She painted several pink stripes on Danielle's ass, though she was very careful not to strike too hard.

"Okay, really good job, girls." Mistress Marjorie placed a hand on Jaime's shoulder. "Jaime, you're still a little timid, but that will improve with experience." Stepping back, she addressed all of them. "Okay, now we'll switch out. Jaime and Lucia, assume the position. Danielle and Katie, take the canes. Ashley, you may continue to instruct."

Jaime handed her cane to Ashley, her heart kicking up a notch. *Please, please, please, let me have Katie*, she begged the BDSM gods. "Danielle, you will work with Jaime, and Katie, you take Lucia," Mistress Marjorie continued, blithely unaware of Jaime's silent plea.

Jaime focused on relaxing her body and mind. *Don't anticipate. Practice acceptance.* The caning began well, the light, steady tapping creating a sensual, steady hum through her blood. She relaxed a little more and drew a deep, calming breath.

The sudden, savage cut across both cheeks struck like a snake, leaving a stinging line of fire in its wake. "Fuck," Jaime blurted involuntarily, the *f* exploding percussively against her teeth, tears blurring her vision.

"What was that?" Mistress Marjorie said sharply, and then, before Jaime could apologize for the outburst, "Oh, dear. Danielle, didn't I tell you no blood today?"

"I'm so sorry, Mistress Marjorie," Danielle said, her tone saccharine sweet. "I didn't mean to."

Jaime's fingers were slippery with sweat and she felt dizzy. Somehow she managed to stay in position, holding on to her ankles for dear life. Something cool and soothing was dabbed gently along the painful line of fire on her ass. "There," Mistress Marjorie said behind her. "You may stand, Jaime." Strong fingers wrapped gently around Jaime's upper arms, helping her to a standing position. "It's a shallow cut, nothing that won't heal quickly, especially with the miracle salve Aubrey makes for us." She turned Jaime so she was facing her. "You look a little pale, dear." She touched the back of her hand to Jaime's forehead. "A little clammy." She turned to Ashley. "Take Jaime over to the recovery couch for a few minutes. Give her some water. The slave boys"—she grinned widely at the term—"will be in shortly for their Sadie Hawkins session." She rubbed her hands together. "I don't know about you girls, but I can't wait."

~*~

Mark remembered something called the Sadie Hawkins Dance back in middle school, where the girls were supposed to ask the boys to the dance. Apparently, in his mother's day, to hear her tell it, such an event was a much bigger deal than in his more liberated time. At his school's dance, as he recalled, he and a gaggle of gangly boys had showed up in a pack, not having been among the chosen few specifically asked by a girl. Like every other school dance he attended until his hormones kicked in sufficiently to override insecurity, he'd stood around, his hands shoved in his pockets, posturing to attempt to impress if a girl moved close enough.

Mark was surprised but pleased to see Lawrence had chosen to participate in the Sadie Hawkins session, signing up for the last of the four available spots that morning. They filed into the room and moved to the yoga mats, as they'd been instructed prior to entering.

Jaime, Katie, Danielle, Lucia and Ashley were standing in a line and Mark's brain did a double take as it struggled to process what was different about them.

They weren't naked.

The slave girls were wearing silky, shimmery lingerie type things, like see-through one-piece bathing suits, except much sexier. Each wore a different color, Lucia in gold, Danielle in cobalt blue, Katie in pink, Ashley in black and Jaime in silver. It was still possible to see their bare, lovely forms beneath, but somehow, perhaps because it was so unusual to see slaves clothed in any way, the effect was extremely erotic.

Mark started to kneel on the mat, assuming that was required, but was stopped by Marjorie. "Welcome, slave boys. Before you kneel and await your instruction, you will strip completely naked. You may leave your clothes in neat, folded piles in the cubbies." She pointed to an area of the dungeon where supplies were kept.

Mark's initial impulse was to balk, but he realized how ridiculous that was. They expected and required the subs to be naked, and they, as subs at least for that morning, should have expected nothing different. He glanced at the other men. Julian, who had already pulled off his shirt, was in the process of removing his boots, a wide grin on his eager face. Anthony was unbuttoning his shirt with a calm, faintly amused expression. Lawrence looked grim, a faint blush moving over his pale face as he reached for the fly of his fine, black leather pants.

Mark, who had dressed that morning in black jeans, work boots and his favorite black leather vest, set about stripping himself as directed. He glanced toward the slave girls, or rather, the Mistresses. All of them were watching the men with rapt attention. Mark smiled as he stared back at them, admiring their lovely, feminine curves, made all the more tantalizing by the shimmery silk. Ashley frowned at him, and he looked away, suddenly aware he'd been behaving in a less than submissive fashion with his brazen stare. This was going to be a *very* interesting morning.

When the men were all naked and kneeling in a relatively neat row, Marjorie said, "Today we will be working in three groups. Your Mistresses have been given carte blanche to fully direct their own scenes. Their plans haven't been discussed or rehearsed. Whatever they say, goes." As she gave them a moment to digest this, Lawrence fidgeted a little beside Mark.

"Anthony," Marjorie continued, "you will be dominated by Mistress Lucia. Mark, you will be claimed by Mistress Katie, and Lawrence, you will submit to Mistress Danielle. Julian, I do believe Mistress Ashley has something wicked in mind for you."

Julian laughed. "Bring it on, Mistress Ashley. I can take it."

Mark's eyes slid to Jaime. As a trainee, she hadn't yet earned the privilege of serving as a Mistress in this scene, but Anthony had mentioned she'd be participating as an assistant and observer. Mark found himself conflicted about whether he wanted her in on his scene. On the one hand, he liked being near her, whatever the circumstance. On the other, she was distracting. It was going to be hard enough to do this particular exercise without having to control his desires, especially given the fact he would be naked. Yes, much better if she wasn't in the way.

"Slave Jaime will assist Mistress Lucia," Marjorie added, and Mark experienced a sudden, sharp letdown that told him he'd been lying to himself.

Katie led Mark to a spanking horse and instructed him to drape himself face down over its back, resting his elbows and knees on the padded supports that ran along the sides of the horse. Lawrence followed Danielle to nearby stocks. Mark watched with amusement as she lifted the hinged top and instructed Lawrence to kneel and place his head and hands in the hollows of the wood. Mark twisted his head but the others in the room were out of his line of vision.

"Stop fidgeting," Katie said, and Mark, chagrined, stilled. As she placed cuffs around his wrists and ankles, a little swoop of adrenaline rippled through his gut.

"Today, slave boy," Katie said in a slightly tremulous voice, "we will begin with a spanking, and then I'll move on to flogging and caning. You will remain still and quiet during the session, except to thank me. Are we quite clear on this?"

"Yes, Ka—, er, Mistress Katie," Mark said, suppressing a smile. He had a fairly high tolerance for pain, and wasn't too worried about his ability to obey her directives. Katie stepped out of his line of vision. He could hear her fumbling about behind him.

He stiffened when he felt the sudden touch of something cold and gooey between his ass cheeks. Katie appeared once more in front of him, this time waving a huge, shiny black butt plug in his face. "To help you enter the proper headspace of a submissive," she continued, her tone less timid now, "I'm going to insert this butt plug into your ass."

Mark barely managed to bite back the immediate, sharp retort that rose in his throat. This exercise in submission was going to be a little more difficult to handle than he had anticipated.

Katie must have seen something in his expression, because she knitted her brows and frowned. "Is there a problem, slave Mark? Are you frightened?" She stroked his head, tilting her own as she peered into his face. "You need to relax—to open yourself to the experience. You need to trust me." She was parroting back words he'd said to her on many occasions during various sessions and, despite the concern on her face, her eyes were sparkling.

She's having fun with it. So should you, he told himself. *This morning is for the slave girls. It's their day to play. Give her what you so easily demand.*

"No, Mistress Katie, no problem," he said sincerely. "Thank you for guiding me, for reminding me." He closed his eyes, took in a deep breath and let it out slowly, willing the stress he was holding in his muscles to leave along with the air in his lungs.

"Much better," Katie said, patting his head.

She stepped out of his vision again, and after a moment he felt the poke of hard rubber against his sphincter. He couldn't help but tense as it pressed its way past the ring of muscle, but it slid in easily enough with the ample lubricant she'd applied. Only the last, wide bit of the plug created a brief, intense pressure that quickly subsided merely into a sensation of fullness.

"We begin," Katie, or rather, Mistress Katie, announced as she brought her hand down on Mark's bare ass. Mark glanced over at Lawrence. Danielle was kneeling in front of him, her face close to his. She'd attached clamps to his nipples, and the chain swung gently below his chest. All at once, she drew back her hand and slapped his face, the sound sharp and sudden, and followed by Lawrence's quick intake of breath.

Danielle tapped Lawrence's hands, which had balled into fists inside the stocks. He uncurled his fingers, his eyes still on hers. She stroked the cheek she'd just slapped with two fingers and then slapped him again on the same cheek, the sound ringing in the air. The two continued to stare at one another. Lawrence's lips were parted. Mark's gaze slid down their bodies, and he observed that Danielle's nipples were fully erect, as was Lawrence's cock.

Well, well, Mark thought, *what the hell is going on between those two?*

He was distracted from his musings by Katie's hard, insistent palm. She was surprisingly strong, and with each smack, the stinging heat rose and spread over Mark's skin. He grunted, tensing in his effort to hold himself in a way that caused the least stress to his body.

He felt a soothing hand on his lower back, though the spanking continued. "Remind him to breathe," Marjorie said, for a moment confusing Mark. Then he realized she was talking to Katie. "See how he's holding himself stiffly, his body taut. He's not relaxing into the spanking. You need to remind him. Talk to him. Bring him along. Ask him how he's doing."

"Oh, gosh. Right!" Mark could hear the chagrin in Katie's voice. She leaned close to his ear, the spanking halted for the moment, which was just fine with him. "Slave Mark," she said softly, "how are you doing? Are you remembering to breathe? To flow with the pain?"

"I'm trying, Mistress," he answered honestly. "This is new for me. Thank you for reminding me."

"You're welcome, slave boy."

Mark smiled at the incongruity of sweet, submissive Katie referring to him as her slave boy, though he managed to hold his grin at bay until she was again behind him.

The smile fell away when her hard palm cracked once more on his now quite tender flesh. It took concentration not to cry out, but he was determined to remain silent and stoic—to take it like a true sub.

When she finally stopped, she demanded breathlessly, "Thank me, slave."

"Thank you, Mistress Katie," Mark replied somewhat breathlessly himself.

The flogger was next, and the sensation was almost pleasant when compared with the sharp, hard sting of Katie's palm. The flogger was a long-handled suede model, ideal for an introductory flogging. She was wielding it in a steady, swinging motion that was more sensual than painful, and Mark began to relax beneath its onslaught. His cock actually rose in response to the erotic pain, rubbed pleasurably against the leather horse with each thuddy stroke. He nearly protested when she stopped, but caught himself in time.

"Thank me," she demanded once more, and he did.

The cane was another story.

Though she began with the traditional light tapping to acclimate the skin, he wasn't ready when the first searing stroke sliced across the top of his ass just below the tailbone. It fucking hurt!

That's the point, he could almost hear himself say aloud, which was what he would have said to a protesting sub if they'd voiced their complaint. The second and third strokes landed with better aim, catching him across the fleshier part of his ass, though the cut was still biting and quite painful. Without the overlay of masochistic hardwiring that made such an experience easier to bear, Mark found himself clenching his fists once more. Though Katie appeared too focused on her task to notice, Mark recognized in himself that he was taking the pain in and failing to release it—to let it go, as he so easily counseled his submissives.

"Breathe," Katie said, stopping a moment to place her hand comfortingly on the back of his neck. "You can do this. You're doing so well, slave Mark. I'm so proud of you."

Mark realized he had, indeed, been holding his breath. He let it out and drew in several calming breaths as she lightly massaged his neck with cool, strong fingers.

But she wasn't done yet. Once more the cane sliced in a line of fire against his ass and thighs. "Stop resisting and give yourself over to the process. Embrace the pain. Become one with it." Struggling to obey, Mark imagined a huge wave coming at him and, instead of stiffening and holding his breath as it crashed over him, he dove into it, seeking to ride it, to let it lift him high in its powerful arms.

"Yes. That's it." Mark was dimly aware of a feminine voice behind him, though he was no longer sure if it was Marjorie or Katie. "Better. Much better."

He could still hear the steady, whistling thwack of the cane as it struck his flesh. He could still feel its sharp, insistent bite. But it no longer hurt. Or, no, that wasn't right. It hurt, but the hurt was bearable. No, it was more than that. The hurt was good. It was necessary. He was riding it now, rather than drowning in panic beneath its undertow. It was lifting him, carrying him, pushing him forward and then...he was soaring, his arms spread wide, his heart lighter than it had ever been, his spirit free...free...free...

"Mark? Master Mark, er, slave boy, Sir? Are you okay?"

Mark slowly opened his eyes. Katie was crouching in front of him, her face twisted with concern. "Oh, phew," she said, blowing out a breath as she pushed her springy curls from her face. "You had me worried there for a second, Sir, uh, slave boy." She grinned. "Are you okay? What happened?"

A slow smile lifted Mark's lips. The sense of utter peace was still there, though amused surprise was now pushing it to the side. "What happened?" he echoed, his smile widening into a grin. "Why, Mistress Katie, I do believe you made me fly!"

CHAPTER 13

Jaime hadn't been able to stop herself from staring as the Masters had stripped in front of them. None of the four had seemed the slightest bit self-conscious about shucking their clothing. Julian was shaven smooth, and sported piercings in his nipples and cock matching those of his slave boy, Hans. Anthony's chest hair was silver like the hair on his head, though his pubic hair remained dark. Lawrence's chest was smooth, his body wiry but muscular, his flaccid cock quite large for his body, over heavy balls.

But it was Mark who had captured and held Jaime's surreptitious attention the longest. He had the long, lean muscles of a natural athlete, his chest hair curling in a dark, sexy V at his sternum and tapering down his flat abs toward his cock and balls. He had those indenting lines on either hip, like a statue of a Greek god, and Jaime wanted to run her hands along the perfect curves and planes of his body in the worst way. She focused instead on his tattoos—one that looked like a piece of Shibari rope running in a circle around his left bicep, the other a small single tail whip, curling around his right hip. She realized she was clenching her fists at her sides in her thwarted desire, and forced herself to relax her fingers and let go of her fantasies.

As the temporary sub boys and Mistresses made their way to their assigned stations, Jaime's position at the rear of the dungeon obscured her view of Master Mark and Katie. That was just as well. It would be easier to ignore her pangs of jealousy and focus on the task at hand—assisting Lucia in dominating the inimitable Master Anthony.

Jaime wasn't entirely sure how she felt about this whole Sadie Hawkins concept. In a way, it didn't feel correct to dominate the

Masters, and yet she understood the need to be prepared to serve as a part-time Domme, should her Master or Mistress require it. Beyond that, she recognized the process reminded everyone at The Enclave that the dynamic of Master, Mistress and slave was a fully consensual and sometimes fluid arrangement.

Turning to Jaime, Lucia asked, "Do you know what this is?" She pointed to a steel apparatus, which was painted a shiny black. Beside it was a tray set on the ground with various cuffs, clips and clamps, along with a small single tail whip and a riding crop. Next to the tray was a large wooden block.

"Some kind of restraint?" Jaime offered, eyeing the torture device, which consisted of a platform, about two feet square, with a sturdy, adjustable rod rising to about waist height from the center, metal ankle cuffs at the base of the rod, a vise at its top. She glanced at Master Anthony. "Uh, for guys," she added, marveling at Master Anthony's calm expression since, presumably, Lucia was planning to place him in this contraption.

"Yes, restraint and also torture," Lucia agreed with a devilish smile, her eyes also flickering toward Master Anthony. "It's called a cock and ball crusher, and with good reason." Her smile widened as Master Anthony grimaced slightly.

"We're going to give Master, uh, *slave* Anthony a taste of erotic suffering this morning." Turning to address him directly, Lucia added, "It can be quite freeing, as you've taught me. The goal is both to transcend the pain, and to harness it, to take its power inside of you."

Master Anthony smiled as if to say *touché,* and Lucia grinned, something sparking between them that Jaime couldn't quite define. "Slave boy," Lucia continued, "position your ankles in the open cuffs." As Master Anthony moved to obey, Lucia explained to Jaime, "The ankle cuffs are adjustable, and so is the rod. " She crouched in front of Master Anthony and adjusted the rod's height until she was satisfied. She reached for his shaft with one small hand, his balls with the other, and pulled his genitals forward into the vise.

Jaime bit her lip in sympathy as Lucia slowly tightened the vise by turning the wing nuts on either side, catching Master Anthony's cock and balls between the metal bars. "Does it hurt?" she asked him, looking up from her vantage point.

"A little, Mistress," Master Anthony replied calmly. "Nothing I can't handle."

Lucia offered another impish grin. "I could make this a lot more interesting by having him stand on the balls of his feet. Then I might adjust the vise so it would hurt like hell if he got lazy or tired and let his feet go down flat." She drew a fingernail along the curve of Master Anthony's balls, her dark eyes sparkling. Normally so quiet and submissively self-contained, Lucia was clearly enjoying her newfound, if temporary, role as Mistress. "But given the limited time and nature of the session, we'll introduce erotic pain in other, more direct ways. The crusher, today, is primarily to keep our slave boy in position and focused."

Jaime glanced at Master Anthony's face to see how he was handling all this. He still looked calm, though a small muscle jumped at his jaw, making Jaime wonder if he were clenching his teeth. Having your cock and balls caught in a vise, even for the most diehard masochist, had to be a definite limit pusher.

Lucia stood and stepped back, her nipples erect beneath the sheer silk of her camisole. "Hands behind your back, slave boy," she ordered. Master Anthony obeyed. Lucia handed Jaime a pair of leather cuffs with a clip already attached. "Secure him," she said. "Then I'll show you what I want you to do."

Jaime moved behind Master Anthony. His wrists were neatly crossed at the small of his back. Jaime closed the cuffs over each wrist and used the clip to attach one to the other. As she turned, the activity at the nearest station distracted her. Julian was stretched out on the padded spanking horse, his knees resting on the support rails on either side, his ass thrust out. He had a black silicone bit gag in his mouth, its strap buckled around the back of his head. Long leather reins were attached to the strap and draped over his bare back. Petite Ashley was standing on a wooden block behind him, the largest strap-on dildo Jaime had ever seen protruding from her groin, its leather belt secured around her small waist.

Ashley was in the process of squirting copious amounts of lubricant over the shaft. Once satisfied, she dropped the tube and gripped her shiny, black cock, stroking it as she coated the rubber dildo with lube. "Spread your cheeks, boy," Jaime heard her say.

Julian reached back without hesitation and pulled his ass cheeks apart, wiggling his butt in obviously eager anticipation. Ashley moved forward, positioning the large cock until the head of it was nestled between his cheeks. Keeping one hand on the shaft, she reached for the reins with the other.

"Hey!" Lucia's voice startled Jaime. "Your focus needs to be here, not there. You're my assistant, remember? Is our sub boy cuffed? Yes? Then get over here. I want to show you how to use the cock whip."

Jaime scurried around to the front of the pillory, where Master Anthony stood tall, chest forced out by his hands cuffed behind his back. His trapped cock and balls jutted forward in the vise, his ankles locked into the cuffs below.

Lucia reached for the riding crop, which she handed to Jaime. "You've had lessons, right? You know how to use this?"

"Yes," Jaime said hesitantly. "But not on a real person."

"I watched you with the cane today," Lucia said. "You have a natural sensibility. The key is to pay attention. Pay attention to the reaction of your sub. Pay attention to what they say and don't say. If you're not comfortable doing something, then don't do it, okay? No pressure. This is about having fun and stretching our boundaries a little, both yours and his, *comprendes*?"

Jaime nodded. She snapped the crop experimentally against her own thigh.

"You got it!" Lucia enthused. "Excellent wrist action. I told you, you're a natural."

Jaime smiled, not at all certain, but pleased with the encouragement.

"Start easy," Lucia continued. "You can touch and tease to get him hard, if he needs the help." She glanced pointedly at Master Anthony's cock, which, unlike a true masochist's would have been in the same situation, was not erect. "Then bring on the crop. The object is to slowly build up the erotic pain, always watching and gauging, always listening to the cues."

"And what will you be doing?" Jaime asked, curious.

Lucia brought over the wooden block and placed it just to the right of Master Anthony. Next she reached down and retrieved a pair of weighted nipple clamps, along with the single tail whip. She flicked the whip in the air with a snap that made both Jaime and Master Anthony flinch. "If I do my job right, I'll be making this slave boy beg," she said, her voice low and throaty, every inch a Mistress.

"Oh," Jaime said, the word uttered involuntarily. Was every sub in this place a switch except for her? Not Katie, surely, she thought, but the rest of them? Or were they just embracing the temporary role assigned to them, taking their submissive duty to the extreme of not merely obeying a dictate, but *becoming* that which their Masters decreed? Would she ever achieve that level of submission?

"We begin," Mistress Lucia announced. She instructed Jaime to kneel on Master Anthony's left side, while she stepped onto the block, which raised her to eye level with the man.

Jaime set down the crop and shifted on her knees to get a better angle. Reaching out a tentative hand, she lightly stroked his balls. They felt hard and smooth, compressed as they were by the vise's grip. She took his shaft in her other hand. As she stroked and gently tugged, it wasn't long before it stiffened in response.

He uttered a soft cry of pain and Jaime dropped her hands, confused. Glancing up, she realized his cry had nothing to do with her. Alligator-style clamps with black vinyl-coated fishing weights dangled from Master Anthony's nipples. "There, there, slave boy," Lucia crooned. "You can take it, I know you can."

"Yes, Mistress," he managed, flaring his nostrils. Lucia stroked his cheek and it seemed to Jaime he leaned into her touch.

Lucia, glancing down at Jaime, snapped, "Focus on your task. You've got the sub boy hard. Now make him suffer."

Jaime looked down at Master Anthony's cock, which was still erect. Picking up the crop, she started with his balls, slapping lightly with the leather rectangle against the taut skin. She shifted her focus to his shaft, using a little more force in her stroke as she smacked at Master Anthony's cock. Despite their directive, she couldn't think of him as a slave boy or sub, or even Anthony. He was Master Anthony to her, and always would be.

His erection flagged a little as she smacked him, the shaft reddening. She gripped his balls lightly in her other hand and continued the cropping. She resisted the urge to lick the head of his cock, not sure what was acceptable in her apprentice position.

The flicking crack of the single tail reached Jaime's ears, followed an instant later by Master Anthony's second tortured cry. Startled, Jaime lowered the crop. Looking up, she quickly realized once again she'd had nothing to do with his cry of pain, though she knew the crop had to sting. It was the single tail, which snapped again as she watched, causing the teardrop-shaped weights at his nipples to sway. She stared, transfixed, as the whip snaked again against his skin, leaving a third red line along his well-muscled chest.

Lucia, whip still in her small hand, glanced down again at Jaime with a reproving look. Embarrassed, Jaime refocused on the man's captured cock and balls. She sought to mix the pleasure and pain, stroking his shaft when it flagged until it hardened once more, and then striking it in a flurry of stinging leather.

Mistress Lucia continued to torture her slave boy above Jaime's head while she focused down below. Master Anthony's limbs had begun to tremble and Jaime could hear the ragged pant of his breathing. Following her instinct, she dropped the crop and wrapped her arms around his legs, resting her cheek against his muscular thigh as Mistress Lucia continued to whip him. Despite what was happening to him, Master Anthony's cock remained hard, bobbing tantalizingly beside Jaime's face.

"Oh, god," he moaned finally. Jaime released her grip and leaned back on her haunches, looking up. "Please, Lucia, I want… I need…" He trailed off.

"I know what you want," Lucia replied in a soft but fervent tone. She dropped the whip and stepped off the wooden block. Standing directly in front of Master Anthony, she fell to her knees beside Jaime. Her chin was lifted, her eyes on Master Anthony's face. "I know what you *need*," she added in a whisper.

Jaime felt superfluous, invisible, as Lucia closed her mouth over Master Anthony's shaft and leaned forward, taking it in as far as she could, given his tethered state. Her hand came up in a tender cup around his compressed balls as she worshipped her Master's cock.

Yes, Jaime thought. Her Master, not her sub boy. Though no words had been spoken, no new directive given, it was clear Lucia had slipped off the mantle of Mistress, her true nature as submissive reasserting itself, her desire for the man before her raw and exposed.

It wasn't long before Master Anthony bucked and shuddered, groaning as he came. No permission was requested and none was needed. Master Anthony took what was offered, what was already his. Lucia, still apparently oblivious to Jaime's presence, rose from her knees, her tongue moving over her lips like a cat licking away the excess cream. Stepping once more onto the wooden block, she took the still-bound man's face in her hands and, without missing a beat, kissed him full on the mouth.

Master Anthony held himself stiffly at first, and then seemed, all at once, to melt against Lucia, leaning into her kiss with a heartfelt sigh. It wasn't the kiss of a Mistress and her slave, or even of a Master and his sub. The two were sharing a lovers' kiss, and Jaime saw the passion and the tenderness, the spark and the raw need. She had become a trespasser, an interloper on something that was too private, too personal, for her to witness.

She had never felt so safe, so accepted and included as she did at The Enclave. They *got* her here. They understood who she was and what she needed. But the community as a whole couldn't give her what she hadn't even known she longed for. She was bereft of love. She had never, not once in her life, been truly in love. Watching Master Anthony and Lucia, it was as if a fist had been shoved into her guts, into the most secret folds of her empty, aching heart.

Blinking back sudden tears, she looked away.

~*~

The scenes had ended, and the Doms had been unbound, released, gently washed and soothed. The men had re-dressed in their black leather and boots, while the sub girls let the silky garments they'd worn as temporary Mistresses fall in puddles to their feet.

Mistress Marjorie and the Masters had left the subs to clean and straighten the dungeon, after which they would have free time until lunch. The girls worked quietly, wiping down equipment and gear, and setting the dungeon to rights.

Jaime stopped what she was doing a moment to watch Lucia neatly coil the single tail, a faraway look in the woman's eyes. "You're in love with him, aren't you?" Jaime dared.

"What?" Lucia looked up from her task. "Who?"

Jaime wondered if she'd overstepped. But since she'd started the conversation, she pushed on. "Come on. I saw the way you kissed him. The way he kissed you..."

"Oh." Lucia shook her head. "No. No, no. I mean, well, maybe a little, but it can't be. It's not meant to be. There's too much history."

"Too much history?" Now Jaime was intrigued. "Between the two of you?"

Lucia glanced around the dungeon. Ashley and Katie were at the front of the room, Danielle nearby but apparently absorbed in polishing the wooden stocks, her back to them. Turning back to Jaime, Lucia said quietly, "Master Anthony was Miguel's mentor."

"Miguel?"

Tears filled Lucia's dark eyes, though she managed a small smile. "My Master. My late husband."

Jaime blinked back her own tears of sympathy. "What happened?" she asked softly. "I mean, if it's not too personal?"

Lucia shook her head. "He had a heart attack, a massive coronary while he was on his construction site—he was a contractor."

"Oh! That's awful!"

She shrugged sadly. "It was completely out of the blue. We had no idea there was even a problem. He never liked to go to doctors. He was strong and in shape, but apparently his heart wasn't."

"I'm so sorry."

Lucia wiped a single tear and then smiled, shaking her head. "We had twenty good years together, me and *mi esposo*. I thought we'd have another fifty, but then, you never expect something like that. Miguel was fifty when he died—ten years older than me.

"It's been nearly three years now. Anthony was a huge support during all the craziness after. He helped me sell Miguel's business and invest the proceeds. Miguel had a life insurance policy too, so I never have to worry about money, and I can help my family." This time her smile was brighter. "Most importantly, he let me join The Enclave anyway, even without my Master. He understood that in order to heal, I needed the comfort and peace of submission and sensual slavery. It keeps me grounded and happy." A solemn but radiant serenity suffused Lucia's expression, though there was still a touch of sorrow in her eyes.

"And it keeps you near Master Anthony," Jaime murmured, shocked at her own nerve in saying it, but certain she was right.

Lucia glanced sharply at her, but then chuckled, surrender in the sound. "It's that obvious, huh? And here I thought I was the master of discretion."

"He loves you, too," Jaime said. "I saw it in his eyes, Lucia."

"No." Lucia shook her head, her arms wrapping protectively around her body. "He sees me as Miguel's submissive. Miguel's widow. I'm not sure he can get past that. And he's got issues with age. Says I'm young enough to be his daughter."

"He needs to get over it," snapped Jaime, and then she clapped her hand over her mouth, her cheeks warming. "I'm sorry. I'm being disrespectful. I know this is none of my business anyway."

"You're right." Lucia grinned. "It's none of your business. Just like the fact that you have a major crush on Master Mark is none of my business, but there you are."

"Oh my god." Jaime brought her hand once more to her mouth as she glanced quickly around the dungeon. Ashley and Katie had disappeared, but Danielle still lingered nearby. "Does everyone know that, too?" she asked worriedly.

"Oh, I don't know." Lucia shrugged. "I think you're fairly discreet, really. But I see it in your eyes when you look at him. And the way your voice kind of softens when you talk about him."

Jaime shook her head, embarrassed to be so transparent. "It's dumb, right? I barely know him. I mean, I don't know how to explain it, but it's like I *do* know him. He seems so familiar to me. Like we knew each other in a past life or something."

"Well, he *is* pretty famous. He wrote all their best stuff, you know. He's a real poet and it might make you think you know the guy, but it's just one part of who he is. We think we know people because of their music, but you really don't know the man behind the musician."

"What?" Jaime wrinkled her nose in confusion.

Lucia, unaware Jaime had no clue what she was saying, continued, "Think how his fans would freak out if they knew the lead singer of Planck Time was also Master Mark of The Enclave, a confirmed sexual sadist who does all sorts of perverted things to willing, eager slave girls?"

"Wait, what?" Jaime struggled to process and make sense of what Lucia was saying. "What are you *talking* about? That grunge band that broke up a while back?" A vision of three young guys in dreadlocks and beards flashed into her mind. She'd liked the band, though she didn't own any of their stuff. They had a dark, intense sound, kind of like that 80's band, Nirvana. She cast back in her mind, recalling the specifics. The lead singer was Mark something. Mark Wheeler…

"Holy shit!" Jaime blurted, understanding finally fully dawning. She realized Danielle was now staring at her, and she lowered her voice. "Master Mark is Mark *Wheeler*? But he looks so different!"

"Amazing what a pair of scissors and a good razor can do." Lucia laughed. "Ashley used to have hair down to her waist when she got here. You wouldn't have recognized her, either, trust me. And Master Mark keeps a very low profile regarding the band. He doesn't like to talk about it."

"You know," Jaime said, "I've heard him a few times playing his guitar out on the veranda in the mornings. He sounded really good, but I just never connected him…" She trailed off, thinking how weird it was she'd been living with and submitting to a famous rock star for the past ten days, and nobody had even said a word. She vaguely recalled some scandal involving drugs, one of the band members dying of an overdose. Poor Master Mark! "This must be like a safe haven for him," she mused aloud. "A place to recover."

"It is, I'm sure." Lucia nodded. "When Anthony met him he was holed up in a house in Charlotte, living pretty much like a recluse. He came out at night to hang out at some of the private BDSM clubs, and that's where they met. The Enclave has given Master Mark the freedom and the privacy to really explore his dominant impulses and his core needs without the spotlight of the media or anything else distracting him. He's only been here a little over two months."

Jaime tried to process the mountain of information being thrown her way. "Wait, so he's not a permanent resident here at The Enclave?"

Lucia shrugged. "He doesn't have an ownership share the way the other Masters and Mistresses do, so yeah, I guess he's not really permanent at this point, though I do know they really like him and want him to stay. So if he decides to make it permanent, they'll work that out, I guess."

Jaime was silent as she pondered this. As her two-week period drew to a close, she knew she would be faced with making a decision, assuming she was offered the chance. She realized she'd been assuming—even counting on—Master Mark as part of that equation.

As if reading her mind, Lucia said quietly, "I didn't come here for Anthony, Jaime. You can't come here for Mark."

Guiltily, Jaime started to protest. "I wasn't—"

Lucia cut her off with a wave of her hand. "I'm not saying you are. I'm just advising you from the heart, because I like you, and I don't want to see you do something stupid. This place isn't about finding a lover or a partner. That does sometimes happen, though most of the couples here were already together when they arrived. But if you sign on at The Enclave as a staff slave, you're making a commitment and promise to serve *all* the Masters and Mistresses to the very best of your ability, every second of every day. Someone might claim you, with your express permission of course, but that doesn't mean they are your lover, and you need to be very clear about that, Jaime. The Enclave is unique, and we subscribe to a lifestyle that suits only a very few. If they offer you the chance to become a member, you had better think long and hard about your decision. If you join The Enclave, it's because you want what we offer here, and because you need to serve. End of story. No Master/husband/boyfriend/lover should enter that equation. You got it, *chica*?"

Jaime swallowed hard and looked away. Something tore in her heart, but she knew Lucia was right. "Yeah," she said glumly, aware Danielle was now openly eavesdropping on their conversation. "I got it."

CHAPTER 14

Jaime turned slowly on her stiletto heels as she admired the room. She set down her bucket and supplies, surveying the space as she decided what to tackle first. She was charged with cleaning all surfaces in the dungeon and making all the gear and equipment shine. As always, just looking at the sexy bondage and torture gear was enough to get her juices flowing. She'd been honored by the cleaning assignment, given the special event to take place at the dungeon that evening.

She surveyed the different stations, letting her mind linger over the bondage table where Master Mark had taken her to the edge with the intense knife play. She had been so scared at the start of the scene, the thought of those sharp, terrifying blades pricking her skin, slicing her flesh, drawing the hot gush of her blood... Yet, as it had a hundred times in the days since that powerful experience, Jaime's mind drifted back to the session itself, and to the amazing man who had so thoroughly engaged every fiber of her being—mental, physical and spiritual—with that intense and incredibly mind-blowing scene.

Ever since her talk with Lucia after yesterday's Sadie Hawkins experience, Jaime had been mulling over and trying to distill her feelings for the handsome, sexy Master Mark. While her newfound knowledge of his status as a rock star was intriguing, she could honestly say her awareness of his fame didn't really impact her feelings for him one way or the other. She was curious about his experiences as a musician and hoped someday they might be close enough where she could talk to him about it. She would love to hear him sing a song just for her. All that, at least for now, was a distant dream.

She thought about Lucia and Master Anthony, about how obvious it seemed to Jaime that the two of them would be a perfect couple, but then, nothing was ever as simple or clear as it might seem from the outside. She recognized that, though she felt a deep and intense attraction to Master Mark, at least some of that had to do with his mastery as a Dom. And she further understood that just because someone was fabulous in a scene and could take you to spiritual and sensual places you never dreamed of, that didn't mean he was destined to be a partner in your life.

She had to laugh at the direction of her thoughts. Lucia was right. Of course she was! If and when Jaime was faced with the decision of joining The Enclave, she would leave Mark solidly *out* of the equation.

She brushed her palms together in a gesture that meant she was washing her hands of the whole thing and picked up a fresh rag, ready to tackle her assignment. She would start with the dusting, and then move on to oiling the leather gear, polishing the chrome and the mirrors, and cleaning the counters and sink. Lastly, she would sweep and mop the floor. She had two hours for the task, and she would use every second to make the place sparkle. Energized, she set to work.

~*~

"We're delighted to have you here with us for a few days, Stefan," Anthony said. "I'm sure I speak for us all when I say I'm excited to see your branding techniques firsthand." Stefan Janssen, a friend of Anthony's, had just arrived from Amsterdam for a brief visit, his reputation as a branding expert preceding him.

Anthony looked down the table to Mason. "Are you and slave Ashley still planning on participating in an actual branding?"

Master Mason nodded enthusiastically. "You bet your ass. Or should I say, Ashley's ass."

There was laughter around the table. Mark quietly studied the diminutive, tattooed girl to Mason's right. She had her eyes on her plate, but a small, secret smile played over her lips. She was one of the most self-contained submissives he'd ever met. Her self-control and high pain tolerance were very impressive.

"What's your take on the subject, Mark? Have you had any direct experience with branding?" Master Anthony asked.

Mark shook his head. "Tonight will be a first for me."

"You are in for a treat," Stefan said eagerly. His accent was barely discernable, notable primarily because of his perfect diction. "As with so much in the scene, it's as much a matter of what is in the head as it is of the body. It's about the anticipation, the fear and the desire, even more than the thrill of burning one's permanent mark into the flesh of another."

Jaime, who sat to Mark's immediate right, drew in a small but audible breath. Mark glanced over at her. "Branding is not your cup of tea, hmm?"

She looked back at him with wide eyes. Her long, wavy dark hair was down tonight, tendrils curling prettily around her cheeks and falling softly over her shoulders. She, unlike Ashley, wore her emotions on her face, and he could see the fear there. "No, Sir."

"So, if I, as your Master, wanted to brand you, to mark you as mine in that way, you would refuse me?" he teased.

Color seeped into Jaime's cheeks, her mouth falling open. "Oh! No, Sir. I mean, yes. I mean, I wouldn't want to disobey but—"

He was immediately contrite that he'd put the trainee in an awkward position with his teasing. "Hey, I'm just kidding. And I'm with you." He flashed a grin. "Branding is not my cup of tea, either." She looked so relieved it was almost comical.

"Permission to speak, Sir?" Danielle, who sat to Mark's left, lightly touched his arm.

He turned toward her. "Yes, slave Danielle?"

"I believe a properly trained slave should *always* submit to her Master's wishes," Danielle said with a lift of her chin. "If you wished me to be branded, Sir, then that is what would please me."

"I appreciate that, Danielle," Mark replied. Something in the girl's tone and countenance reminded him of a particularly smug teacher's pet he'd known in middle school, but he pushed the ungallant thought away. "While I recognize that branding can be a valid and powerful expression of ownership and submission, I would never ask my sub to alter herself in such a permanent way for me, unless it was something we both agreed was right for us."

Danielle lowered her thick fringe of lashes and echoed softly, "*Us*. Yes, Sir. Thank you for teaching me. I understand." Mark had the momentarily unpleasant feeling Danielle had deliberately misunderstood him, but he decided to let it go.

When dinner was cleared, dessert and coffee on the table, Stefan turned to Anthony. "I would like to take a look at the facilities and get set up before the demonstration. Is that possible?"

"Of course." Anthony looked to Lawrence. "Would you accompany Stefan?"

Lawrence pushed back his chair, dropping his napkin to his plate. "Of course. Slave Jaime," he said, looking over Danielle's and Mark's heads. "I haven't had a chance to inspect your handiwork. You will come with us."

"Yes, Sir." Jaime pushed back her chair and stood. Her bare breast, round and soft, brushed Mark's shoulder as she stood, sending a jolt directly to his cock. He was glad his napkin hid his sudden arousal, and he kept his eyes down as she moved away.

~*~

Jaime followed the men out of the dining room, through the main living area and along the wide hallway to the dungeon. Master Stefan carried a large gear bag over his shoulder. Jaime tried to imagine what must be inside—branding irons, a blowtorch to heat the metal designs that would be burned into the flesh, soothing balms to treat the wound that would eventually heal into a symbol of servitude and devotion.

She shivered slightly as she imagined the searing pain of the white-hot brand, and the sizzling stench of burning flesh. *Not for me. No way, no how.* But then another thought slipped in right behind the first. *Never say never*, and she knew this was true. If someone had told her before Master Anthony's astounding proposal back at the Garden only a few weeks ago that Jaime would willingly subject herself to complete sexual, submissive servitude at the hands of a group of dominant strangers, she would have dismissed the idea as completely absurd—utterly impossible!

Yet since she'd been at The Enclave, her life had slowed from a frenzy of busywork, struggling to make ends meet and always looking ahead and ahead and ahead, never living for the moment, never content. For the first time in her life, she was living each day purely on its terms, taking in each experience and letting it lift and carry her, taking her where she needed to go.

They reached the double doors to the main dungeon. "Jaime is in training," Master Lawrence said to Master Stefan as he pulled open the doors. "She has prepared the dungeon for tonight's demonstration." They stepped inside, Jaime just behind them, her heart executing a small loop-de-loop in her chest.

She had learned firsthand that Master Lawrence was an exacting man. She had done a tiptop job cleaning the dungeon, but if Master Lawrence was determined to find fault with her work, she knew he could find something to criticize.

"What a marvelous space," Master Stefan said as he moved into the room. He stumbled forward suddenly, his hands thrust out as he struggled to keep his balance. *"Wat de hel…"* he cried. Fortunately, he regained his footing and didn't fall.

Master Lawrence rushed forward and then stopped suddenly. "Slave Jaime! What is this on the floor?" His tone was angry and Jaime's heart clutched in her throat.

"What is it, Sir?" She stepped forward.

He pointed to the floor. There was a puddle of what looked like floor wax directly in front of the door. Jaime stared at it uncomprehendingly. "Unacceptable," Master Lawrence barked. She started to reply, to explain there was no way she'd left that there, but he cut her off. "Silence. Don't move."

He turned away from her where she stood frozen to the spot, confusion and horror short-circuiting her brain. "Stefan, are you all right?" he asked solicitously, moving toward the older man.

"I'm fine. It's nothing," Master Stefan said quickly.

"I'm so sorry," Master Lawrence said. "I should have inspected the dungeon before bringing you here, but the day got away from me. This trainee was permitted to do this task unsupervised"—he flashed Jaime a venomous look—"and evidently failed to finish the job."

Jaime opened her mouth once more to protest, but then closed it, recalling his order that she stay silent.

"Oh dear," Master Stefan said, gesturing toward one of the counters. "A bit of a mess here, I'm afraid."

Jaime stared in mute horror. The dildos, cuffs, gags and other paraphernalia she'd meticulously dusted and neatly arranged were in a jumbled pile on one end of the counter, some of them in a heap on the floor beside it, as if someone had used their arm in a sweeping gesture along the surface.

Dread moved with an icy finger along her spine. Someone had done this—someone had deliberately made a mess of all her hard work. Her gaze shifted, her eye caught by something white beside one of the St. Andrew crosses. There sat a bucket, a wet rag hanging over its side, another puddle of soapy water on the floor beside it. A dildo was perched on the seat of one of the bondage chairs, a tube of lubricant beside it, as if someone had masturbated there and forgotten to clean up.

The whole thing was such an obvious setup it was ridiculous, and again Jaime opened her mouth. This was insane. She had to tell Master Lawrence. "Please, Master Lawrence," she said urgently. "Permission to speak."

"Denied," he barked, whipping his head back to glare at her. His face was purple with fury. "You were given a simple task. How dare you treat this incredible training opportunity with such disdain? We have a guest here! What were you thinking?"

"Lawrence," Master Stefan interjected, placing his hand on Master Lawrence's arm. "Perhaps you're overreacting? Please don't worry on my account. You mentioned she is still in training. Perhaps she didn't properly understand the assignment?"

Master Lawrence pressed his lips together in a thin, hard line. "Perhaps," he said, his tone calmer now, some of the blood draining from his face. His lips lifted into something resembling a smile, though his eyes were like chips of blue ice. "If you don't mind waiting in the living room for a few minutes, we'll get the dungeon properly prepared for you to set up."

"Not a problem," Master Stefan said, flashing a sympathetic look in Jaime's direction. "I'm sure this is easily remedied."

Turning back to Jaime, Master Lawrence spoke in a measured tone, though Jaime could feel the anger just beneath it. "Get your ass to the punishment room. Close the door behind you and kneel down in the offering position. Wait in that pose until I come for you."

"Please, Sir!" Jaime cried desperately. "I didn't—"

"I did *not* grant you permission to speak." His voice was sharp as a knife's edge as it cut across hers. "If you speak out of turn again, you will be dismissed from this training program. Do. You. Understand."

Jaime swallowed hard, tears springing to her eyes, her hands clenched into fists of frustration. Someone had done this, and she had an idea who it must have been. She also recognized, even in her turmoil, that Master Lawrence was embarrassed in front of Master Stefan for the apparent failure of his trainee. Surely once they were alone, she would be able to explain what must have happened, and he could seek out and punish the actual culprit.

"Yes, Sir," she managed. Not knowing what else to do, Jaime bowed her head, turned on her heel, and left the room. She walked in a daze through the empty living room, glad at least there was no one there to witness her humiliation.

She entered the punishment room and flicked on the overhead light. "This isn't fair," she wailed to the empty room. "Why wouldn't he let me tell him?" Tears of frustration rolled down her cheeks and she angrily wiped them away.

She took in the small cage beside the cross and shuddered. One of her hard limits during casual BDSM play had always been confinement in very small spaces. But she hadn't been asked about hard limits here at The Enclave. She had blindly, blithely trusted that Master Anthony and the others would intuitively understand and respect her limits, and so far, that had been true.

No safeword.

She could turn around and walk out. She wasn't an *actual* slave with no recourse or rights. The clothing she'd had with her, along with her duffel containing her cell phone and other personal items, had been neatly stowed in the bottom drawer of her bureau. She could go there right now—there was no one stopping her—and get her things. She could call a cab and leave this place, never to return.

The thought nearly broke her heart.

She didn't want to leave.

She would make Master Lawrence understand. He would have to listen to her. Hope fluttered like a trapped butterfly in her chest as she knelt on the floor as directed, wrists crossed, arms stretched out overhead, forehead touching the ground, ass in the air.

She no longer bothered to wipe away her tears as they splashed on the floor. She closed her eyes and focused on recapturing the blissful feelings she'd experienced during the Shibari exercise. She reached for the warm, sensual memory of Master Mark's arms around her on the veranda and wrapped it around her senses. She thought about his tender, loving gaze after she'd soared during the edge play session, and the feel of his hand on her cheek as he brought her gently back to earth.

Patience, obedience, submission, grace.

She heard the door open. Her pulse, which had slowed during her meditation, leaped to life. Her heart thumped against her bones. She heard footsteps on the wooden floor and then a hand gripped her hard by the hair and yanked her upright. Master Lawrence's face was suddenly close to hers, his breath hot on her face.

"You will be punished now, slave Jaime. Sloppy work is never tolerated here at The Enclave." He pulled her to her feet, using her hair as a handle. Jaime winced in pain.

He dragged her toward the cross and yanked her right arm upward, locking it into a cuff before she could react. He quickly secured the second cuff. She whipped her head in his direction. "I didn't do it," she said fiercely.

He grabbed her hair again and jerked her head back, making her gasp with pain.

"Enough of your excuses. You are on very thin ice right now. Very thin, indeed. You can't seem to keep that pretty mouth of yours shut, so I'm going to shut it for you." He lifted his free hand and pressed something against her lips. He wasn't going to let her explain. He didn't care what she had to say.

She smelled the rubber of the ball gag and instinctively tried to turn her head away. She had to make him understand. But he was much stronger than she, and just as determined. Letting go of her hair, he gripped her jaw hard, forcing her mouth open. With his other hand, he pushed the ball of the gag into her mouth. Moving behind her, he buckled it tightly into place.

He stepped away and a moment later she heard the terrifying whistle of bamboo whipping furiously through the air. "Twenty strokes with the cane," he said in a tight, hard voice.

Before Jaime could prepare, mentally or otherwise, the cane cut across her ass several times in fiery succession. She screamed but the sound was pushed back into her throat by the gag. The cane sliced into her thighs. More strokes of fire snaked along her calves. Tears streamed down her face.

When the cane met her back, Jaime couldn't entirely process what was happening. There wasn't a trace of eroticism in this punishment— just pure, fiery, agonizing pain. She tried to draw in a breath, but she had forgotten how to breathe. Her heart felt like it was exploding in her chest. There was an odd ringing sound in her ears and the room began to spin. A misty, gray film moved over her vision.

It took Jaime a second to realize she must have passed out, and as she came to her senses, she felt the cuffs being pulled from her wrists.

Her knees gave way and she fell back into the arms of her tormentor.

"Dog!" Master Lawrence said sternly. "Now!"

At first Jaime had no idea what he was saying. Then she realized he was referring to the slave position. Dog meant she was to drop to all fours, ass thrust up, legs wide. When she didn't immediately react, he pushed her roughly to the floor.

"Crawl," he commanded. He pointed toward the small cage. Again, when she failed to react, he reached down and grabbed her by the collar and jerked her roughly toward the cage. Jaime instinctively tried to twist away, all at once on high alert, her heart smashing painfully in her chest.

"Get in there." With strong, deliberate movements, he pushed her into the tiny space. "You will stay there and think about what you have done while the rest of us watch the branding demonstration."

His words hit her like a tight fist. "No," she screamed as she struggled against him. "No!" Though it came out as a gurgle, her shaking head and rigid limbs had to convey her meaning. Her back was to the room, and he reached into the cage, pulling at her arms so they were behind her as she lay on her side. Her wrists were pulled together, cuffs clipped into place around them. She could hear the cage door closing and its latch sliding home. Panic rose like bile in her throat.

"You will start once more with a clean slate once your punishment is complete, but I would caution you—this sort of behavior will *not* be tolerated. You've disgraced The Enclave."

Jaime could barely hear his words over the rush of blood in her ears. His voice came from far away, as if he were talking through a tube. "Someone will return for you within the hour." His footsteps echoed away from her along the hardwood floor. The door clicked closed and she was left alone in a small cage, her mouth plugged, her arms twisted uncomfortably behind her back, her skin in tatters, her mind blank with terror.

~*~

Mark stood near the door of the dungeon, too distracted by what Master Lawrence had told him to concentrate on the branding ceremony about to take place between Master Mason and Ashley.

It wasn't the first time Master Lawrence, The Enclave's resident disciplinarian, had found fault with a cleaning task and punished the errant submissive for his or her transgression. Mark hadn't even realized what was happening until two staff slaves had been dispatched to put right what Jaime had apparently left wrong in the main dungeon.

Mark hoped the punishment hadn't been too severe. Perhaps Jaime hadn't understood what was expected. The whole thing didn't sit quite right with Mark and made him wonder. That kind of carelessness didn't seem like the Jaime he'd gotten to know. Was it possible he was letting his attraction for the woman cloud his perception of her as a sub?

He watched as Master Stefan heated the metal brand clamped in a pair of insulated pliers with the blue flame from a propane torch. Ashley was kneeling up beside Master Mason, her expression calm as she watched the heart-shaped brand glow a fiery red.

He thought about Jaime's reaction at the dinner table to the prospect of being branded, and Danielle's assertion of accepting whatever her Master meted out, no matter her own feelings on the matter. Master Lawrence and Danielle would make a good couple, it suddenly occurred to Mark. He thought back to the Sadie Hawkins session, recalling the intensity of their connection, both physical and emotional, during their scene. Master Lawrence favored that sort of dictatorial, all-knowing Master approach and, at least to hear Danielle tell it, so did she.

As he took in the people sitting, standing and kneeling throughout the dungeon, all eyes fixed on the proceedings, Mark's thoughts veered again to Jaime. She should have been there, kneeling among the other subs.

He placed his hand on the doorknob and turned it. Pulling the door quietly open, he slipped out of the room and headed down the hallway. He knew the rules about interfering with another Dom's punishment arrangement, but he didn't care. Suspecting Jaime might be in need of a little TLC, given what he knew of Lawrence's methods, Mark made a quick detour to the kitchen, where he grabbed a clean dishtowel and snagged a bottle of water from the refrigerator.

The punishment room door was closed. He opened it and stepped inside. For a second he didn't see her, and then his eyes fixed on the cage. Jaime was huddled into a fetal ball inside it. She was trembling, her wrists cuffed behind her back, which was crisscrossed with welts, two of them wet with blood.

"Fuck," he breathed softly, his heart constricting as he strode quickly to the cage. Tossing aside the water and towel, he crouched down, pushed back the latch and yanked open the cage door. Reaching inside, he pulled loose the Velcro cuffs at Jaime's wrists. To hell with Lawrence and the rest of them, too, if they had a problem with his actions. He was taking her out of there.

Slipping his hands carefully beneath her trembling body, he drew Jaime gently from the confines of the small cage and took her into his arms. Jaime turned her tearstained face toward him and he saw the ball gag wedged tightly between her teeth. Reaching behind her head, he quickly unbuckled the gag and pulled it from her mouth, dropping it onto the floor.

Careful of her ravaged back, he drew her closer. Reaching for the towel, he dabbed lightly against her wounds. They would need to be properly cleaned and treated, but not now, not yet.

Jaime hid her face in his chest and began to sob. Mark held her gently, his heart cracking as she cried. While he understood the two-week initial training had to be rigorous in order to weed out the players and wannabes, Lawrence had gone too far this time.

Mark was clenching his jaw and he made a conscious attempt to let go of his fury, which served no one. "Shh," he murmured, focusing on the girl in his arms. "It's okay, Jaime," he murmured soothingly. "You're okay." He began to hum a tune his mother had sung to him when he was a child, while he gently rocked the girl in his arms.

Eventually Jaime's trembling subsided, as did her sobs. She pulled back from Mark and he let his arms fall away. They sat facing one another in the middle of the small room. Mark reached for the bottle of water that had rolled nearby. "Here. Have some water." He twisted the cap off the bottle and handed the water to Jaime. After she had drunk her fill, he took the half-empty bottle from her and set it down.

He handed her the towel, waiting as she wiped her tear-stained face. "What happened, Jaime? Why did Master Lawrence punish you so harshly?"

"I didn't do it," she whispered, her eyes dark with misery. "I didn't." Tears sprang again into her eyes. Speaking louder, she continued, "It wasn't me. But he wouldn't let me tell him." Her voice cracked. "He wouldn't let me explain."

"Hey, it's going to be okay. Stay calm. Take a deep breath. We'll get to the bottom of this."

With a nod, Jaime drew in a shuddery breath and let it out. Mark reached once more for the water bottle and held it out. Jaime accepted the bottle and took another swallow. "Thank you, Sir." Jaime managed a wan smile.

"Better," Mark said. "Now tell me, what didn't you do?"

She pushed her hair back from her face and tucked it behind her ears in a way that made him want to kiss her. "I didn't leave the dungeon in that condition," she said. "It was spotless, I swear. I never would have left puddles and buckets and a mess on the floor. I promise you, Master Mark. Someone came in after me. Someone deliberately made it look like I left that mess."

Mark wasn't sure what he'd expected, but that certainly wasn't it. To blame someone else for your failures as a sub was the consummate no-no at The Enclave. Mistakes were tolerated, even expected, but excuses were not. Yet what she said made sense. Who in their right mind would be so stupid as to leave their task half finished, especially when they knew they would be the focus of keen attention and judgment? Jaime wasn't a stupid woman, nor did she seem the self-destructive type.

But if she didn't do it, then who?

All at once he knew.

"I believe you, Jaime," he said.

"Thank you, Sir," she whispered, and the light returned to her eyes.

CHAPTER 15

Mark placed his hands lightly on Jaime's shoulders, pulling her closer so their faces were almost touching. All at once the door of the punishment room flew open. Lawrence stood there, fury washing over his face as he took in the scene. "What the hell is going on in here?" he spluttered indignantly. "How dare you interfere—"

Jaime froze, her eyes wide with fear, her back still to the door. Lawrence stopped abruptly as a large hand clamped firmly on his shoulder, and Mark saw Anthony just behind Lawrence. Taking in the scene, Anthony dropped his hand and pushed past Lawrence into the room, his expression grim. Lawrence crowded in behind him.

Anthony, his eyes fixed on Jaime's welted back, spoke in a quiet but firm voice. "What happened here?"

"I did my job, that's what. You saw the condition of the dungeon," Lawrence snapped. "The trainee humiliated the entire house in front of Stefan and then tried to cover up her mistakes with excuses and lies. She got what she deserved and Mark had no right—"

"That's enough." Anthony's voice had turned to steel. "Lawrence, please go wait in my study. I'll be there directly."

"What?" Lawrence retorted. "I'm in charge of discipline and—"

"I said"—Anthony interrupted, a hard look Mark had never seen before entering his face—"go wait in my study. Now."

Color rose in Lawrence's face. For a moment Mark thought he would refuse, but then, with a curt nod, Lawrence turned on his heel and disappeared. Addressing Mark, Anthony said quietly, "Please get

Marjorie and Aubrey while I talk to Jaime a moment. Ask Aubrey to bring her doctor's kit. She's just finishing up with Ashley's aftercare."

Mark didn't want to leave Jaime but he didn't protest, instead pushing himself to his feet. "It's gonna be okay," he murmured to Jaime, reaching down to stroke her cheek. "I promise."

The rest of the household was still in the main dungeon. Ashley was seated in Mason's lap, a large gauze bandage on her upper back, Mason's newest mark of ownership no doubt just beneath it. Aubrey stood behind them, in the process of closing up her medical kit. Marjorie was nearby with Brandon and Stefan, the three engaged in conversation.

Mark approached Aubrey first. "Excuse me, Aubrey, but you're needed in the punishment room. Please bring your medical kit." He turned toward Marjorie, who had an expression of concern on her face that told him she'd just heard what he said. "Sorry to interrupt, Marjorie, but Anthony asks if you could come too. Jaime needs some help after a punishment that went a little"—he caught himself and stopped. Why sugarcoat it?—"a *lot* awry."

He filled them in briefly, the women letting him talk without interruption as the three of them hurried through the house. There wasn't room for them all in the small space of the punishment room. Anthony stepped out and spoke quietly with Marjorie for a moment, though Mark couldn't hear what they were saying. Then the women entered the small space, clucking and crooning as they took Jaime under their maternal wings.

Anthony turned to Mark. "Jaime told me what happened. Thank god you had the foresight and sense to stop this when you did." Mark nodded, not quite trusting himself to speak. Anthony continued, "Let's go talk to Lawrence and sort this out."

Mark thought the best way to sort this out would be to give Lawrence some of his own medicine. He briefly fantasized about caning the shit out of Lawrence and then stuffing him into a cage. He knew even as the fantasy inserted itself into his brain that it was unworthy of a Dom—unlike Lawrence, Mark would never punish a sub, or anyone else, out of anger.

Anthony's study was large and comfortable, a distinctly masculine space with dark wood paneling and floor-to-ceiling bookshelves. Anthony sat in a wingback chair and gestured toward the sofa, where Lawrence was perched ramrod straight on one side, his lips compressed in a thin line, his arms crossed over his chest. Mark settled on the other side.

Anthony sat quietly for a time, his gaze moving from Lawrence to Mark and back again as he composed his thoughts. "You know," he said slowly, looking now neither at Mark nor Lawrence, but rather staring off into the middle distance. "During training, a lot of focus is placed on getting at a submissive's emotional core. Submission is about truth, about revealing yourself. If you simply demand obedience without understanding a sub's true motivations and needs, even if the sub obeys every command to the letter and every aspect of every scene, they're just going through the motions, and so are you."

"Yes! That's it!" Mark blurted before he realized he was going to speak. "That's it. That's what makes this place different from the BDSM club scene and the players you find there. Or at least, I'd thought so." He shot a dark look at Lawrence, who glared back.

"You thought right, Mark," Anthony replied, favoring him with a nod. "And you, Lawrence, I think this is what you've been missing, what's lacking in you." Lawrence, who still held his defensive posture on the edge of the sofa, stiffened further but remained quiet. "You have to listen not just to a submissive's words and physical cues, but to the heart and soul that lie beneath. They are giving you a gift, and it's your responsibility to cherish rather than abuse it. It's not just an exchange of power, you see. It's an exchange of trust. You have to trust them as much as you ask them to trust you."

"This is all very well," Lawrence said through clenched teeth, "but I don't understand what this has to do with what happened tonight. I thought you brought us here to explain to Mark what he did wrong, but instead I'm hearing that you have a problem with what *I* did, and I have to say, I resent that. I did what I always do in my role as disciplinarian at The Enclave. I punished the trainee for misbehavior. Mr. Rock Star here"—he shot a withering glance at Mark before looking back to Anthony—"decided he knew better than I did what she needed, and took the matter into his own hands. Now Jaime is no doubt completely confused about our expectations, and it's all his fault."

"No," Anthony shouted, the word accompanied by his fist, which he smashed against his knee for emphasis. The outburst was so unexpected in the normally imperturbable man that both Lawrence and Mark startled.

"Excuse me?" Lawrence managed, his eyebrows lifted in surprise.

"No," Anthony repeated, though he lowered his voice. "That is *not* why we're here, Lawrence. I invited Mark to join us because I want him to understand the serious nature of what has transpired here. He was witness and thus this affects him. Mark is still considering if he'll join us permanently here at The Enclave, and I want his decision to be a fully informed one." He glanced at Mark, and the tight coil of tense worry in Mark's gut unwound for the first time since he'd found Jaime in the cage.

Anthony returned his attention to Lawrence. "It's true Mark intervened directly in a punishment when he might have come instead to you to suggest a different course of action. Be that as it may, he reacted based on what he saw in the moment, and in my estimation, he reacted appropriately. You left a trainee alone in a cage with her hands bound and a gag stuffed in her mouth, her back torn and bloody. You didn't tell anyone else what you had done. Whatever Jaime did or didn't do regarding her duties earlier today when cleaning the dungeon, you failed to *listen*. You didn't let her speak—you simply assumed she was lying. You reacted with anger, Lawrence. You behaved in a reckless way that endangered another person, and quite frankly, it's grounds for immediate expulsion from this community."

"Anthony!" Lawrence interjected in a shocked tone, the color draining from his face. "You can't be serious. My life is here. I belong here!"

Anthony held up a hand. "And I want you to stay, Lawrence, but there are conditions. The first of which is you need to agree to counseling."

"Counseling?" Lawrence furrowed his brow. "Like with a shrink?"

"Yes," Anthony concurred. "Precisely. I believe you have some emotional and anger issues that are going to prevent you from becoming the Dom I know you want to be. Issues that, if I may be so blunt, are keeping you from finding the love and connection I know you long for."

Lawrence's eyes skittered toward Mark and then away, and Mark understood Lawrence had confided in some way about his personal hopes and dreams, and perhaps his failures, to Anthony, just as Mark himself, and probably every man at The Enclave, had done at one time or another. Anthony was that kind of person—at once father-figure, mentor and best friend. You just felt safe baring your heart to him. Mark wondered if Lawrence regretted sharing those confidences—if he believed it now made him vulnerable. Mark realized his fury toward the man had subsided. He no longer wanted to beat him to a pulp. He understood Lawrence was weak and frightened, as bullies generally were when you scratched just beneath the surface of their swagger.

"I know an excellent therapist who works with people in the BDSM community," Anthony continued. "He has an intimate knowledge and understanding of the kind of issues we sometimes face in this lifestyle. It's not easy being a good Master, and we all work at it. You're having trouble balancing the power of your position with the grace and love that must accompany that power. I want to get you the help you need to start to deal with those issues from the inside out. Do you agree to some counseling sessions as a condition of remaining here?"

Lawrence swallowed hard, his jaw working. Finally he nodded. "Yes. If it means I can stay, yes, I agree."

"Good." Anthony said. "I'll call him first thing in the morning. In addition, I'm going to put you on probation until you demonstrate you've attained the understanding and internalized the philosophy of The Enclave to my satisfaction. You're obviously highly skilled in the mechanics of being a Dom—that was never at issue here. It's the spiritual aspect that we'll focus on during your probation."

"How long?" Lawrence whispered. "How long will I be on probation?"

"That's up to you, Lawrence," Anthony said, his voice now gentle. "I'll let you tell me." He stood, adding, "I need to talk to Danielle."

"Just what I was going to say," Mark concurred.

"Danielle?" Lawrence queried, clearly confused.

"She's the real culprit here. I'll bet my bottom dollar on it," Anthony replied. "I believe Jaime that she's innocent. She didn't leave the dungeon in that condition. I've thought it over and Danielle is the only one of our staff slaves capable of this sort of behavior. As much as I don't want to think it's true, there is no other conclusion I can draw."

"Danielle?" Lawrence repeated stupidly. A play of emotions moved over his face, and Mark saw he, too, was finally putting two and two together. Understanding dawned with a lift of the eyebrows, and then shame crumpled his face, his mouth falling open as Lawrence finally seemed to grasp the full extent of what he'd done. "Jesus," he whispered, "why would she do that?"

"I suspect it has to do with our rock star here." Anthony glanced toward Mark with a mirthless grin. "Danielle's been dealing with the age-old issues of attraction, loneliness and insecurity that afflict the young and stupid. Or no," he amended, "they afflict us all, young people just tend to do a much worse job of disguising it. Danielle's been lonely and scared since Alan abandoned her, and who can blame her? Now I wonder about the wisdom of letting her stay on once he'd left. I felt sorry for her, but I see now I made a mistake."

"You can't send her away!" Lawrence burst out.

Anthony raised his eyebrows with obvious surprise. "You're defending her actions?"

"No, I'm not defending what she did, if in fact we find out that's the case. Like you said, she's young and stupid. She's made some poor decisions, but I see something in her. You did, too, or you wouldn't have allowed her to stay on when Alan left. You're giving me another chance. Why not her?"

Anthony was quiet a moment as he regarded Lawrence. "As soon as we're done here, Marjorie and I are going to have a long talk with Danielle. I will take your suggestion into serious consideration, Lawrence. You're right. She's young and stupid, but she's been dealing with issues by herself that perhaps we should have been more sensitive to. I do believe in second chances." He stood, and Mark and Lawrence stood as well.

"If we decide it makes sense for her to stay," Anthony added, "she'll be on probation, same as you."

"Understood," Lawrence said, his anger and arrogance drained away. "Thank you, Anthony." He turned to Mark. "And thank you."

Mark, stunned, could only nod.

~*~

Jaime sipped the hot, fragrant tea and let the soothing sound of rushing water lull her senses. She was exhausted—the weariness permeating not only her body but her psyche. Mistress Marjorie sat on a nearby chair, Aubrey having excused herself once she finished ministering to Jaime's wounds. Her back barely hurt now, the welts cleaned, Mistress Aubrey's miracle salve smoothed over the broken skin. She'd been permitted to speak freely, to explain what had happened, and she had been listened to and, most importantly, believed.

Tentatively, she leaned back against the soft towel Marjorie had thoughtfully placed along the back of the deep, overstuffed sofa in the meditation room. It was her favorite room in the house, especially the slate and copper waterfall that covered an entire wall, with its soothing sheet of water cascading down in an infinite cycle.

When she'd been curled into herself in the small cage, left alone with her thoughts and her pain, she'd vowed she would not spend another night at The Enclave. When Master Lawrence let her out, and surely he had to eventually, she would pack her meager belongings and call a cab. Her time so far at The Enclave had shown her she required a life of sensual submission, but not at a place where she couldn't feel safe or heard.

Now she no longer knew what she thought or felt. Too much had happened, too fast. "You don't have to decide anything right now," Mistress Marjorie had counseled. "Just rest and recover. We still need to understand this whole situation. Master Anthony should be along directly."

As if summoned by her words, there was a light knock on the door. At Mistress Marjorie's, "Come in," it opened, revealing Master Anthony in the doorway. As he stepped inside, Jaime saw Danielle just behind him, a defiant, petulant expression on her face.

Master Anthony pointed to a floor cushion. "You will kneel there, slave Danielle. I want you to tell Mistress Marjorie and Jaime what you just told me." Jaime stiffened at the sight of her. She bit her lower lip to keep from saying something she might later regret.

Danielle moved toward the cushion and knelt as directed, while Master Anthony took a seat on the sofa near Jaime. He placed his hand lightly on Jaime's shoulder as he gazed into her eyes. His look and his touch eased some of the tension Danielle's presence had triggered, and she managed a small smile.

Master Anthony dropped his hand and turned his attention back to Danielle, who was staring at the ground. "Go on, Danielle. Tell us what you told me a moment ago."

Danielle lifted her head, the defiant look still on her face. "I told Jaime she was going to get in trouble if she did such a crummy job, but she said no one would notice. It's not the first time she's cut corners during chores. I haven't said anything because I don't like to tattle on others. It's not my fault she got punished. I don't know why everyone thinks this is somehow my fault." She lifted her chin, clearly waiting to be challenged.

Master Anthony stared at her until she lowered her eyes once more. Turning to Jaime, he said, "Stand up, Jaime, and turn around. Show Danielle your back."

Reluctantly, Jaime stood and walked to where Danielle was kneeling. She turned until her ravaged back was to Danielle. Danielle drew in a sudden, audible gasp. Master Anthony nodded toward Jaime. "You may sit down."

He returned his focus to the kneeling woman. "I wanted you to see that, Danielle. It's quite possible some of those wounds will scar. It's possible Jaime won't finish her training, as traumatizing as this experience has been for her. In addition, we are considering asking Master Lawrence to leave the community, as his methods don't coincide with how we do things at The Enclave."

Danielle brought her hands to her mouth, a look of fear mingled with horror on her face. "I didn't— I wasn't…" She trailed off, a beseeching look on her pretty face as she moved her gaze toward Mistress Marjorie.

Mistress Marjorie leaned forward. "We understand you're scared right now, Danielle. We need to hear from you directly, what part you actually played in this. This kind of thing goes beyond girlish jealousies and competition. People's lives have been negatively affected. There will be consequences, of course there will be, but they will be much worse if you can't find a way to tell the truth. We value what we have built here at The Enclave too much to let this go unaddressed. I know it's been hard since Alan left you, but that's no excuse for your behavior."

A sob welled up in Danielle's throat, a yelping keen, and she dropped her face in her hands. "I'm sorry, I'm sorry," she wailed. "I didn't mean for it to get so out of control." Between hiccupping sobs, she managed, "Everything was perfect till she showed up. I almost had him. He was going to make me his personal slave. I just know it. Now he can't stop mooning over *her* with those bedroom eyes, and it just made me so furious. It's not fair! I've worked so hard for this. I can't bear to be humiliated again."

"Master Mark?" Mistress Marjorie queried, echoing Jaime's unvoiced question. Danielle, still crying, nodded, her unexpected words whirling in Jaime's brain. Had Master Mark been mooning over her? Where had she been while this was going on? In spite of Danielle's damning admission, in spite of the girl's breakdown and Jaime's exhaustion, her words sent a thrill through Jaime's being.

Master Anthony reached for a tissue from the end table by the sofa and stood, moving toward the crying girl. He crouched beside her and handed her the tissue. As Danielle wiped her eyes, he said, "I do appreciate, very much, that you've admitted you were the one who set this terrible chain of events in motion. You'll feel better, too, once you calm down, to know your actions won't continue to taint an innocent person."

He stood and returned to the sofa. Once seated, he leaned toward Danielle, his hands on his knees. "Danielle, I don't think The Enclave is the place for you," he said earnestly. "I do believe you're sincere in your desire to submit, but I think your focus on finding a mate since Alan left has made you lose your way on your submissive journey."

"No, please," she begged, "don't make me go! I'll be good, I promise. I'll do anything. I'll stay in the shed out back, just please, please, don't send me away. I have no place to go." Her voice turned suddenly bitter. "Alan, that bastard, cleared out our account when he went back to his ex-wife. He left me penniless."

Master Anthony shook his head while Jaime processed this tidbit of information. "Staff slaves are here because of their love and commitment for the lifestyle, not because they need a roof over their head or a particular Master to own them. Do you see that, Danielle? Yes, there are couples here, but that isn't the purpose of this community, merely a happy byproduct. Alan came highly recommended by someone I know in the scene, but I didn't know him personally when I allowed the two of you to join. I won't make that mistake again. Nor will I compound it by keeping you here out of pity."

Danielle started to protest again but Master Anthony silenced her with a raise of his hand. "I have a place in Asheville where you can stay while you get on your feet. And in point of fact, you are not penniless. Staff slaves draw a significant monthly salary—we keep it in escrow for you. You'll have full access to your money. You're a licensed massage therapist, as I recall. Mistress Aubrey is well connected with physical therapy clinics in Asheville and I'm sure she can help you get a job, if you choose to remain in the area."

"No, no, no, no," Danielle moaned, dropping her forehead to the floor and throwing out her arms in subjugation. "Please, Sir, please

Master Anthony. I'm sorry. I'm so sorry." She lifted her head, turning her blotchy, tear streaked face toward Jaime. "Please, Jaime, forgive me. It was a horrible thing I did, and the hiking boots, too. I've never known how to get along with other girls. It's always been about getting the guy, no matter what, but I don't want to be like this anymore."

She turned next to Mistress Marjorie. "Please, Mistress, don't let him send me away. Give me a chance to make it up to everyone." She turned back to Master Anthony. "Even if you don't let me stay, please give Master Lawrence another chance. I don't want to mess up his life because I was an idiot. Please." Her voice trailed to a whisper, the tears rolling steadily down her cheeks. "Please."

Jaime stared at the girl, stunned at her admissions and apology. It occurred to her Danielle was, perhaps for the first time in her life, being utterly sincere. The room was silent for several long beats, save for the rushing sound of the waterfall. Finally Master Anthony broke the silence, startling Jaime by addressing, not Danielle, but her. "What do you think, slave Jaime? Does Danielle have what it takes to rebuild our shattered trust? Can you find it in your heart to forgive her? Do you think I should give her another chance?"

Danielle looked down, her shoulders sagging, and Jaime realized she thought she knew what Jaime's answer would be. And really, wouldn't it be best to send this girl packing, after all the damage she'd done? But Jaime knew what it was to be lonely and afraid; and she knew, too, what it was to make stupid, impetuous decisions that came back to bite you in the ass. She also recognized Danielle's genuinely submissive plea. She'd expressed her longing not only with her words, but through a visceral, physical response that couldn't be faked. While Jaime doubted she would ever come to like Danielle, her heart ached for the miserable, defeated girl kneeling there before them. In the end, she, too, believed in second chances.

"Yes," Jaime replied, half surprising herself. "I do."

CHAPTER 16

The next morning after breakfast Jaime was directed to present herself in Master Anthony's study. When she arrived, Master Lawrence was sitting on the sofa along with Master Anthony.

"Good morning, slave Jaime," Master Anthony said with a kind smile. "How are you this morning? How is your back?"

"Better, Sir, thank you," Jaime replied, her eyes darting toward Master Lawrence, who was looking down at the ground. She dropped into a kneeling-up position on a floor cushion in front of the men and waited.

"That's good to hear. I asked you here this morning because Master Lawrence needs to speak to you. He has something to say."

Jaime's stomach lurched unpleasantly. What now? Hadn't he done enough damage already? Her spine stiffened and she drew in a breath through her nostrils, willing herself to remain calm.

Master Lawrence looked up at her. To her astonishment, she saws tears in his pale blue eyes. "Slave Jaime," he said, his voice cracking a little. "I'm sorry."

The words hung in the air between them while Jaime's confused brain struggled to process their import. Master Lawrence, *sorry*? Had she somehow entered a parallel universe?

Turning to Master Lawrence, Master Anthony prodded gently, "Go on, Lawrence. Tell her what you told me."

Master Lawrence swallowed hard, his Adam's apple bobbing at his slender throat. A faint flush had moved over his face and neck, and Jaime sensed his discomfort. As he blew out a breath, she also sensed his resolve. He met her eyes squarely. "I ask your pardon, slave Jaime. I failed as a Master to you and to The Enclave when I refused to listen to you. I punished you in anger. I promise that will never happen again. Please accept my apology."

Jaime realized she was staring, her mouth fallen open in shocked surprise. As she'd lain awake the night before, she'd fantasized about just such an apology, savoring her imagined victory as Master Lawrence groveled in shame before her. But now, faced with the actual man, with the fallible, humbled man before her, all she felt was gratitude and relief.

"I accept your apology, Master Lawrence. Thank you."

Master Lawrence smiled. "Thank you, slave Jaime."

"And I thank you as well, Lawrence," Master Anthony added. "Humility is as important for Dominants as for submissives, if not more so. We must always remember that the exchange of power is a gift and should never be abused."

"Yes, Sir," Master Lawrence said quietly. "Thank you, Sir."

As Jaime's last few days of training progressed, Danielle was given the most menial of service tasks, including washing out dirty gutters on the outside of the house and scrubbing the floors on her hands and knees, using only a rag and bucket of soapy water for her task. Her free time was spent in a punishment corner holding a penny against the wall with her nose. Jaime found her crying in the laundry room one morning as she was ironing a huge stack of linen napkins. Jaime took no pleasure from the girl's obvious disgrace, but when she tried to offer comfort,

Danielle vehemently shook her head. Though her dismissive, snarky behavior had stopped, Danielle had resisted Jaime's few attempts at friendliness since her apology. "No. Please go away. I just need to be alone right now." With an inward shrug, Jaime had let her be.

Master Lawrence, too, remained on probation. He still attended training sessions, though Jaime hadn't worked directly with him since the cage incident. From what she could observe, and from what Katie shared, he was working hard at his rehabilitation and seemed genuine in his desire to be a better Master. That, as much as anything, swayed Jaime in a positive direction as she mulled over what her answer would be, given the opportunity to remain at The Enclave as a full-time staff slave.

Her final Friday afternoon found her sitting in a meditative trance as she stared at the golden coins of sunlight dancing on the rippling lake water. Her back had healed surprisingly well in the four days since the punishment caning, and Mistress Aubrey had reassured her there would be no scarring. Her training had progressed well, the slave positions nearly automatic now, her ability to withstand and even embrace erotic torture with grace definitely improved. She still had trouble with controlling her orgasms, both the withholding and the coming on command, but she understood the process better now and knew with time and practice she would get there.

"Hey there."

Jaime's heart gave a pleasant jolt at the sound of Master Mark's voice.

Turning from the rippling, sun-dappled water, she smiled up at the handsome man.

"Hello, Master Mark."

"I was looking for you," he said, taking a seat beside her on the bench. "I wanted to let you know I have to leave The Enclave for a few days. My little brother's getting married. He roped me into being his best man."

Master Mark didn't seem especially happy at the prospect. Not sure what to say, Jaime offered, "Congratulations. I mean, it's a good thing, right?"

"Oh, yeah. Sure, yes, it's good, but the timing is lousy, with your final assessment coming up tonight. The actual wedding is tomorrow but the rehearsal dinner is this evening. I kind of have to be there."

"Of course, Sir. I understand." Though Jaime didn't want him to leave, it warmed her that he had sought her out to tell her.

"I didn't want to leave without seeing you once more. I needed to talk to you."

Jaime held her breath.

Master Mark stared into her eyes for several long moments, as if trying to decide where to begin. In the sunlight, she noticed there were tiny dots of blue deep within the green of his eyes, with brown underneath, as if his eyes were soil and grass and sky.

He looked reached for her hand, which rested on the bench between them. Turning it over, he ran his thumb over the fleshy part of her palm. His touch sent a warm, buttery shudder through her body, all her nerve endings zinging.

All at once, he let go of her and turned to face the water. "I'm sorry." He ran a hand over his face. "I shouldn't be doing that. It's not fair to you. We aren't on an equal footing right now, with me still your trainer and all."

"Permission to speak, Sir?"

He glanced back at her, as if startled by the question. "What? Oh, yes, of course. Please."

"What's going on, Sir?" Jaime asked quietly, watching him. His touch had been that of a lover, not a trainer. "You said you wanted to talk to me."

"Yeah. I do. I guess I'm just not sure how to begin."

"At the beginning?" Jaime teased with a smile, and Master Mark laughed, a hearty, satisfying sound that made Jaime laugh too.

"You're something special, slave Jaime," he said, sobering, and Jaime's heart twisted with longing. "The thing is, I won't be here this evening for your final assessment. There are some things I wanted you to know in the event you are asked to stay." He paused, gathering his thoughts. "I don't need to tell you how intense a trainee's experience is, without throwing someone else's emotions into the mix. I've worked with two other trainees since I've been here. They were both good, worthy subs, it just wasn't the right fit for The Enclave. In those instances, I didn't have any trouble keeping my emotions—my heart—out of the equation. But with you—" He took her hand in his once more and squeezed it. "With you, it's been different. I think you know that. I've been doing my damnedest to keep my feelings, or at least the actions resulting from those feelings in check, but I couldn't leave without telling you, without acknowledging there's something between us, even if we can't act on it right now."

"Oh, Sir," she breathed, unable to look away from his serious, sweet gaze. She felt as if her body had been pumped full of helium, as if she might float right up into the sky if he let go of her hand.

He smiled again, a little ruefully, it seemed to Jaime. "The thing is, this isn't fair to you."

"What?" Jaime blurted, not understanding. "What isn't fair?"

"Me laying it out there like this. It's a timing issue, I guess. I don't want any feelings there might be between us to cloud your decision. If they offer you the opportunity to stay, you need your mind free and clear of clutter. What I'm trying to say is, it shouldn't be predicated on anything that might or might not develop between you and me. If we decided to move forward, to get to know each other on a personal level, that shouldn't be a factor that affects your decision to join The Enclave or not."

Jaime nodded, getting it now, though it was hard to focus, the excited little girl inside her shouting, *He likes me! Oh my god, he likes me!* "What you're saying makes sense," she said in her best imitation of a mature adult. He was still holding her hand, and he leaned toward her, their faces now nearly close enough for a kiss. She closed her eyes, her lips tingling—

A sudden burst of electronic bells startled her. Her eyes flew open and they both pulled back, Master Mark dropping her hand. He snorted and shook his head. Reaching into his pants pocket, he pulled out his cell phone. "My alarm," he said with a grin. "It's telling me not to do anything stupid." He touched the screen and the sound stopped. "Seriously, though, I better get a move on. If I'm late for this dinner thing, there'll be hell to pay."

Standing, he placed his hand lightly on the top of her head. "See you soon, slave Jaime?" It came out as a question.

She nodded. "Yes, please, Sir," she said softly.

His answering smile lit her from within.

Once dinner was over, the subs stood at attention behind their chairs while the Dominants filed from the room. Tonight before the evening play session, the focus would be on Jaime. Earlier, Master Anthony had instructed her to wait on a floor cushion in the living room after dinner until the dominant members of the community had assembled to conduct her final assessment. Gene, who was standing to Jaime's right at the table, gave her shoulder an affectionate squeeze once the staff slaves were alone in the room. "Good luck, Jaime," he said. "I hope they ask you to stay."

"Me, too," Katie piped up from across the table. "I feel like you've always been here."

"You're a *braves mädchen*—a good girl," added Hans.

Lucia and Ashley had already disappeared into the kitchen, which left only Danielle. To Jaime's surprise, Danielle said in a small voice, "I hope you stay, Jaime. You're a true submissive."

Warmed and encouraged by their words, Jaime took a deep breath and smiled. "Thank you."

Heart kicking up a notch, she entered the living room and moved to a large silk throw pillow in front of the couch where she'd had her first inspection upon arrival at The Enclave. Katie was right—in a way it was as if she'd always been here. Yet it had only been two weeks, barely a drop in the bucket of her twenty-seven years on the planet. Was that really enough time to make such a momentous decision as would be asked of her tonight?

Yet, if she were honest, hadn't she made the decision already? Hadn't she known the answer the moment Master Anthony had posed the question—the tightly furled bud of submissive longing in her heart opening like a rose in a time-lapse video at his first offer that night at the Garden?

Jaime couldn't stop thinking about Master Mark and his revelations by the lake. In her excitement and delight to know her feelings for him were returned, she hadn't really had a chance to tease out how much of a decision to stay at The Enclave was based on those feelings, and how much on a heartfelt, pure desire to serve and submit. He'd said her decision shouldn't be based on anything that might or might not develop between them, but what did that mean exactly? She wished they'd had more time, say an hour or a week or maybe a few years, to figure this all out.

Hearing the sound of approaching footsteps, she knelt quickly on the floor pillow, assuming the at-ease position, hands resting lightly on her thighs, eyes downcast, heart pumping at an accelerated pace as the Masters and Mistresses settled on the couch and chairs in front and on either side of her.

"Slave Jaime," Master Anthony said, and Jaime lifted her eyes to meet his. "I know you've been waiting all day for our decision, and I don't want to make you wait any longer. You have behaved in an exemplary fashion during your training period. You've learned and grown as a submissive and, while there is always more to learn and strive for, we believe you are well on your way to achieving true submissive grace. As such, our decision is unanimous—we would like to invite you to join The Enclave as a full-time staff slave."

Jaime looked at each member, feeling Master Mark's absence keenly, despite her rising euphoria. All of them seated there, Master Anthony, Master Brandon, Mistress Marjorie, Master Mason, Mistress Aubrey and even Master Lawrence, were smiling encouragingly at her. "Oh gosh!" she exclaimed, her hands coming together over her heart. "Thank you all so much. Oh, wow! I was hoping this would happen, but I wasn't absolutely sure. I mean, you know—"

She clapped her hand over her mouth, furious with herself for gushing, heat washing over her cheeks and throat. Damn it, she'd practiced a somber, sophisticated response in her head all through dinner—not a school-girly gush of *oh goshes* and *wows*, for heaven's sake.

They were all still smiling, some of them now absolutely grinning, but Jaime remained mortified. She looked down as she tried to compose and organize the rush of her thoughts. Fortunately, Master Anthony continued as if she hadn't just made an ass of herself. "We're very glad this has been a good experience for you, Jaime. We know it hasn't always been easy, and it hasn't always been fair to you, but hopefully you've come to see during the process that we're all human here. No one is infallible, but we can all learn from our mistakes." He shifted his gaze from Jaime to Master Lawrence, who nodded soberly.

Master Anthony turned his gaze back to Jaime. "We would love to have you join our community, but we recognize we're asking for a major commitment, and it's not one you want to make lightly. After only two short weeks, we're asking you to give up the life you had before—your apartment, your friends, the right to come and go at will, the freedom to live your life purely on your terms. As a staff slave, while you can get permission to leave The Enclave for family visits and things of that sort, you are basically entering a consensual agreement of sexual and service enslavement. You will no longer have access to your own finances, though money will be set aside for you every month and will be available to you if and when you need it. You will no longer be permitted to make decisions about your body, your daily life or your submissive and masochistic choices. We, as your Masters and Mistresses, will decide for you. There are no hard limits here, no safewords. Once you sign on as a staff slave, you abdicate all rights. The only choice left to you will be the choice to leave, should you decide you are unhappy here. In that case, your connection with The Enclave would cease, and you would not be allowed to return."

He paused a moment, scrutinizing Jaime's face as he allowed her to absorb his words. "With that in mind," he finally went on, "we want you to take a few days to think this over, removed from the intensity of life here at The Enclave. Take your time. Even if you think you know the answer, let it germinate and rest inside you. It's also a good time to think about what steps you'll want to take to get your previous life in order, if you make the decision to join us. We'll help with the details of closing up your apartment, paying off your car, things of that nature. We have a storage facility here on the property where you can keep your belongings, if you wish. Tomorrow morning Hans will drive you back down the mountain, and I'll give you a call on Monday morning to get your answer. Does that suit you, slave Jaime?"

She smiled inwardly, aware that, as usual, Master Anthony was at least one step ahead of her. He was right, of course. Despite her initial impulse to shout, "Yes! I'm in, I'm in!" it was better to take a little time, a few days, to sort things out. She needed to let the excitement settle, to make a decision with a clear mind, and without distraction.

Lifting her chin, Jaime fixed her gaze resolutely on Master Anthony. "Yes, Sir," she replied. "That suits me just right."

~*~

Mark drummed his fingers on the steering wheel in time to the music as he made the drive back from Charlotte that Sunday morning. The wedding had gone smoothly, and his brother and new wife were on their way to Hawaii for their honeymoon—Mark's wedding gift to the two of them. He'd left Charlotte as soon after the Sunday breakfast as he could, eager to get back to The Enclave.

His thoughts had veered constantly to slave Jaime over the course of the weekend. Had he done the right thing in telling her his feelings? Should he have left those things unsaid? Had he, rather than making matters clearer for them both, just confused the issue? He'd wanted her to understand her decision to join The Enclave shouldn't be predicated on whatever might be developing between them, but had he just muddied the waters for her? Should he have kept his mouth shut?

Used to making decisions and then moving forward without too much agonizing, Mark became annoyed with himself. This new uncertainty was not to his liking. What was his problem, anyway?

"The problem is you care about her," he said aloud as he drove. "She's either going to sign up as a staff slave at The Enclave, or she isn't. She knows how you feel, and hopefully she gets it that you'll continue to feel that way, whether or not she joins the community. You should let her be while she makes that decision."

Newly resolved, he reached for the tuner knob and changed the station. A Planck Time song was playing, one of their top hits, and Mark decided this was a good omen. Turning up the sound, he sang along with himself as he headed west on the highway.

He had intended to take the exit toward the mountains, but found himself continuing on to Asheville, a part of his brain apparently making decisions for him without his express knowledge or permission. He told himself he might stop at the new BDSM gear store he'd heard about, but even as the thought flitted through his mind, he knew he was lying.

Anthony had told him in advance of their intention to offer Jaime a position as staff slave. He'd further shared his intention of having Jaime leave The Enclave for the weekend while she considered her response, which Mark thought was very sensible. He had also appreciated this time away to think about his own future without the intensity of life at The Enclave coloring his decision.

He'd read Jaime's slave file, which included her address in Asheville. He had her cell number too and could have called, but decided against it. Instead, he headed toward Pasqual's Bakery, a little spot Mason had told him about, which made the best buttery, melt-in-your mouth croissants he'd ever had in his life. He realized as he pulled into the small parking lot that he was hungry, having had only a cup of coffee, several glasses of juice and a few pieces of bacon at the breakfast, a little hung over from too much champagne the night before.

Cutting the ignition, he climbed out of the car, a man on a mission. The smell of freshly baked bread and melted chocolate assailed his senses as he entered the place. Pasqual, a small, rotund man with rosy cheeks, stood behind the counter busily placing rolls and croissants in a large cardboard box for the customer in front of Mark. When it was his turn, he chose three plain croissants, three chocolate and three with raspberry cream.

Bakery box in hand, Mark returned to his car. It wasn't too late to change his mind. He could do the mature thing and bring the croissants back to The Enclave, giving Jaime the space she needed to make up her mind without distraction.

"Oh, what the hell," he said to his image in the rearview mirror. "Maturity is overrated."

~*~

Two weeks really wasn't that long in the scheme of things, but when you unplugged yourself from social media during that time, it could seem like a lifetime. Jaime found ninety-seven unread emails and a billion notifications on her Facebook when she booted up her laptop for the first time in two weeks. Most of it, she was happy to realize, was junk, spam or the unimportant chatter of a generation that grew up posting its trivia online as if that somehow lent it importance.

She toyed with the idea of calling Amy, the closest thing she had to a friend in Asheville, to discuss what might be the biggest decision of her life, but couldn't think how she would broach the conversation with someone who had no clue about the lifestyle. She thought about trying to contact some of her play partners from the Garden, but knew she would not.

It made her realize how far she'd come since training at The Enclave. She was no longer a club sub, using the people and gear to get her kinky thrills, and basically topping from the bottom in the process. There was nothing wrong with being a player in that kind of scene, but she no longer felt at home there. It was like splashing in a blowup baby pool in the backyard, when you'd become used to swimming in the ocean.

How odd it had been to put on her clothing for the trip back to Asheville Saturday morning. How quickly she'd come to appreciate the freedom and grace of being nude, the only adornment her leather slave collar. Once she'd worked through the initial shyness, she found being naked while her Masters and Mistresses were clothed kept her centered—a constant and sensual reminder of her status as a submissive.

The minute she returned to her apartment she'd shucked the now-unwelcome garments. Master Anthony had allowed her to keep her slave collar, which was still around her neck. It was a warm, comforting reminder of the place she had begun to miss the moment Hans had driven out of the large gates that marked the property entrance.

As she'd lain down to sleep the night before, she'd had to stop herself from reaching for the cuffs and chain she had become used to placing on her wrists each night of her stay at The Enclave. When she had woken earlier that morning she'd known before even coming fully conscious that she wasn't where she was supposed to be.

The sun was moving across the sky and yet she'd done nothing but daydream since she'd awoken several hours before. She wanted to get up and moving, but couldn't quite summon the will. Instead she remained sitting on the edge of her unmade bed, staring out the window at the parking lot and convenience store across the street. She touched her lips, recalling their almost-kiss. She closed her eyes, summoning the vision of the lake, lit gold by the setting sun, the feel of his hand, strong and sure around hers, the tremble inside her body as her eyes fluttered shut—until that stupid cell alarm interrupted everything.

Somehow, impossibly, the alarm was chiming once more, the sound popping her daydream like a bubble. It took another fraction of a second to process that it was in fact her doorbell that was ringing. Who the heck could that be?

Jumping up, she grabbed a sundress from a hook in her closet and slipped it over her head as she hurried to the front door. She looked through the peephole, expecting perhaps a deliveryman at the wrong door or a neighbor who'd locked themselves out.

Jaime drew in a sharp breath when she saw him standing there, a white box tied with red string in his hands, a smile on his handsome face. Fumbling briefly with the lock, Jaime pulled the door open wide. "Master Mark!" she cried, "I thought you were in Charlotte. What're you doing here?" Afraid she had sounded rude, she stepped back, gesturing him inside. "Please, come in."

"Hi, Jaime." Master Mark entered her small living room, giving it a quick glance. "I hope it's okay I stopped by. I was in the neighborhood…" He trailed off, grinning. "These are for you." He held out the box. "In case you were hungry."

Master Mark's apparent discomfort startled her. The masterful, fully-in-control Dom at The Enclave was out of his ken, on her turf, not certain of his welcome.

She accepted the proffered box with a warm smile. "Thank you, Sir." The bottom of the bakery box was still warm and she lowered her head to inhale the aroma. "Hmmm, whatever's in here smells yummy," she said as she looked up at him. He still seemed a little nervous, his hands shoved in the back pockets of his jeans, his teeth gripping his full lower lip. "Would you like some coffee?"

"Yeah, coffee would be good, thanks," he replied quickly, grabbing onto her suggestion as if it were a lifeline. "Those are from Pasqual's. The best."

He followed her into the kitchen. Jaime set the box down on the counter and untied the bow of red string. She opened the box and saw the pile of flaky, fragrant croissants inside. "Oh, yum," she enthused. "I smell chocolate."

"You look different," Master Mark said from behind her.

Jaime turned toward him with a laugh. "Not used to seeing me with my clothes on, Sir?" she teased.

"Yeah," he said, a small smile lifting the corners of his mouth. "That must be it." He moved closer, so close they were almost touching. Instinctively, she stepped back, bumping against the kitchen counter. He reached for the straps of her sundress, drawing them down her arms. "I think you should take this off," he murmured as he guided her arms out of the straps. The dress puddled to the floor at her feet.

He gripped her shoulders. "I've been wanting to do this forever. Since that first day when I saw you kneeling at the door." He lowered his face and this time no cell phone alarm chimed, no doorbell rang. Jaime had stopped breathing, and when his lips touched hers, she moaned against his mouth, the sound primal and yearning.

As they kissed, he wrapped his arms around her, pinning her between his body and the counter so that her feet barely touched the floor. She lifted her legs and brought them around his hips, crossing her ankles at his lower back. Cupping her ass with both hands, he lifted her into his arms. Turning, he carried her out of the kitchen and through the living room into the single bedroom, kissing her as they moved.

He dropped her onto the bed and stood before her, his earth-and-sky eyes never leaving her body as he unbuttoned his shirt, kicked off his shoes and yanked down his jeans and underwear. Jaime stared back hungrily, actually salivating as she drank in the lean, muscular lines of his body. His cock was thick and long, fully erect, a pearl of pre-come beckoning at its tip.

He made a sound, something like a growl, as he fell onto her, his mouth finding hers once more as he pinned her to the bed beneath him. His cock was rock-hard against her thigh. Her legs fell open in wanton invitation.

"Please," she begged.

His mouth covering hers, he pushed into her sopping wet cunt, his hard cock sending shooting spirals of nearly unbearable pleasure that radiated from her core and spread throughout her being. She groaned, arching up to take him deeper, to pull him into her until they became one being.

He held her tight as he swiveled and thrust, his pelvic bone grinding just so against her engorged clit. It seemed like only seconds before she was ready to come. They were in her apartment, far from The Enclave, but she was still slave Jaime and he very much her Master Mark. "Please, Sir," she panted, "may I come?"

"Yes. Come for me."

She let the wave crash over and through her, dragging her along in its relentless wake. Master Mark held onto her throughout, keeping her grounded and safe as she keened her pleasure.

When she was able to catch her breath, Master Mark, who still hadn't come, raised his body a little, letting the cool air in the room move between their sweaty torsos. Slowly, languorously, he reached for her wrists, bringing them together in one hand. He pressed them into the mattress over her head and brought his other hand to her throat.

He framed her jawline with his forefinger and thumb, pressing until her breath caught in her throat, and then pressing harder still. She felt her face reddening, the pressure building behind her eyes and nose. She was frozen in his grip, utterly at his mercy, his hard cock still pulsing deep inside her. She stared into his eyes, her entire body trembling with primal, delicious, erotic anticipation, her being suffused with a wrenching desire like none she had ever known.

When he finally released his chokehold on her throat, she drew in a deep, shuddering breath, letting it out in a sigh. Her wrists still caught in his powerful grip, his eyes still fixed on hers, he began to move again inside her. Her cunt spasmed and clung to him as he pulled nearly out and then plunged deep into her.

He held himself just over her, their bodies touching only at the groin. His body was sheened with sweat, his breath rasping in his throat as his hips moved in perfect rhythm. Arching suddenly, he let his head fall back. She focused on his neck, on the vein pulsing at its side, and the masculine curve of his jaw. He climaxed with a cry, his hand still tight on her wrists, and then collapsed against her, his hand falling away. She could feel the rapid thump of his heart, beating like a drum against her chest.

They lay that way a long time. Jaime floated in a kind of fugue state, only returning to full consciousness when Master Mark carefully disengaged himself from their tangle of limbs and flopped onto the bed beside her. Turning toward him, Jaime lifted herself on one elbow.

Master Mark regarded her with a sleepy, satisfied grin. "I think you killed me," he announced.

"Then I hope there's an afterlife," she teased back.

He sat up with a laugh. "And I hope there are croissants from Pasqual's when we get there. Say, is that offer of coffee still on the table?"

"Yes, Master Mark, Sir," Jaime replied, suddenly ravenous. "It most certainly is."

CHAPTER 17

They sat on the narrow balcony of Jaime's third floor apartment perched on folding chairs, a plate of warmed croissants and two mugs of coffee on the small, round, wrought iron patio table between them.

It was one of those perfect, crisp late summer days that hinted at the autumn to come, with a cool breeze wafting lazily toward them from the mountains, the sun gently beaming on them from a china blue sky. The coffee was hot and strong, the croissants flaky, buttery and as delicious as he remembered them.

Their impromptu lovemaking had been every bit as amazing, if not more so, than his many fantasies over the past two weeks. During the drive from Charlotte he'd thought about a slow, sensual seduction involving rope, a satin blindfold and candlelight, but he'd known the moment she'd opened her apartment door he couldn't wait another second.

Even now he wanted to reach across the little table and rip the flimsy material of her dress from her lovely body so he could take her there and then. His cock perked eagerly at the thought. To distract himself, he selected a chocolate croissant from the plate and held it out to Jaime, who so far had only sipped at her coffee, not touching the food.

Jaime took the pastry with a smile of thanks. When she bit into it, her eyes fluttered shut in ecstasy and she gave a small groan of rapturous appreciation.

Mark grinned with pleasure. "Good, huh?"

Her eyes opened and she smiled. She licked a tiny dab of chocolate from her lip, the gesture almost painfully erotic. "Oh, yes, Sir," she breathed, and with that one word—Sir—the mood shifted from friends or even lovers to something deeper, something better.

Slipping easily, effortlessly, into dominant headspace, Mark said quietly, "Tell me, slave Jaime, how long have you been aware you were a sub?"

Jaime set down what remained of her uneaten croissant, a lovely sort of serenity washing over her features as she replied, "Ever since I can remember, Sir."

"What's your earliest submissive memory?"

Jaime tilted her head back as she contemplated the question, her gaze turning inward. "I was probably six or seven. It was one day at recess. I hadn't managed to make it to the swings in time to get one, so I was standing around waiting for a turn when I noticed a group of older boys nearby. They were playing pirates, brandishing sticks and swaggering around. One of them noticed me watching and yelled 'Capture the wench! We'll make her serve us on the ship!' They all started running toward me and instinctively I ran in the other direction."

Jaime shook her head, a look of wonder moving over her face. "I will never forget that first powerful rush, the intense thrill when one of them caught me in a bear hug from behind, pinning my arms to my sides. It felt so good, so *right*, to be held that way, caught in his grip, under his control." She met Mark's eye, her expression at once yearning and shy.

Responding to her unspoken question, Mark replied, "I understand, slave Jaime. You needed, even then, what the boy was offering, even if for him it was no more than a game. You need to be possessed, controlled, owned."

Something in her face softened, a shine entering her eyes. They were an unusual shade of blue gray, the hue different depending on the light. Now the irises were like luminous gray silk rimming her pupils, the sunlight sparking them almost to silver. "Yes, Sir," she whispered. "Yes, Master Mark."

Mark reached across the small table for her hand. "I want to be that Master for you, Jaime, and more." He turned over her hand and brought it to his lips, lightly kissing her palm. A tremor moved through her frame, and his cock rose hard in his jeans. Forcing himself to focus, he continued, "Whatever's happening between us right now isn't about The Enclave. Yes, that's where we made this connection, but the decision you face this weekend shouldn't be impacted by you and me."

"It shouldn't?" Jaime looked confused.

"No," Mark replied, taking a moment to formulate his thoughts so he could get his point across. "What's happening between us is independent of whether or not you return to The Enclave."

"What do you mean?"

"I'm not sure what all you know about my situation at The Enclave. I've been there living and working as a Master, but until now I haven't signed on for full-fledged membership. Anthony has been encouraging me, and the time away this weekend has really helped me solidify my decision. I'm ready to make that commitment, but that doesn't change what's been happening between us.

"What I'm saying is, I'm planning on living at The Enclave and serving there as a full-time Master, but I'd still have plenty of time to myself—time to spend with you here in Asheville, even if you decide becoming a part of The Enclave community isn't right for you. We can still have a relationship, however that relationship evolves between us."

"And if I do decide to join the community?"

"If you accept Master Anthony's offer, you would belong to the community, and be expected and required to serve there, much as you have been during the candidacy training. But I would want to claim you for my own, as well, if that's something we both agree we want."

"Oh, Sir," Jaime breathed. "Yes. Please."

Mark's heart warmed, happiness suffusing him. At the same time, he recognized they were moving fast, maybe too fast, their emotions perhaps getting the better of them. "Don't decide yet," he cautioned. "Let's take the time Anthony has given us. When he calls on Monday, that's when you'll know for sure. That's when you can tell him, and me, of your decision."

Jaime was quiet a long while. Finally she nodded, turning a smile on him that was like a burst of pure sunshine. "Yes, Sir. Thank you, Sir."

Mark stood and held out his hand. Jaime accepted it, allowing him to pull her upright. "Now," he said, his balls tightening with anticipation, "about that continued exploration…" Reaching for Jaime, he scooped her into his arms and carried her through the open slider back into the apartment, heading directly for her bedroom.

~*~

The second time they made love was even better than the first. Their bodies fit perfectly together, the eager desperation of their first time segueing into a slower, more fully realized sensual dance. At one point he rolled from her, pulling her along as he moved and positioning her so she was on top. Even astride him, ostensibly the one in control, Master Mark subtly shifted the balance of power back his way by reaching for her nipples, capturing and twisting them as he ordered her to ride his cock to orgasm. She was more than happy to comply.

Afterward they dozed together in a pleasurable fog of post-orgasmic bliss, entangled in one another's arms. When Mark's breathing became deep and even, Jaime pulled carefully away. As her mind began to boot up, the huge decision that loomed before her came once more to the fore. She had thought she was certain of her decision to remain as a staff slave the moment Master Anthony had made the offer, but she recognized at least part, perhaps the most significant part, of her decision was colored by her feelings for Mark. Now that she understood they could be together whether or not she signed on at The Enclave, she had to rethink her decision, probing and analyzing it to make sure her motivations and desire to be a full-time staff slave were pure.

Lifting up on her elbow, she regarded the sleeping man beside her, her eyes moving lovingly over the muscular curves of his body. On an impulse, she leaned over and ran her tongue lightly over the rope tattoo that circled his left bicep. He didn't stir. She moved her hand softly over his chest, following the pattern of curling chest hair along his sternum and down his flat belly, veering away from his lovely, resting cock to the tattooed whip that graced his hip.

"Hmmm," Mark said sleepily, his thick fringe of lashes fluttering as his eyes opened and focused on her.

"When did you get this?" Jaime asked as she stroked the black ink image.

Mark reached for her. She rested her head on his chest, snuggling against him as he pulled her close. "I got the whip back in my early twenties when I was still relatively new to the scene. My Mistress wanted me to get it. It was her farewell gift to me."

Jaime was silent a beat as her brain tried to compute the words she must have misheard. She lifted her head to see Mark's face. "Wait, what?"

Mark chuckled and nodded. "Yeah. You heard me right. When I first was exploring BDSM, I tried it both ways. I wanted to understand the experience from all angles. I met this older woman at a BDSM underground club in Charlotte and she invited me to spend a weekend with her in her dungeon. She believed in total immersion, and she kept me naked and chained the entire time. She was heavily sadistic and had lots of whips and canes, every single one of which she used on me during that long, amazing weekend. She controlled my every move and action, from when I ate, when I used the bathroom, when I could ejaculate—everything."

"Wow," Jaime blurted, trying to imagine Master Mark in such a position, and failing. "How did you handle all that?"

"The same as you handled Sadie Hawkins Day at The Enclave, I suppose," he said with an amused smile. "Remember, I wasn't there against my will. I wanted to experience the passion of D/s from the other side. I'm not sorry I did it. Not for one second. The experience was very intense and very involving. I feel like it's given me a better understanding of the true courage and enormous trust it takes to submit fully to another. It also firmly solidified for me what my own needs and desires are. I understood by the end of the weekend that my orientation lay squarely on the other side of the spectrum. I need to be the one in control, the giver of erotic pleasure and pain, the Master of the situation."

Jaime was quiet as she absorbed this fascinating aspect of Mark's story. It made her love him just a little more, if that was possible. "What about a tat relating to your career as a musician? Do you have some hiding somewhere I haven't seen?" Raising her eyebrows, she flashed a grin.

Master Mark shook his head. "You know, I've been asked that before. My band mates had plenty of them, enough for all of us, I guess." He rubbed his chin, as if still pondering the question. "I guess we get tattoos, which are permanent, to honor the things that mean the most to us." He met her gaze. "As weird as it is to say, while I love music and writing songs, the whole band and touring thing—it was never really right for me. It was a constant struggle, if you want to know the truth. Even if Jake hadn't"—Mark paused, a spasm of pain moving over his features—"if he hadn't died, we still would have broken up the band. It was time. I was done."

"Maybe you could keep the part of it you love," Jaime suggested gently. "You can still sing and write songs, even if you don't go touring, right?"

"Yes." Master Mark smiled. "You're right, Jaime. I can keep the part I love. Thank you for reminding me."

They were both quiet for a time. Eventually, Jaime began to trace the tattoo on Master Mark's arm. "What about this one? Did another Mistress order you to get it?" she teased.

Master Mark grinned and shook his head. "I just got that this past year when I was attending a Shibari workshop in Houston. I'm fascinated with the power of erotic bondage, especially as practiced by the Shibari Masters. It goes beyond the physical act of restraint, and even beyond the visual beauty of the precise placement of rope, body and limbs. I love the emphasis on sensuality and vulnerability, and also of strength. I got the sense when we introduced you to Shibari that you share my sensibility on this."

"Yes," Jaime breathed, her skin suddenly tingling with longing for the rope. "Though I'm new to it, that session with you and Master Anthony was one of the most intense bondage experiences of my life. It's like the rope became an extension of your hands. It was so—so intimate."

"Yes, exactly," Mark agreed, holding her tighter. "I love your description of the rope as an extension of my hands on your body. That's exactly how I visualize it."

She twisted toward him so their pelvises were touching, her breasts smashed pleasantly against his muscular chest. In spite of the fact they'd made love twice in as many hours, she felt the swell of his cock between them and her cunt moistened in instant response. "I never travel without my rope," Master Mark murmured in her ear. "I left my duffel just inside your front door. I want you to get it and come back as fast as you can. I think a Shibari session is in order, slave Jaime."

"Yes, Sir!" Jaime didn't try to hide her broad, happy grin as she scampered from the room.

~*~

Though the weekend alone had been wonderful and affirming, Mark was excited to begin their new life together, no matter what Jaime's decision might be. As he reentered her apartment that Monday morning, a bag of warm croissants and some fresh raspberries in tow, he heard Jaime's cell phone chime from the bedroom. "Hello?" came her sleepy reply and then, considerably more alert, "Oh! Hello, Sir. Good morning, Master Anthony."

Mark moved closer in the silence that followed as Jaime listened to whatever Master Anthony was saying on the other end. "Yes, Sir," Jaime said, a quiet determination entering her tone. "I have made my decision."

Though he'd meant it when he'd said he would find a way to fit her into his life, whether or not she joined The Enclave on a full-time basis, in his heart of hearts he wanted her there 24/7. He wanted to share her grace and submissive charms with the people he'd come to regard as his family. And at the same time he wanted to possess her fully, to keep her in his bed at night, and by his side or on her knees in front of him when she wasn't serving the needs and pleasures of the household. The days away from The Enclave, both at his brother's wedding and over the past two days with Jaime, had solidified for Mark his desire and intention to make a full-time commitment himself to The Enclave. As a fellow musician had once said to him when marrying his true love after two decades on the road, Mark was ready to unpack his suitcase and put his shoes under the bed. In a word, he'd found his home. Now, with all his heart, he fervently hoped Jaime had come to the same conclusion.

Mark stood stock-still, forgetting to breathe as he waited to hear what she would say.

"I want to return to The Enclave, Master Anthony," Jaime said, her voice clear and sure. "I want to serve."

CHAPTER 18

Strings of tiny lights twinkled in the leafy branches overhead, the sky velvety black above the canopy of the trees. The effect was magical, like a scene from one of Jaime's favorite childhood stories about a secret fairy garden where a lonely little girl was transformed into a princess. White wooden folding chairs had been arranged in a semicircle in front of an arch cobbled together with wooden beams. The arch resembled a wedding canopy, except instead of white gauzy curtains and garlands of flowers, it was hung with rope, leather restraints and whips. A folding table had been set up to the side of the arch, piled with gear Jaime knew would come into play later in the evening. A large plastic bowl had been placed underneath the table.

Throw rugs had been scattered on the ground over the area to accommodate bare feet and knees. The staff slaves knelt on the rugs, three on either side of the arch, their backs tall and proud, their hands resting lightly, palms up, on their thighs. They were all looking at her and smiling encouragingly, even Danielle. Jaime would have smiled back, but her lip muscles weren't cooperating at the moment, and it was all she could do to remind herself to breathe.

Lucia and Katie had helped Jaime with her hair and makeup earlier that afternoon, Lucia creating a beautiful, elegant updo to rival actresses on the red carpet, Katie applying Jaime's makeup in a way that left her looking dewy fresh and natural, only better. Master Anthony had reviewed the basics of the ceremony with her beforehand, including her expected behavior and responses, which were simple enough, as long as she kept her mind clear and focused. Mistress Marjorie had led her through a meditation just after dinner to help her focus and relax.

Before she took her place with the other slaves, Jaime would have to walk the gauntlet between the Dominants, who stood before her in two lines, four on each side. Master Anthony and Master Mark were at the head of the line. Master Anthony gave her a solemn nod, his dark eyes fixed on hers, his lips lifted in a hint of a smile. Master Mark's smile was broad, his eyes fiery with pride and love. She could feel his positive, encouraging energy moving through her, easing away at least some of her jitters. She smiled back, took a deep breath and stepped forward.

Master Brandon and Mistress Marjorie were first in line, standing across from each other. They both held single tail whips, which they raised as Jaime approached. Master Brandon spoke first. "Will you take my mark, slave Jaime, as a symbol of your submission and service to The Enclave?"

"Yes, Master Brandon," Jaime said, her voice quavering a little as she faced him.

"Offer your right breast to me," he commanded.

Jaime placed her hand beneath her right breast and lifted it, trying to hold onto the sense of grounding Master Mark had given her a moment before. The single tail landed with a crack against the top of her breast, leaving a line of white-hot pain in its wake.

"Thank you, Sir," she said through gritted teeth, "for your gift."

"You're welcome, slave Jaime."

She turned toward Mistress Marjorie, the welt on her breast now a dark red line. "Will you take my mark, slave Jaime, as a symbol of your submission and service to The Enclave?"

"Yes, Mistress Marjorie."

"Offer your left breast," the Mistress instructed. Her stroke landed with the same fiery, welcome pain, creating the symmetry of a second welt.

"Thank you, Mistress," Jaime managed, "for your gift."

"You're welcome, slave Jaime."

Mistress Aubrey was next. She had a pair of clover clamps in her hands held together by a thin black chain. "Will you wear my clamps, slave Jaime, as a symbol of your submission and service to The Enclave?"

"Yes, Mistress."

"Offer your nipples, slave Jaime."

Jaime lifted both welted breasts, her nipples tingling with anticipation. Mistress Aubrey gripped her right nipple first and opened one of the clamps, letting it close on either side of the distended nipple. The intense pressure was immediate and explosive, and Jaime couldn't stop the hiss of pain that escaped her lips. Unperturbed, Mistress Aubrey gripped the second nipple and closed the clamp over it, sending another seismic tremor of erotic pain through Jaime's nerve endings.

"Thank you, Mistress, for your gift," Jaime breathed as she struggled to process and handle the tight, unyielding bite of the clamps.

"You're welcome, slave Jaime."

Shakily, Jaime turned to Master Julian, who stood across from Mistress Aubrey. To her dismay, she saw he held a fat butt plug already shiny with lube. His eyes crinkled with amusement as his gaze moved over her face. "At least pretend you like it," he teased.

Embarrassed, Jaime struggled to arrange her features into welcoming submission. "Please pardon me, Sir."

Still smiling, Master Julian intoned the ritualistic words, "Will you take my plug, slave Jaime, as a symbol of your submission and service to The Enclave?

"Yes, Sir."

"Turn around and bend over."

Jaime did as she was told, determined to finish the gauntlet without another graceless hitch. She spread her ass cheeks and closed her eyes, focusing on her breathing as the hard rubber pushed its way inside her. When it was firmly in place, Jaime stood and turned to face Master Julian once more.

"Thank you, Sir, for your gift."

"My pleasure, slave Jaime."

As she approached Master Lawrence, Jaime's gut clenched with residual fear, despite her awareness of Lawrence's sincere efforts to become a better Master. He gripped a long, thin cane by its black-suede-covered handle with one hand, stroking its length with the other as he stared into her face with his icy blue eyes. "Will you take my mark, slave Jaime, as a symbol of your submission and service to The Enclave?"

Jaime's eyes fixed on the long, lethal rod. Determined to bear its stroke with as much grace as Master Lawrence had shown with his apology to her, she, too, squared her shoulders. "Yes, Master Lawrence. I will."

"Offer your ass."

Jaime turned and bent, the chain of the clover clamps swaying between her nipples. The stroke was quick and broad, the cane catching her along both ass cheeks, the force of the blow nearly making her stumble. A cry of pain rose in her throat like a sob, but she managed to bite it back to a whimper.

Breathing hard, she stood and turned to face Master Lawrence. "Thank you, Sir, for your gift."

"You're welcome, slave Jaime," Master Lawrence said, stunning her as he added, "We're all glad to have you here. You'll be a good addition to the community." He actually smiled.

Jaime realized her mouth had fallen open and she clamped it shut. Finding her voice, she replied with complete sincerity, "Thank you, Sir. I appreciate it very much."

Master Mason grinned at her as she turned to face him. He, too, held a pair of clover clamps. Jaime regarded the clamps, confused, until the direction of Master Mason's hooded gaze made his evil intentions clear. "Will you wear my clamps on your pretty little cunt, slave Jaime, as a symbol of your submission and service to The Enclave?"

Jaime tried to swallow away the lump that had risen in her throat. Failing that, she still managed to reply, "Yes, Sir." She spread her legs wide and arched her hips forward to give Master Mason easier access to her tender folds. The clamps bit into her flesh, but it was actually less painful than the initial throb at her nipples, filled as they were with so many more nerve endings than her outer labia.

"Thank you, Master Mason, for your gift."

"You're welcome, slave Jaime."

She turned next to face Master Anthony, though she could feel Master Mark's warm, intense gaze on her. Master Anthony held a silver leash. "Will you wear this chain, slave Jaime, as a symbol of your submission and service to The Enclave?"

"Yes, Master Anthony," Jaime breathed, much of the tension that had coiled inside her unspooling beneath his calm, steady gaze.

Master Anthony clipped the leash to Jaime's collar and led her to the row of kneeling slaves, indicating she should kneel in the spot at the center, the space reserved just for her. He draped the leash over her back as Jaime, still clamped and plugged, sank to her knees between

Danielle and Lucia.

The Dominants, save for Master Anthony and Master Mark, had moved to sit on the chairs facing the arch. Jaime bowed her head as she struggled to get a grip on the emotions churning within her—the thrill and honor of being accepted as a staff slave warring with the excited, anticipatory fear of what was to come next.

Master Anthony stood in front of the row of slaves and faced the seated members of The Enclave. "It is my pleasure and honor to welcome Jaime as a full-fledged staff slave." There was applause and a few cheers. In spite of her jitters, Jaime felt her face warm with happiness.

Master Anthony smiled broadly at Master Mark and then turned to face the Dominants. "There is more good news. After living and working with us these past months, Mark has agreed to join the community as a full-fledged Master."

"Yeah!" called out Master Mason, amidst laughter and more applause.

"I tell you this during Jaime's ceremony," Master Anthony continued, "because I have very special news to share with regard to these two young people. Slave Jaime will be joining us not only as our communal property, but as Master Mark's personal slave. To commemorate their union, Master Mark and I have chosen a boundary-pushing experience, with the full knowledge and consent of slave Jaime."

Murmurs of excitement and approval rippled through the space, and Jaime's heart began to pound. At a nod from Master Anthony, the other slaves rose and moved to stand in a neat row behind the seated Dominants. Master Mark appeared beside Jaime, his long, leather-clad legs so close she could have wrapped her arms around them.

Reaching down, Master Anthony tugged gently at the leash, and

Jaime rose, striving for the grace she'd practiced in Mistress Marjorie's training room, in spite of the fact her legs had turned to rubber. He handed the leash to Master Mark, and Jaime turned with the chain to face the man she'd fallen in love with in so short a time. He looked gorgeously dominant, dressed in full leather from his boots to the leather vest he wore over his broad, bare chest.

She forced herself to resist the urge to melt against his body, fully aware she needed to muster all her courage for what was planned next. Though she had participated in the planning, and agreed to what was to come, that didn't stop her heart from smashing like a crazed bird against the window of her chest. How could a heart pound with fear and croon with joy at the same time?

Master Anthony stepped away as Master Mark led Jaime to the center of the arch. Looking down into her eyes, he reached for the nipple clamps "Are you ready?" he asked quietly.

Jaime stiffened but nodded. "Yes, Sir," she whispered, as ready as she would ever be. She managed to stifle the cry of pain as he released the clamps, allowing the nerve endings to shriek to life as the blood flow returned. Master Anthony stood nearby, the plastic bowl in his hand. Master Mark dropped the nipple clamps into the bowl and turned his attention back to Jaime.

The removal of the labia clamps wasn't as difficult to handle. Depositing them in the bowl, Master Mark gestured with his hand for Jaime to bend over. Happily, the butt plug slid easily from her body after the initial tug and was added to the bowl for later cleaning and sterilization. The two men moved together toward the table. They returned a moment later holding several coils of Shibari rope.

"Arms behind your back," Master Mark commanded, and Jaime obeyed. The two men worked quickly as they wrapped and twisted the supple rope around Jaime's arms, binding them together from elbow to wrist. Moving to stand in front of her, Master Mark coiled the ropes in pleasing patterns and knots around her breasts, her nipples jutting like ripe cherries at their centers. Jaime could feel Master Anthony's steadying hands on her shoulders from behind. A potent mixture of sensual peace and throbbing lust wove its way through her blood as it always did when she was properly bound.

Master Mark walked toward the folding table, returning with the piercing kit he'd shown her earlier that day, along with the small black velvet box that contained the nipple rings he wanted her to wear as a symbol of his ownership and her submission. Even her untrained eye could tell it was fine jewelry, exquisitely made. The hoops were twisted into a delicately wrought knot of gold, a conscious nod to the Shibari rope they both loved.

As he opened the kit to reveal the piercing equipment, Jaime's stomach lurched, but the snug, comforting embrace of the ropes, Master Anthony's reassuring hold on her shoulders and Master Mark's warm, loving gaze all gave her the courage to face what was to come.

The clearing was silent, save for the slight swish of the leaves above caught in a gentle evening breeze and the hoot of a distant owl. Jaime could feel all eyes trained on her but she kept her focus squarely on her Master as he swabbed her nipples with a pre-treated gauze pad to ready them for the needle. Setting the gauze aside, he stroked her cheek. "Are you ready, slave Jaime? Will you take my needle and wear the jewelry that symbolizes my ownership of your body and soul?"

"Yes, Master Mark." Jaime had meant to speak loudly for everyone to hear, but her voice sounded as if it were coming from a distance, reedy and wavering.

Master Mark regarded her, his eyes moving over her face as if he could read the thoughts and fears in her head. "You can do this," he said with quiet certainty. "You are my strong, brave girl. You were born to submit, slave Jaime. And I was born for you."

With those words, the last of her fear snapped inside her, like a lock springing open. She watched with an almost detached calm as Master Mark pulled her right nipple taut with the forceps. She closed her eyes when the sharp point of the piercing needle touched her nipple. Though she was no longer frightened, dizziness suddenly assailed her, making her sway. Again she felt Master Anthony's steadying hands on her shoulders.

"Open your eyes," Master Mark commanded, his voice soft but firm. "You will watch the needle pierce your flesh. This is your gift to me, and mine to you. You will participate fully, slave Jaime, as I claim you for my own."

His masterful words centered her once more. The dizziness left her, her balance and poise returning, her courage rising once more to the fore. "Yes, Sir," she said, her voice steady. "Yes, please."

The pain as the needle pierced her flesh made stars explode across her vision. She would have screamed, but the shock to her nerve endings took her breath away. Mercifully, he was very quick, both nipples pierced and threaded with the jewelry in a matter of seconds. As she looked into Master Mark's eyes, a joyous lightness of being suffused her. She imagined she might float away but for the ropes that crisscrossed her body and held her arms tightly behind her back.

Master Anthony stepped from behind her and stood in front of her as Master Mark stepped aside. Master Anthony regarded her with a serious gaze, though his eyes were twinkling. "Welcome to The Enclave, slave Jaime. You belong to us all now. I hope you will serve with all the grace and submission I know you possess."

I will, Sir. I promise," Jaime said fervently, tears popping into her eyes, which she blinked rapidly away.

With a nod and a smile, the silver-haired man stepped once more behind Jaime. As he untied the knots and unwound the rope, blood flow returned with tingling insistence to her arms and fingers, which she flexed to ease the sensation. The release of the buckle at the back of her neck startled her. Why was Master Anthony taking away her slave collar, which she'd only removed, and then reluctantly, in order to shower? Of course, she was too well trained to ask or resist, but her neck and throat felt naked without the comforting wrap of leather, her world suddenly oddly out of balance.

Master Mark appeared in front of her, an oblong velvet case she hadn't seen before in his hands. He opened it to reveal a beautiful leather collar dyed a lustrous pearly blue-gray, a single diamond sparkling at its center.

"Oh," Jaime breathed, transfixed. "It's beautiful, Sir."

"Master Brandon outdid himself with this one," Master Mark said, glancing toward the leather master with a smile. "The leather captures the color of your eyes perfectly, and the diamond symbolizes the strength and endurance of the bond we're forging together."

Jaime glanced shyly at Master Brandon, who beamed back at her from his seat. She closed her eyes, the world righting itself as Master Mark wrapped the soft leather collar around her neck and buckled it into place. The group erupted into spontaneous applause and happy laughter.

Master Mark dipped his head close to Jaime's ear. "Welcome to The Enclave, slave Jaime," he murmured. "Welcome home."

Available at Romance Unbound Publishing

(http://romanceunbound.com)

A Lover's Call
A Princely Gift
A Test of Love
Accidental Slave
Alternative Treatment
Beyond the Compound
Binding Discoveries
Blind Faith
Brokered Submission
Cast a Lover's Spell
Caught: Punished by Her Boss
Claiming Kelsey
Closely Held Secrets
Club de Sade
Confessions of a Submissive
Dare to Dominate
Dream Master
Enslaved
Face of Submission
Finding Chandler
Forced Submission
Frog
Golden Angel
Golden Boy
Golden Man
Handyman
Heart of Submission
Heart Thief
Island of Temptation
Jewel Thief
Julie's Submission
Lara's Submission

Masked Submission
No Safeword
Obsession: Girl Abducted
Odd Man Out
Our Man Friday
Pleasure Planet
Princess
Safe in His Arms
Sarah's Awakening
Seduction of Colette
Slave Academy
Slave Castle
Slave Gamble
Slave Girl
Slave Island
Slave Jade
Sold into Slavery
Stardust
Sub for Hire
Submission in Paradise
Submission Times Two
Switch
Switching Gears
Texas Surrender
The Auction
The Compound
The Contract
The Cowboy Poet
The Inner Room
The Keyholder
The Master
The Solitary Knights of Pelham Bay
The Story of Owen
The Toy
Tough Boy
Tracy in Chains
True Kin Vampire Tales:
Sacred Circle
Outcast
Sacred Blood

Connect with Claire

Newsletter: http://tinyurl.com/o6tu4eu

Website: http://clairethompson.net

Romance Unbound Publishing: http://romanceunbound.com

Twitter: http://twitter.com/CThompsonAuthor

Facebook: http://www.facebook.com/ClaireThompsonauthor

Printed in Great Britain
by Amazon